Praise for Sarah Glenn Marsh and *Fear the Drowning Deep*:

"Haunting—gripping—beautiful. So powerful!"

—Tamora Pierce, #1 *New York Times* bestselling author of the Beka Cooper trilogy

"*Fear the Drowning Deep* is gorgeous. Lyrical. Atmospheric. Magical. Sarah Glenn Marsh's debut is perfect for anyone who's ever looked out at the sea with awe, and wondered what kind of creatures lurk in the deepest places. Utterly haunting."

—Jodi Meadows, author of the Incarnate trilogy, the Orphan Queen duology, and *My Lady Jane*

"Beautifully-written with mysteries and love lurking within the pages as dangerously as an ancient evil waits in the drowning deeps of Sarah's unique setting on the Isle of Man. Don't miss this one!"

—Martina Boone, author of *Compulsion* and the Heirs of Watson Island trilogy

"Readers will be swept away by Bridey's love story, every bit as thrilling and mysterious as the Isle of Man's deep, dark sea."

—Tricia Rayburn, author of the Siren trilogy

"Sarah Glenn Marsh's debut is a captivating tale of love and loss, fear and doubt, monsters of the sea and inside ourselves, and the strength it takes to endure and conquer them all. Hauntingly written with a richly developed setting of the Isle of Man in the early 1900s, you can smell the salt of the sea with every page you hungrily turn."

—Lori Goldstein, author of *Becoming Jinn* and *Circle of Jinn*

FEAR
the
DROWNING
DEEP

FEAR
the
DROWNING
DEEP

SARAH GLENN MARSH

Sky Pony Press
New York

Sky Pony Press books may be purchased in bulk at special discounts for sales promotion, corporate gifts, fund-raising, or educational purposes. Special editions can also be created to specifications. For details, contact the Special Sales Department, Sky Pony Press, 307 West 36th Street, 11th Floor, New York, NY 10018 or info@skyhorsepublishing.com.

This is a work of fiction. Names, characters, places, and incidents are either the product of the author's imagination or used fictitiously.

Sky Pony® is a registered trademark of Skyhorse Publishing, Inc®, a Delaware corporation.

Visit our website at skyponypress.com.

Books, authors, and more at www.skyponypressblog.com

www.sarahglennmarsh.com/

10 9 8 7 6 5 4 3 2

Library of Congress Cataloging-in-Publication Data is available on file.

978-1-5107-0348-3
eBook ISBN 978-1-5107-0349-0

Cover design by Georgia Morrissey
Cover art © Shutterstock

Printed in the United States of America

Interior design by Joshua Barnaby

For my sister, Lindsey.
If you ever have a monster in need of slaying, call me.

"I am not afraid of storms, for I am learning how to sail my ship."

–Louisa May Alcott, *Little Women*

Chapter One

May 15th, 1913
Isle of Man, near Peel

They found her body at dusk, washed up in a tide pool with a handful of sea urchins and a slender green starfish. As they lifted the girl, her dark hair wrapped around her neck like seaweed. Fat drops of saltwater rolled off her body and kissed the cold sand. I shivered in sympathy, though, of course, she didn't feel the bitter wind tugging at her gown. Her waxy skin appeared paler than the full moon, which had risen early in the lavender sky.

Old Mr. Gill pushed the girl's hair back, revealing milky, grayish eyes. I couldn't begin to guess their true color. Cradled in his arms, the girl looked like a nymph, or one of the mermaids my mam loved to paint.

A neighbor standing beside me shrieked, sending a chill rippling down my back. Other women sniffed. They reminded me of a flock of guillemots, the way they'd perched themselves on the lowest cliff overlooking the rocky shore. They shared handkerchiefs and made little hiccuping sounds.

Not one of them noticed me lingering where a girl of sixteen shouldn't have been.

Many heads bowed in respect as Mr. Gill and several fishermen carried the girl up the steep incline leading to town. Had she come from the other side of the island, or one of the smaller islands around us? I'd never seen her before, and in our close community that was rare.

One of the women turned to follow the procession back to town, dabbing at her eyes with a scrap of linen. Her graying hair was pinned on the top of her head, and even with the pervasive air of sadness, she stood tall and proud.

Before I could consider hiding—a near impossible task on the barren cliffs—the woman's shrewd brown eyes spotted me. Despite her age, my neighbor Mrs. Gill rarely missed a thing. Folk said she was as clever as Morag, the ancient sea-hag who lived on the swell of land above town. I thought she was just nosy, though I didn't dare say it. Her husband had been the self-appointed leader of Port Coire for as long as I could remember.

Mrs. Gill broke from the procession and bustled in my direction, frowning. "Bridey Corkill, this is hardly a sight for young eyes! Shouldn't you be helping your mam put on supper, child?"

"I'm not a child," I protested, though without force behind the words. No one argued with Mrs. Gill unless they wanted everyone else in Port Coire to hear about it. "Mam sent me to buy bacon from Mr. Vondy."

"Yet, I see you're sadly empty-handed." Mrs. Gill eyed my windswept hair, and I resisted the urge to pat it down. "How'd you end up here, when the market is on the other side of town?"

"I followed the screams." I glanced around. The crowd had almost dispersed, but a few curious souls—all young, fit men— were scuttling down the cliffs by way of a narrow, winding path to a stretch of beach flecked with tide pools.

The Gills' nephew reached the bottom first. He stared into the pocket of saltwater that had, moments ago, held the girl's body, as though he might find answers bubbling to the surface simply because he'd willed them to appear. In the early moon-washed dusk, he wouldn't be able to see anything there for much longer.

"Wonder if this has anything to do with all the fish disappearing lately," one boy muttered to his companions.

"How could it?" the Gills' nephew scoffed. "Something like this would attract all the sharks from here to Britain."

"Bridey?" Mrs. Gill's voice cut over their muted conversation. "Have you heard a word I've said?" She sighed. "I know this is upsetting. I can only imagine what your mam will say when you have one of your night terrors after the sight of the poor lass. . . ."

"I won't. I swear." I drew myself up taller and squared my shoulders as the sea breeze crashed into me. "But who do you suppose the girl is? Could she have come all the way from— from Ireland?"

Mrs. Gill shook her head. "Certainly not. She would've made a fine supper for some hungry creature long before she reached our shores." She pulled her black shawl tighter around her shoulders. "Where are your sisters?" She looked past me as though searching for more errant girls.

I clenched my hands at my sides, hiding my fists in the folds of my skirt. My sisters' whereabouts were none of the old biddy's business. Clearing my throat, I answered sweetly, "Grayse is scrubbing potatoes. Liss is hanging the wash. And Mally's out with her sweetheart, having a picnic."

"Is she still sweet on Adam?"

"I think so. Or Artur. I can't exactly recall, but I'm certain his name starts with *A*."

Mrs. Gill pursed her lips. "Your poor da. Sometimes I wonder how he manages to keep his head in a house full of high-spirited women."

"He says most days it's like treading water. Taking lots of deep breaths, and praying for rescue." Much like I felt at that very moment. I hoped my tart reply would be enough to encourage Mrs. Gill to go pester someone else.

"Marta?" Mrs. Kissack, the baker, called from a short distance away. My rescuer. She took a step forward, but paused and licked her lips.

"What is it?" Mrs. Gill asked.

Mrs. Kissack gestured to a few waiting neighbors, the last of the onlookers. "We were just wondering what time we'll be gathering."

Of course. The town leaders would want to plan a search for the drowned girl's kin. Perhaps they'd even make funeral arrangements.

Mrs. Gill nodded. "Let's meet in an hour, at my place. Right after supper." She looked from Mrs. Kissack back to me. "I'd best go." She heaved a long-suffering sigh. "Now I have to clean the house, on top of everything else."

Turning back to the churning water, I took a deep breath. My lungs filled with briny air, and the salt on my tongue made my stomach squirm. I was probably the only islander in existence who couldn't stand the grit of salt and sand in everything she owned, and who felt nauseated whenever she smelled fish.

But perhaps it wasn't so strange, hating the sea's very existence when it had taken my grandad from me much too soon. Just like the Gills had never quite forgiven the sea for stealing their oldest son many years ago.

"Bridey!" Mrs. Gill shouted over the billowing breeze. She stood at the top of the cliff, leaning on a weathered post. "I suggest you head straight home after visiting Mr. Vondy's." An unfamiliar shadow crossed her face. "You shouldn't tarry after dusk, especially not here."

I nodded and took the path at a run, legs swallowing up the distance between the cliffs and the heart of town.

"Evenin', Bridey!" a girl called as I passed the first group of shabby wood and stone houses. Nessa Daley stood in her front yard, clutching a handful of scraggly white-and-yellow flowers, wearing a smile as brilliant as the sun on water.

She hadn't seen the men bearing the girl's body into town, then. Keeping my word to Mrs. Gill, I didn't stop to tell Nessa about the grim scene by the cliffs. I gave her a halfhearted wave and hurried on.

As I ran, I pictured Mrs. Gill's face as clearly as though she still stood in front of me, wearing that unsettling expression. I hadn't seen her so troubled since her sister passed away five years before. Or since she'd heard my account of how Grandad died.

Had the sight of the drowned girl bothered Mrs. Gill more than she cared to admit?

Opening the door of our cottage, I inhaled the familiar scents of home: hearth smoke, the earthiness of dried sage, and the metallic smell of Mam's paints. The tang of freshly skinned fish wafted toward me a moment later. I wrinkled my nose and fought the urge to gag.

Shedding my cloak as warmth washed over me, I crossed the main room and entered the bedroom I shared with Grayse and Liss.

"Bridey? Is that you, bird?" Mam called.

"Of course," I answered, lighting the greasy fish-oil lamp on my dresser. By its muted amber glow, I located my sheepskin slippers half-hidden under the bed. Grayse had left her entire collection of ragdolls strewn across our quilt, where a trail of suspicious-looking spots suggested the dolls had been subjected to another tea party with real tea.

"Well, hurry with the bacon, unless you've decided to have fish like the rest of us."

Rusty old lanterns rested on every available ledge of the kitchen, creating a bright glow, though none sat too close to the cantankerous stove in the corner of the narrow room. The stove's innards blazed as it greedily consumed the wood I'd chopped for Da last week.

"You're late, love," Mam chided, turning away from a boiling pot. She swooped down to kiss my cheek. Her lips were dry against my skin, chapped from the cool, salty air. "Where's the bacon?"

I thumped the package down on the counter. "Would you fry it? Please?"

"You'll have your bacon as I make it. And tonight, that's boiled with the fish and potatoes. I don't have extra pots to spare for picky daughters." Mam wiped her damp brow with a rag and unhooked the latch on the window.

A breeze ruffled my hair, coiling around my shoulders like an unwelcome embrace.

I glanced sideways out the open window as the frigid fingers of a northern wind penetrated the hot kitchen. Far below, restless gray waters rolled and crashed, sending up a furious spray. I couldn't see it through the dark, but the sea crowded in around us, writhing with the pull of the tide like blood pulsing through a body.

I imagined walking out to the edge of the nearest cliff and diving into the thick sea foam that masked the deadly rocks waiting in the shallows. Would I feel the impact when I hit them? Or would I be too numb with cold?

Swallowing with a lump in my throat, I tried to banish the sickening thought. I didn't want to die, truly. But ever since I saw Grandad jump to his watery death, the view from our small window never failed to give me terrible visions.

Ever since Grandad jumped, I'd turned my back on the sea and all the wicked things it hid below its jewel-bright surface.

"Hungry, Bridey?"

I whirled away from the window, grateful for a distraction.

"Want some?" Grayse smiled around a mouthful of the crusty bread Mam had set out for supper, revealing the dark gap of a missing front tooth.

"No, thanks, little fish." I ruffled my sister's light blonde hair.

"Don't do that," Grayse scolded, smoothing her hair down. She leaned back in her chair, which creaked a warning. Da had fashioned our table from wood left to rot in the harbor, and every time Grayse swung her scrawny legs, I worried she might cause the whole thing to collapse with one poorly placed kick.

Head still spinning from my vision at the window, I drew out a chair next to her and sank into it with a sigh.

"What kept you, Bry? Did you see Catreena at the market?" Liss asked from across the table. She held a boning knife in one hand, and the grim remains of a fish clung to the chopping block in front of her.

Though she was a year younger than me, she looked older. Or at least more respectable. She kept her dark gold hair in two neat plaits that fell past her waist and, despite the amount of time she spent toiling with Mam in the kitchen, her apron was always spotless.

"Bridey, I'm speaking to you." Liss frowned.

"Sorry," I said, sitting up straighter and focusing on her pale hazel eyes.

"Well, did you meet Catreena, or were you off in the woods again on one of your *adventures*?"

"No." I arched a brow, ignoring Liss's taunt. "Haven't you heard the news?" Most days, gossip traveled between houses faster than I could run.

Mam joined us at the table, a tiny crease forming between her brows. "What news?"

"A girl—a stranger—washed up with the tide. Drowned. And not too long ago, by the look of her."

Mam's eyes narrowed. "It sounds as though you saw the body."

"Only for a minute. The Gills were there, too." I dropped my gaze, pretending to study a scorch mark in the floor.

"Oh, Bridey." Mam laid a hand on my back. "Are you worried you'll have nightmares?"

"She has enough of them already," Liss muttered.

I glared, opening my mouth to respond, but Mam spoke first.

"Enough, girls! Bridey, you've told me plenty. I'm sure Marta will tell me the rest later." She shifted her attention to my sisters. "Grayse Sharlott Corkill, you're not to repeat a word of this to your friends, understand?" The rest of her warning hung in the air: *because everyone in town thinks we're strange enough as it is.*

Grayse nodded and helped herself to more bread.

"Good girl. Liss, be a love and help me serve. . . ." Mam and Liss walked to the stove, their voices fading to murmurs.

"What killed the girl?" Grayse whispered, leaning in. "Was it . . . the same thing that took Grandad?"

My heart swelled with gratitude for my sister's willingness to believe my account of what had happened on that terrible day, even when no one else in the family would. Even when the past eight years had dulled the memory enough to make me sometimes wonder if I hadn't, in my nine-year-old mind, somehow twisted the truth of what had really happened.

"I don't know, Grayse. Wish I did." I lowered my voice to the barest whisper. "All I saw that night—or thought I saw— was something white, like a ghost made of ocean mist. And all I saw today was a washed-up stranger, solid as you or me."

"All right." Grayse put down her bread and met my eyes. "But I'm gonna say extra prayers tonight. Just to be safe."

"Thanks. You know, you're quite clever for your seven years."

Grayse giggled. "You're clever, too."

"If she were *really* clever, she'd be eating this delicious cod she used to love," Liss countered, shoving in between us to set down our bowls. I rolled my eyes and said nothing. Liss only plagued me with such remarks when she really wanted to get under my skin.

The scrape of our spoons was the only sound as we ate, our eyes fixed on the meal. I swallowed the occasional lump of fish without complaint, focused on thoughts of England, Ireland, France—even America. Someday, I would leave this rock and make my home miles from the sea. Cities or towns, fields or mountains, anything but here would do. I could learn a new language, try new foods, and hear the constant buzz of voices instead of the lonely rush of waves.

"Mam?" Grayse said, breaking the silence.

"Yes, little fish?"

"When's Da coming home? He's been gone for *two whole days*." Grayse pushed her empty bowl aside and gave Mam her best pout.

"He's *always* gone for a few days at a time, Graysie," Liss muttered.

Mam gave her a look, then smiled at Grayse. "He'll be back tomorrow morning. And hopefully this time, his nets will be bursting with scallops and big, fat lobsters for Mally to sell at the market."

I tapped Grayse's shoulder. "We'll wake up early and greet him at the harbor," I suggested in a falsely cheery voice. "How's that sound?" I'd rather eat a whole pot of fish than set foot in the harbor where Da and the others moored their boats, but more than anything, I wanted to make Grayse happy.

She gave a smile that stretched across her whole face, showing off her missing tooth again.

"I'll take that as a yes."

After helping to clear the table, I stood by the sink before the open window to take my turn washing the dishes. Bowing my head, I tried to ignore the cold breeze mussing the top of my hair. I added the wind to the growing list of things I longed to put behind me.

I was about to dip my rag in the water when Mam appeared at my side. She closed the window and latched it. Not for the first time, I wondered why that window had a latch at all. It wasn't as though anyone would want to climb through it in the middle of the night. There was no crime in Port Coire. Not until today, anyway.

The shutters rattled as the wind forced its way through the cracks. "I want you to latch your bedroom window, too, bird." Mam's voice sounded higher and thinner than usual. But when she saw my frown, she smiled and swatted my arm with a rag. "Now get to work!"

I lay awake long after Grayse and Liss had drifted off on either side of me. Their warmth made me drowsy, but my eyes wouldn't stay shut. I shifted until I could see moonbeams streaming through the latched window.

A knot formed deep in my stomach as my thoughts returned to the drowned girl. She hadn't looked like a murder victim. There had been no bruises or grisly wounds visible. Yet remembering the sight of her drenched limp figure made my skin damp with cold sweat.

How did she end up in the water? Had her boat capsized in a storm? Had someone pushed her in? Or had she—like Grandad—dived for the water with a look of ecstasy on her face, as though summoned by some invisible force?

The sea did strange things to people. It played tricks on the mind. Its vastness hid things . . . Bodies. Secrets. The deadly bulk of icebergs.

A month ago, people on both sides of the Atlantic had mourned the one-year anniversary of the sinking of the *Titanic*. People had called the giant ship *unsinkable*, but the sea had proven them wrong. Maybe she didn't like being challenged. Maybe that's why she took the ship and most of its passengers to a place no one living could follow, in a tragedy that continued to haunt me from the pages of the newspapers Da brought home.

I turned away from the moonlight and closed my eyes. Even with the window shut and Liss's familiar breathing in my ear, I was sure I could hear someone wailing away on his fiddle, playing a mournful tribute to all those lost to the sea. And along with the melody came the unmistakable sound of water slapping against the rocks far below us, slowly eroding the foundation of Port Coire and everything I loved.

CHAPTER TWO

I've had this dream so many times. Often enough to know I'm dreaming, but helpless to wake myself, even knowing what's about to happen.

Knowing, and dreading.

I'm nine years old again, walking along the cliffs at Grandad's side, hand in hand. Mine is small and sticky, his huge and leathery. Together we navigate the sweltering summer dusk, eavesdropping on seabirds' conversations. We have to strain to hear them over the hiss and roar of the ocean below.

The persistent breeze has already dried my tears and cooled my burning face, but Grandad and I keep walking away from town. He seems to know that I'm not ready to go home and face Liss just yet. She thinks I cut her favorite doll's hair—the expensive, irreplaceable one Gran gave her for her birthday—but it was really Mally. She'd wanted to give the doll the latest style.

The fight that ensued had everyone, even Mam, in tears.

It's a good thing Grandad had come for supper. He scooped me up, letting me bury my damp face in his shirt, and brought me out here to clear my head.

"I'm never talking to Liss again," I announce as we pause beyond a rise that hides town from view.

The first stars are just appearing, sprinkling Grandad's worn face with pale light and making his once-gold hair look even whiter as he smiles and says, "Ach, that's going to make life rather difficult don't you think, my Bridey-bird? I remember when I was a lad, my older brother . . ."

His words trail away as he glances toward the sea, his head tilted, listening.

"Grandad?" I tug his hand, wanting to hear the rest of his story.

"Hmm?" He blinks, like I've startled him. Like he's seen a ghost. "I'm sorry. What was I saying, my little love?"

"About your brother," I reply helpfully.

But he's looking to the sea again. Still clutching my hand, he walks slowly toward the nearest cliff, leading me forward until we're teetering on the very last bit of rock before a long drop into the open water.

Fresh tears well in my eyes. Normally, the sigh of the sea calms me, like the voice of an old friend, but now its hissing sounds like a threat. With both my hands gripping one of Grandad's, I use all my strength to try to pull him back from the edge.

"Don't you hear it?" Grandad asks, shaking away my grasping hands. His voice sounds distant, and as his misty eyes stare into the far-below waves, I have a sinking feeling he has gone somewhere I can't follow.

"Hear what?" I whimper. There's no answer. "Hear what?" I beg, louder.

"The music." He makes the slightest motion forward, kicking pebbles from the cliff into the crashing surf.

"You're scaring me!" I sob, grabbing fistfuls of his shirt. "Grandad!"

"It's so beautiful," he murmurs. "Sweeter than fairy song, even." He smiles, a broad grin that sheds years from his face, his gaze never wavering from the restless sea. It's as if he can't hear my pleas. As if I don't exist in whatever world he's drifted to.

"I have to go now." Still smiling, he raises his arms and arcs his body into a diver's pose.

The motion knocks me to the ground. I cough and hiccup and grasp at air.

Grandad leaps from the cliff with a swan's grace, looking happier than I've ever seen him.

Somehow I manage to push myself up onto my knees. My hands claw at the dirt to keep me anchored as I lean over the edge, my frantic heart hoping for a sign of Grandad. The moon aids my search as I scan the blurry expanse of dark water before me.

He surfaces for the briefest moment, not near the rocks as I'd feared, but already farther out than I'd thought him capable of swimming. He closes his eyes, that strange broad smile still plastered on his face, and lets the waves swallow him one last time.

And then, soft as a whisper, the whine of a fiddle reaches my ears.

Or perhaps it's my own keening cry, tossed back to me by the wind. There aren't any fiddlers out here on the cliffs. No one who hears my cries and screams for help.

A flash of white draws my gaze back to the water. At first, it appears to be the transparent figure of a tall man—Grandad's spirit?—watching me from above the waves. But when I blink, there's only a whitecap, rolling through the empty space where Grandad disappeared.

A flock of white birds darted around Grayse's head as she stood at the end of the harbor dock, tossing crumbs of cheese in the air.

I sat cross-legged a few feet away, shivering at the water's nearness, my gaze flicking between the unchanging horizon and my sister. I kept hoping for a glimpse of movement, a speck growing larger as Da approached, but the sea maintained its morning calm. Flecks of light played across the harbor's tranquil waters and a breeze made tiny ripples around the dock. Under a clear sky, with my sister humming a lively song, the sea appeared innocent. Almost.

Grayse's humming was broken by a sudden cry, and I leaped up. "Stop it, birdies!" she yelped, dropping the cheese to cover her face with her hands.

The sun glinted on sharp beaks and talons. I ran toward Grayse, making shooing motions at the birds. "You've given them enough, little fish! We aren't running a charity for the guillemots."

The spark of an idea flashed in her eyes as she retrieved the cheese.

"Grayse," I groaned, inspecting her face and hands for cuts. "Promise me you won't start collecting scraps for them. When you tried to start a charity for the porpoises last year, all the donations amounted to were a couple of fish heads and an old boot, remember?"

Grayse mumbled something that sounded like "I remember."

We lapsed into silence, listening to the rustle of birds' wings as they flapped across the water to seek their fortunes elsewhere. To our right, a rusted dinghy bobbed alone in the harbor, rocked by the breeze.

"Bry, do you think there's a monster hiding under the dock right now?" Grayse asked, peering through gaps in the battered wooden planks.

"I don't know. But if something tries to grab us, I'll tell it to eat me first." I plopped down on the boards again, trying not to think about what foul things might be curled in the shadows below.

Grayse gave a halfhearted smile. "D'you think Mally will get married soon?" She broke the cheese in two and offered me a piece. "I hope she chooses Thomase."

"What? Why him?"

"He gave me the fish heads for the porpoises. And he's *handsome*."

I laughed and bit into the sharp cheese. "You shouldn't know about 'handsome' yet. Besides, Mally has her heart set on Artur. He's promised to take her to England someday."

"Not him!" Grayse shook her head as though trying to clear away the image of the lad who wore drab colors and calculated numbers in his head for fun. "Why don't you marry Thomase then?"

I choked, spraying my skirt with bits of cheese. How could I explain to her that marriage would be another tie to a place I dreamed of leaving behind? Not to mention what a git Thomase was.

"Mam says it's time you found good work or a good husband."

"I know what Mam says."

I didn't like hearing her lectures repeated by my sweetest sister. After all, Mam's idea of good work was selling her paintings during Tourist Season, which was finally upon us, to supplement the living Da made for us with his fishing. Mermaids. Selkies. Pearly pink octopi swirling through the deep. Each day Mam trapped her strange dreams on canvas, yet she expected me to do mindless work while she indulged her whims. I intended to find a job soon, but it would take years to save up enough money for a one-way ride on a sturdy boat.

I tipped my head back, letting the sun warm my face. My eyes fluttered closed and my breathing slowed as I imagined being miles from the sea.

"Look!" Grayse poked me in the ribs with her bony elbow and scrambled to her feet. "Da! Over here!" She bounced on the spot as though she were attached to springs.

I looked out over the water. A shape separated itself from the horizon and coasted toward us. Da's boat. From such a distance, he wouldn't be able to hear our shouts, but Grayse continued to call to him.

By the time Da was close enough for us to see the stubble on his chin, Grayse had worn out her voice. She smiled and stood with her arms outstretched, signaling she was ready to catch the line.

"My girls!" Da beamed as his boat approached. His cap had fallen off, and the wind was ruffling his dark hair, giving him a wild appearance. "Ready, Grayse?" he called as he tossed her the heavy rope.

I tried to assist as little as possible, but Grayse didn't protest when I shouldered some of the weight of the line.

"How's everything at home?" Da asked. He sat in the boat with his arms folded, giving Grayse time to tie the rope to the dock's metal cleat. "Your mam? Liss and Mally?"

"Everything's fine. Not much changes here in three days." We exchanged a smile, and my arms itched to embrace him. "Only . . ." I took a deep breath and tried to quell the squirming in the pit of my stomach. "Mr. Gill and a few other men found a girl's body on the beach yesterday. No one we know. Were there bad storms? Her boat might've hit the rocks."

Da sucked in a breath and pressed his lips together. "You can tell me."

I glanced at Grayse, whose head was bent over the cleat, then back to him.

As Da swung himself up onto the dock, I was all too aware of the murky water waiting to swallow him up if he took a wrong step. My shoulders only relaxed once he landed on the worn dock with a dull thud.

Da wasted no time wrapping me in a tight hug, and I buried my face in his shirt. The scent of fish guts and sweat overwhelmed me, crawling in through my nose and trailing down my throat. I sneezed so hard the boards beneath us groaned in protest.

"Steady there, Bridey-bird!" Da made a show of wiping off his already filthy shirt before beginning to haul his catch out of the boat.

Studying the mess of buckets, nets, and rods as he pulled them up, I realized everything looked grimier than usual. "There *was* a storm, wasn't there?"

He nodded, showing me a couple of empty buckets. "Aye. It started the morning of my second day out. A nasty squall blew up, and I lost nearly half my catch."

I peered in the bucket he plunked down closest to me. A meager handful of prawns sat within, glistening under the sun. I turned my head away before the stench could make me gag and focused on Da's many nets. I couldn't spot a single lobster in any of them.

"I didn't see a girl, though," Da added before I could ask. "Just a few of the fellas heading for deeper water." He bowed his head. "Poor lass. I wonder if she was trying to sail out too far on her own."

"That's a lecture you'll never have to give me," I said, but the sight of an empty bucket, then another, wiped away my smile. "Is this really all you caught?"

A frown spread across Da's weathered face. "The sea's a fickle mistress, bird, and sometimes the places where I've fished in the past . . . well, they dry up. The fish stop coming, and I have to try elsewhere. But, I'll not deny that *everything* seems scarcer lately. For everyone." His shoulders sagged. "I'm afraid this town is headed for hard times."

I looked away, my stomach sinking.

Grayse gave a triumphant—and rather hoarse—shout as she finished her knot, distracting Da and sparing me from attempting to say something falsely cheery.

"Let me check what you've done there, little fish . . ." Da hurried toward Grayse, but rather than inspecting the joining of the line and cleat, he swept her into his arms and spun her around.

I turned, ready to abandon the dock for the safety of firm ground, when a glimmer of something pinkish-white in Da's fishing gear caught my eye. I crouched for a closer look. A round object about half the size of a chicken egg rested in a tangle of coarse netting. I tugged at the pile, hoping to jar it loose.

The thing rolled across the dock boards, its surface splashed with the many hues of a rainbow as sunlight caught its angles.

Once the marble-like object came to rest against a bucket, I reached out, straining my arm until my fingers closed over its slick sides. I gazed down at what looked like a giant pearl. It felt like a pearl, too, cool and smooth against my palm. But pearls were never this large. Why hadn't Da noticed this bright beauty, with so little else in his nets?

I stuffed the pearl in my pocket, deciding to surprise Mam and Da with it later. That way, I could see both my parents' delighted expressions at once. Maybe Da could find more like it when he went back out to sea tomorrow.

"Bridey," Da called from the opposite side of the dock. "Care to join us?" He was helping Grayse feed the birds the rest of our cheese.

"I'm fine right here, thanks."

I glanced down through a wide gap in the boards just in time to see something stirring in the shadows below. A large black fin sliced through the water, making ripples as it swam away. My heart gave a nasty jolt, and I suppressed a shriek. The creature made a splash as it dived under.

"Da!" I finally managed.

His careworn face turned toward me, along with Grayse's, and a flush crept into my cheeks. "Let's head home, shall we? Bet you're ready for a nap, Da." My pulse fluttered as I tried to form a clear picture in my mind of the creature under the dock.

Da shook his head, oblivious to my discomfort. "I can't leave my catch sitting here. The guillemots would have a feast before I had a chance to haul it to the market. Why don't you take your sister for lunch at Ms. Katleen's?"

He searched his pockets and produced a pair of moldy-looking coins.

Grayse's lip trembled. "I want to stay and help!" She gazed imploringly at Da. "And I had enough cheese to last me till supper."

Da smiled. "Can't argue with that. What about you, Bridey? Are you in the mood to sort prawns for me?"

"Not today, I'm afraid." I glanced from my bare feet to Grayse's. I couldn't stay here with something lurking in the water. Da would insist I'd seen a dolphin or a seal. And if Grayse heard mention of her finned friends in the harbor, she'd want to take a closer look.

"Go eat." Da handed me the coins. "Then help your mam with the housework."

"*Gura mie ayd.*" Distracted, the Manx *thank you* slipped from my lips.

As Da and Grayse returned to the boat, I assured myself they'd be safe. The morning was giving rise to a rare cloudless day, allowing light to reach deep into the water, which meant Da would be able to spot any dangerous creatures lurking around the dock.

I trudged uphill alone, watching the ground closely—one stray fish hook in my path would keep me out of my beloved woods for weeks—but my thoughts remained with the black fin under the dock.

What fish had fins like that? Could it have been a seal with a deformed tail?

"Morning, Bry!" a lad called.

I glanced up, startled, and found myself gazing into the faces of my two best friends.

"Have you heard the news? Isn't it *awful*?" Catreena gushed, latching onto my right arm. Ever since I'd known her—since the day she tripped a beautiful English tourist who'd made me feel as inferior as day-old fish and become my best friend in an instant—Cat had possessed an insatiable appetite for gossip.

"She hasn't talked about anything else all morning," Lugh grumbled, moving to my other side and taking my hand. My skin tingled as he laced his fingers with mine. Lately his closeness made me flustered. I tried to focus on Cat's voice.

"Can you imagine? Drifting through the water, fish nibbling at your toes . . ." Cat's dark curls tickled my cheek as she whispered the last few words in my ear. "Her funeral's in two days. On the cliffs, above the spot where they found her. I heard my mam talking about it last night."

"Really? What else did she say?" I tried to keep my voice steady, but judging by the slight crease between Lugh's brows, I hadn't succeeded. "Did they find any trace of a boat, or . . . or anything?"

Cat shook her head, her curls bouncing around her shoulders. "Not that I've heard. But Nessa Daley didn't show up to work this morning. She's never missed a day."

I stared at Cat as a chill crept up my arms. "Is she ill? I saw her only yesterday, and she looked fine."

"That's the thing," Cat dropped her voice to a whisper and widened her eyes. "No one's seen her since supper yesterday, not even her new husband. She seems to have vanished in the night."

The chill in my arms seeped into my chest. I didn't know Nessa well—not beyond exchanging the occasional hello—but she didn't strike me as the type to leave town without a word. No one in Port Coire ever just vanished.

"Maybe the sea-witch took her." Cat shuddered, turning several shades paler. "Maybe old Morag needed her hair or her bones for a spell."

"Or Nessa finally ran off with that tailor from Peel who's always visiting. She's fancied him for ages." Lugh directed a glare at Cat from over my head. He was easily a foot taller than either of us. "Let it go now. It's a terrible subject. And no more talk of witches."

I gripped Lugh's hand tighter, and he squeezed mine back. Warmth enveloped me, banishing the cold. I hoped that wherever Nessa was, she sent a letter to her poor husband soon. For his peace of mind, and everyone else's.

"What're you two doing out here, anyway?" My voice came out breathier than usual. "Looking for Nessa?"

Lugh ran his free hand through his shaggy red hair and grinned. "Looking for you, actually. Mrs. Kissack gave Cat the afternoon off. Want to grab a bite with us?"

"I'd love to." I reached in my pocket to retrieve the money from Da and my sweaty fingers brushed against the pearl. "My treat." I showed Cat and Lugh the coins, but the pearl remained my secret for now.

We continued up the path, my friends on either side of me. "What do you fancy today?" Cat asked as we crested the hill.

I considered our options, which were quite few, but Lugh said, "We'll share a bucket of oysters. Sound tasty, Bry?"

I stuck out my tongue at him.

After supper, a glimpse of one of Mam's paintings hanging in the hall—a mermaid wearing nothing but tiny silver pearls—reminded me of the treasure still in my pocket. Nessa Daley's sudden disappearance and the afternoon spent with my friends had driven it far from my mind.

I had changed into clean clothes before supper, so I slipped away from the table to find the pearl.

The dress I'd worn earlier was hanging in my wardrobe beside a few similar ones, but I recognized it by the years-old stain on the bottom. I put my hand in the pocket and grasped the round, smooth object, then hurried to surprise my parents.

They sat on the lumpy sofa in the main room, their heads bent together as they spoke in low voices.

I moved toward them, clutching the pearl and thinking of how I'd share my good news. But the words died on my tongue as I overheard snatches of their conversation.

". . . savings are gone. And Grayse will need new clothes soon. We can't ask Mally to spend more hours at the market," Mam said.

"Or Liss to wash more dishes at Katleen's. Her hands look too much like mine already," Da grunted. "But I tell you, something's scaring all the damned fish away. I'm not catching half what I used to, nor are the other lads."

I lingered in the shadows, hardly daring to breathe.

"What about Bridey?" Mam said suddenly.

"What about her? She's only fifteen, Mureal. It wouldn't be—"

"Bridey's almost seventeen. Liss is fifteen. And Liss has been working since the summer."

I stared at the floor, ashamed for the second time today. *Was I so useless?* At least I had the pearl. I uncurled my fingers, eager to be reassured by the pearl's swirl of colors, and gasped.

An unremarkable stone rested in my hand, bumpy, dark, and dirty.

I rushed back to our room to search the pockets of my other dresses.

Nothing. The pearl must have fallen out during my adventure with Cat and Lugh. But wouldn't one of us have noticed such a beautiful thing rolling away?

When I returned to the main room, Mam and Da were still talking. This time, I cleared my throat to announce my presence. They flinched and scooted apart. Sighing, I perched on the edge of the armchair.

"I overheard you." I let them feel the full weight of my stare before I continued. "I'd be glad to find work."

"Really?" Mam smiled, but shadows rimmed her eyes. Perhaps she'd had one of her headaches today. They always accompanied the dreams that inspired her paintings, and sure enough, a new canvas lay glistening on her easel. It was one of her most unusual paintings yet, of what looked like a black horse with deep blue eyes and a dolphin's tail, swimming beneath an unsuspecting boat. It wasn't the shape of the creature that made it seem so unusual, though. What struck me as odd was that its eyes seemed somehow *human*, full of an intelligence I'd never seen a horse or dolphin possess.

Recalling the eerie image, I shuddered.

"If you're sure about this, Bridey"—Mam's voice drew me back to the present as she rubbed her temple and exchanged a glance with Da—"I know just the thing."

"I'm sure." I tried to return her smile, but my lips only twitched. "It's past time for me to start contributing to the family."

Unlike the pearl from Da's net, that wasn't an empty, glittering promise.

Chapter Three

Bathed in the early morning gloom of the front hallway, Liss and I shivered as we donned our thickest cloaks. The howling wind that had woken me around sunup showed no sign of relenting. Sighing, I turned up the high collar of my cloak, grateful that whoever had sewn it knew the island's fickle weather well.

"Here, bird. Take this." Mam offered me a scarf, but I merely glared.

"Isn't there somewhere else I could work? I could chop wood for Ms. Katleen at the tavern, or . . ." I shrugged, at a loss for ideas.

Jobs were as scarce as fish lately. At least for a girl who wouldn't go near the sea.

Mam rubbed her temples. "This is the only position I could arrange for you on such short notice. And Morag Maddrell is a sweet, harmless old dear. You'll be a great help to her, assisting with errands and tidying her cottage." Mam frowned when I pressed my lips together. "You'll want to walk quickly in this weather, as she lives above—"

"I know where she lives!" My throat stung. I hadn't meant to shout, but every child in Port Coire grew up hearing of Morag's strangeness. And everyone feared the witch's house. It sat on a big hill at the far end of town, crouched deep in the woods like a barnacle clinging to driftwood. Liss and I used to dare each other to see who would venture closest without shrieking and running away. Even now, with my most practical sister by my side, I dreaded the thought of going there.

Mam pressed the scarf into my hands and, for a moment, I wanted to shout again.

Instead, I took a deep breath and let it out through my nose. The promise I'd made to my parents just two nights before echoed in my thoughts. Work meant more food on our table, and with the sea's bounty evading the nets of Da and the other fishermen, my family needed me.

"Let's go." I exchanged a grim smile with Liss, then put a hand on the doorknob and glanced at Mam. "You'll be rotten with guilt when we never come home because Morag decided to use our bones in a spell like she did with Nessa Daley."

"You watch your tongue!" Mam's face was ashen. "I can't imagine a killer among us, least of all Morag. Now, off with you!"

I stepped outside, Liss at my heels. Since the mysterious girl had washed ashore, my life bore a strong resemblance to Da's fishing—it had taken a turn for the worse.

Liss was silent as we climbed the steep path to the witch's cottage. The trees lining the way had grown so that their branches had intertwined, creating a shady canopy that blocked the cold sea breeze.

This chill weather always reminded me of Grandad. He said it made him feel more alive. He was always trying to convince us to take walks with him on mornings like this one, sometimes to look for seashells, other times just to talk.

I shook my head to clear it. Every once in a while, something still made me miss him.

A few more steps brought us within sight of a rotting cottage huddled in the woods. It reminded me of a scab I'd had once, a giant black blemish on my knee that I had taken great pains to peel off.

I glanced at Liss, and hesitated. "I'm not sure I can go through with this." I didn't know how Liss could, either. But the moment she'd learned where I was to work, she had insisted on seeing me safely inside.

She smiled thinly now. "We're not children anymore, Bry. We can't let some mean old witch frighten us." With that, she marched up to the cottage and rapped on the door.

"Jus' a moment!" barked a woman's scratchy voice.

Liss stumbled over a fallen branch in her haste to back away but quickly regained her balance. The leaf-filtered light made her face appear greener than usual. Or perhaps she was more nervous than she cared to let on. She joined me by a copse of ashes, eyeing the small knife I had pulled from my pocket. The blade's edge dripped with sap from the nearest tree.

"Want some?" I licked my sticky thumb. Grandad had told me more than once that eating ash sap was the best protection against witchcraft.

Liss swiped her index finger along Da's knife and sniffed the clear liquid. "It smells stale."

"Just try it."

She touched her tongue to her sap-covered fingertip. "Strange!" She grinned. The unexpected blend of earth and sugar was enough to put a smile on anyone's face.

"And what spell is it you two need protecting from? Perhaps I can help."

We froze at the sound of the rough voice. Through lowered eyes, I glimpsed a foot dragging along the ground as Morag shuffled closer.

"Nothing." My hands trembled as I clutched the knife, unsure whether I should try to hide the blade. "We can look after ourselves, thank you very much."

"I see."

Liss edged toward the trees, but my fear evaporated, replaced by a hot, prickling annoyance. I drew myself up and looked into the face of Port Coire's resident witch for the first time.

I'd expected her leathery, age-spotted skin; her hunched posture causing her to stand only as high as my shoulder; her baggy dress, sewn from old flour sacks, and feet filthier than mine. But her intense blue-green eyes startled me, and I staggered back.

Morag advanced on me and I finally noticed her scent—a mixture of salt and seaweed. She continued to scrutinize me with her sea-foam eyes.

Perhaps this was what Pastor Quillin meant when he said in his sermons that we should "search our souls" more often. Perhaps the witch could see mine, and she was trying to form an opinion on it.

Her eyes narrowed. I stared back, wishing I could sink into the ground and disappear. Morag came so close, she had to tilt her chin up to keep looking at my face. Only the basket she carried created any space between us.

She shifted her eyes to the right where Liss was cowering behind a tree, before settling her gaze on me. "You must be Mureal's girls. You frown like her—with your head tilted slightly to the left." Her breath reeked of whiskey, like Da's did on the rare night once or twice a year when he got to visit the tavern with his friends.

The smell made my stomach flip. "Aye, we're her daughters."

"Well then, welcome to my home." Morag's lips cracked open to reveal a mouth full of crooked, grayish teeth. She lifted her basket higher and twitched back the cloth covering.

I retreated farther. I didn't want to see whatever was inside.

"Biscuit?" Morag chirped. She reached into the basket and pulled out a lumpy, black-bottomed piece of bread that didn't look remotely like my favorite dessert.

"I . . ." My mind raced for a way to decline her offer without causing offense. "Thank you, but I have a dreadful stomach-ache." It wasn't a lie.

The witch's smile widened. "There's ginger jam in the house. That should settle your stomach. Now come in, come in." She hobbled partway to her cottage, pausing to look over her shoulder at the trees. "You too, shy one."

A noise between a sigh and a whimper issued from behind a nearby tree and Liss reappeared. "Why did she bother carrying the biscuits out of her house?" she whispered.

"I don't know. Better not to dwell on it. And I'd not ask her, if I were you." I studied the two long braids trailing down Morag's back, so like Liss's, though the witch's were the color of tarnished silver and not done up nearly as neatly.

Morag opened her door, which squealed like its hinges had never been oiled, and soon the cottage's dim interior cloaked her in shadows. She dropped her basket behind her to keep the door ajar.

"You'd think if she's lived here for a few hundred years, she'd have hired someone to spruce up the place before now," Liss muttered, squinting at a rotten spot in the floorboards. Saplings and vines sprouted from the eaves. "The inside is bound to be worse, but I suppose we'd best go in."

With a lump in my throat, I entered the cottage, silently repeating my promise to Mam and Da. Liss followed on my heels, shutting the door once she had crossed the threshold.

I wished she hadn't. A dwindling fire provided the only light in the one-room dwelling. Thick curtains covered the cottage's only windows.

I leaned against the door at my back and groped with one hand until my fingers brushed the knob, which I held for extra security. If things turned too unpleasant, Liss and I could flee anytime we wanted.

Morag puttered in a corner to my left. Plates clinked as she took them down from a shelf.

"Oooh, *what* is that?" Liss dug her fingers into my arm as a musty, sour smell assaulted our noses.

I was amazed I hadn't noticed it sooner. Perhaps the offending scent belonged to the witch, though she hadn't smelled this awful outside. Maybe it was just the reek of decades of clutter.

Whatever the stench's source, I would rather have dunked my head in a bucket of week-old fish than stand there for another moment breathing it in. "May we open the windows?" I asked in the dulcet tone that usually earned me an extra scone at Mrs. Kissack's.

Morag sniggered as she flung plates carelessly onto her hulking monstrosity of a table. "You're my new caretaker, aren't you? Or is it the shy one?"

Liss huffed.

I gripped the doorknob tighter and tried to make out Morag's features in spite of the deep shadows. By the time my eyes adjusted to the low light, the witch had turned away.

"I am. I'm Bridey. But you didn't—"

"If you think the windows need to be opened, then open them, Apprentice Bridey." Morag limped toward the hearth where a kettle hung over glowing embers.

I glanced at Liss, who nodded encouragingly, then I moved slowly through the room. The ruddy firelight made the witch's furniture seem more menacing than ordinary objects should. I passed a large table on my left, a cabinet on my right, and banged my shin on a stool. Bits of dried herbs and straw stuck to my feet, marking one of the rare occasions on which I wished everyone on the Isle—myself included—wore shoes every day.

"I thought she'd have more dead things hanging about," Liss whispered.

I yelped, shoving her away without thinking, and she staggered back and bumped the table with her hip.

"What was that for?" Liss narrowed her eyes, rubbing her side.

"You scared me." I glanced at Morag. She was focused on coaxing the fire to burn brighter and hadn't appeared to hear the noise. "You know, now that we've seen her, I don't think she's a day over eighty. And if she has any spell books in here, they're lost under all this other junk."

Liss chuckled, but kept her wide-eyed stare.

"Will you help me with the windows?" My eyes watered as the house's putrid smell grew stronger.

"As long as you don't push me again." Liss frowned. "But then I'll have to be on my way. Ms. Katleen is expecting me before the lunch crowd."

Those were the words I'd been dreading, though I couldn't blame Liss for wanting to escape.

The flimsy shutters opened at my slight touch, but the motion sent a cloud of debris into my face. I leaned out the window, coughing, and gulped clean forest air until the tightness in my chest eased.

"Splendid!" Liss smiled as she admired her work on the other window. Somehow, she'd found the means to tie back the curtains on her side. The curtains nearest me hung in tatters, raising puffs of dust as they shifted in a breeze.

"Maybe we should swap jobs."

"Not a chance, dear sister." Liss pecked my cheek. "See you tonight." She walked calmly to the door.

"Leaving already?" Morag asked without looking up.

Liss paused in the doorway, silhouetted by daylight. "I'm afraid so. I have duties to attend in town. Good day." I wished she'd added: *and I'll cut out your tongue if you attempt a single spell on my sister.*

My stomach sank as I watched Liss go. So far, the old woman didn't seem as forbidding as the rumors claimed, but what if her demeanor changed now that we were alone? I stood stiffly, hands at my sides, wondering what Morag wished me to do first. I didn't have long to wait.

A rhythmic thumping accompanied the witch as she made her way from the hearth to the table holding a kettle. "Come pour our tea, lass."

I opened my mouth to ask whether she'd seen Nessa Daley recently, then closed it. Morag would probably just laugh creakily. Although her cottage smelled like death, with so much rubbish, there was little room left to conceal a body. Maybe Nessa really had run away to make a life for herself in Peel with a handsome tailor.

Sighing, I lifted the kettle.

"You're strong," Morag muttered, pinching my arm. I jerked away. "How'd you get muscles like that? Your sister didn't look capable of lifting so much as a chair."

I arched my brows, rubbing my arm. "I chop a lot of firewood for my mam. Da's almost always at sea, and my sister Mally's never been up for the task."

"You'll make a good apprentice, then." Morag slouched in a seat and pushed two mugs toward me. I wondered if they held moths and spiders. "I doubt I'd find many other girls in town chopping wood."

"I don't mind. It always helps clear my head." I peered into the mugs, surprised to find them spotless. "Do you take sugar?" Remembering my surroundings, I amended, "Do you *have* sugar?"

"I like my tea plain and piping hot, lass."

I served the witch's brew and, after seeing her glance more than once at the second mug, filled it, too. Taking the only other chair at the table, I stared into my murky tea, remembering the sight of the drowned girl and the black fin under the harbor dock.

Finally, the witch set her tea down and blinked. "Are you afraid of tea?"

I wanted to ask how she thought I'd be comfortable having tea with her after seeing the state of her kitchen. Instead, I replied, "No ma'am. But I'm not here for tea. I'm here to work."

She acted as though she hadn't heard. "This particular blend is birch bark and chamomile. It'll make your pretty hair grow longer."

I looked from my mug to the witch. "How lovely. But—"

"Tell me, were you born under a full moon?"

"I have no idea."

"I'd wager you were. It's the only explanation for hair as light as yours. Someone must have told you how unusual it is. I've seen it just once before, on your . . ." Morag blinked as though she'd surprised herself. "Well, never mind."

I pressed my lips together and tugged on a strand of hair tickling my cheek. No one commented on my white-blonde hair anymore. To me, it was dull and unremarkable unless the light struck it just the right way, and then my hair would glow with a tender pink sheen, like the inside of a seashell.

"What will I be doing here?" I asked. "Weeding your garden? Dusting your—er—everything? Scrubbing your cauldron?"

Morag smiled. "Scrubbing what?"

"Your cauldron. Witches have cauldrons, don't they?"

"Oh, I don't need a cauldron to work my magic." Her thin lips twitched. "However, all spells require quality ingredients to work. That's why I need you."

"Pardon?" Looking into her vivid eyes made my head spin.

"Your mam told me you know the woods well. That'll prove useful, but I'll also need you to go to the beach on occasion. There's treasure to be plucked from the flotsam."

My hands clenched around my mug. Mam hadn't mentioned anything about the beach when she'd described the apprenticeship. "I won't go to the beach. I'll do everything else you ask—I'll even scrub your outhouse, if you ask it of me—but I can't go near the sea."

"You're my apprentice," Morag snapped. "You'll go whether you like it or not."

I lifted my gaze from the table to glare at her. "What do you mean, *whether I like it or not?*"

"It means exactly what you think it does, lass. Ye ken?" Her accent thickened as anger warmed her voice, and she matched my glare with a scowl that made the lines on her face deepen. "There're things I need down there. Important things."

I gripped the table's edge, silently cursing Mam for apprenticing me to a witch. "Why not go yourself, then?"

Morag thrust her weak leg out from under the table. "I'd fall down the cliffs, never to be seen again." Perhaps she sensed that I didn't think this would be such a great tragedy. She narrowed her eyes. "Besides, I don't like being near the water if I can help it."

"Why not?"

"I don't like the sea. I respect it, mind, but I don't like it."

"Why not?" I repeated, watching anger and frustration at war on Morag's face. And for a moment, as she mutely shook her head, I thought I saw a tremor rush through her.

"Well, I'm sorry, but I won't go to the beach. I don't like it, either." I crossed my arms. "I can clean or garden or fetch your bread and milk. I'll find you herbs in the woods. I know at least fifty different kinds of flowers, and I can learn more. But it's not safe to be near the water right now. A girl drowned just this week, and another's disappeared."

A shadow crossed Morag's face, reminding me of Mrs. Gill's expression after seeing the dead girl.

I leaned across the table, hoping she wouldn't put a curse on me over a simple question. "Do you know how that girl drowned?"

Morag gave me a look. "She must've gotten too much water in her lungs, mustn't she? Now, if you want to see any of my coin, you'll do as I ask. No trips to the beach, no pay."

I gritted my teeth and nodded, resigning myself to my fate. I imagined being found face-down in the sand like that stranger, and cold broke over me.

"I won't send you there without protection," Morag added curtly, her gaze still sharp. "Now drink your tea."

I lifted the mug and feigned a sip. "*Please* tell me what you need me to do today, so I might begin." I'd already wasted half the morning pretending to drink tea, when I could've been visiting Cat at the bakery or playing puppets with Grayse.

Morag slid off her chair and moved toward a tall, narrow cupboard. "You know, it might not be so bad for you here, if you've an open mind." She paused, turning to me. "Your mam liked working for me well enough."

I slammed my mug down. "Mam worked here? And she—liked it?"

"Indeed. She used to help me, back when she was about your age. Still does, on occasion." Morag returned to the table, holding a pole with straw sloppily fixed to one end.

"What's that?"

"A broom. I trust you've seen one before. And somewhere in this death trap, there's a dustpan to accompany it. Since you're so eager to get to work . . ." She snapped her fingers, looking pleased with herself. "Hop to it!"

I jumped off my chair and grabbed the broom. If Mam had done this, so could I. Liss worked. I just needed to decide where to start. The layer of crumbs around the table seemed as good a place as any.

While I swept, Morag wandered off again, presumably in search of the elusive dustpan.

"*Shoh slaynt*," I said to the witch's back in a mock salute. *To your health.*

CHAPTER *four*

"Tell me about the witch." Lugh sounded out of breath, weighed down by the produce our mams had charged us with fetching from the market. "I still can't believe your mam sent you up there yesterday. And that you didn't tell me you were going!"

I frowned over the top of the egg custard Mrs. Kissack had given me in exchange for one of Mam's recipes. The custard wobbled ominously with each step. "Is this how you thank me for keeping you out of harm's way, Lugh Doughtery? I thought setting foot on her property might get me killed by one of her spells—no sense in both of us dying."

"I would've protected you."

"And, pray, how? Anyway, she's just a tetchy old lady who lives in a filthy hovel. If she knows any magic, she'll never share it with me."

I thought of the sneering faces of the older lads who'd first told us stories about Morag. "If you want to do me a favor, hit Jenken Cowell about a bit for telling us she drinks children's blood. And blacken Homlyn Murray's eye for saying she flies over our houses at night to peer at us while we're in bed. And—"

Lugh laughed, which made his face look even more hand-some. "You've made your point, Bry. Then she's not a real witch?"

"No more than you or I. Her house smells something dreadful, but she didn't have a cauldron, and she doesn't seem keen on hurting me." I scrunched up my nose. My arms were sore from yesterday's work. "Though cleaning her house might finish me off."

"Folk might not think such wild things about her if she would just pop into town now and then."

"She can't. Her leg's bad." Lugh gave me a curious look. "She didn't tell me why. And I don't plan on asking."

"Sounds like you're intending on going back, then."

"Tomorrow. Besides, if I put in enough hours, I might be able to save enough for a ticket someday."

Lugh bowed his head, but I didn't miss his wince. "Do you know where you'd go? Where you'd sleep? What sort of work you'd do to feed yourself?"

"I'd rent a room above a London shop. Maybe even a coffeehouse. Can you picture it? Me, a shopgirl?" I tried to keep the excitement from my voice for fear of offending Lugh. "Imagine—hot tea and biscuits whenever I wanted! And I'd find a library where I could read as many books as I pleased. It wouldn't be an easy life, I'm certain, but it would be all my own. And far from the sea."

Lugh frowned harder. "You've really thought this through. Is it so miserable here?"

I sighed.

"Let's see: it's too salty, too damp, too cold, too—"

"Full of people who care about you?" Lugh stopped without warning, nearly losing his grip on a basket of potatoes. He shifted it higher in his arms and signaled for us to continue on. "What about your family? Your friends? Everything you know is here."

"There are plenty of folk I'd miss. Some especially so." I gave him a pointed look. "I hope they'd miss me just as much, and that they'd come to visit often. It's not as if I plan to move to China. Or the moon."

The corners of Lugh's mouth twitched, but he said nothing more.

As we rounded a bend, I raised my eyes to avoid the sight of the rolling waves. One glance at the steely sky told me the ocean would be equally dark. Closely guarding its secrets. And though I hadn't seen the black fin since that day in the harbor, I had a gnawing suspicion the creature was making itself at home here. A creature that size might be responsible for scaring away fish from our shores.

"Bry? Are you all right? You're staring at that custard like you want to hurl it into the trees."

I turned my head to hide my burning face. "I'm fine. I was just thinking about—" I paused, casting around for a topic other than mysterious water-dwellers. "—Da's knife. I borrowed it to take to Morag's and brought it home covered in sap. He said the blade's ruined. But you know Da. He's never harsh. He just told me we'd save up for a new one when there're more fish in his nets again."

Lugh grinned. "Wish my da was more like yours."

"What're you going on about? Your da's always been kind. Quiet, I suppose. At least folk don't whisper behind your back about how he's too soft."

"I just meant he expects a lot of me—being his only son and all. And, anyway, no one wags their tongues about you. Not that I've heard. Your da gives you girls so much freedom, I think the others, they envy you, even if they don't realize it."

"Really? They envy Mally's trysts and my prowling the woods?"

I doubted Da would mind if responsible Liss was more like Mally and me. Mam, on the other hand, would have minded our antics a great deal more if her headaches didn't so often confine her to her room.

By the time Lugh and I reached the row of proud stone homes that hid our older, shabbier cottages from view, the gray day was being replaced by a breezy, indigo night.

"Thank you for accompanying me today." I debated quickening my pace, longing to free my hands of the bothersome custard, while wanting to spend more time at Lugh's side.

"Anytime." Lugh flashed a smile, then looked from the road to the grassy slope on our left. "I know it's late, but how do you feel about taking a not-so-shortcut?"

We ambled toward home by way of the slope, navigating a swath of wildflowers and reedy grasses. I kept my eyes trained on the ground as I trampled weeds, still aware of the sigh of the sea.

I tried to distract myself with conversation. "Do you think someone will hear from Nessa Daley soon? Or the dead girl's kin?"

Lugh shrugged. "Mr. Gill and the others have been searching for Nessa for days now. If she didn't run off—"

I shivered and cut in, "If Mr. Gill has put together a search party, he doesn't think she ran off. He thinks—and so do I, for that matter—that some terrible fate's befallen her."

"Or he's trying to remind everyone what a strong leader he is by solving a problem that doesn't exist." Lugh must have noticed me frowning. He hurried to add, "I'm sure she'll turn up eventually. With a babe in her arms and a long apology for her husband. He—"

A deafening *crash* erupted over the water, much louder than the usual meeting of wave and rock. Almost a thunderclap, or what two prows colliding must sound like.

Lugh gave a shout of surprise, dropping baskets as he threw his arm out to create a barrier between me and the sea far below. The crash reverberated in my ears as we spun to face the water. I scanned the ocean for the source of the noise, my lips shaping a hurried prayer that Da wasn't anywhere near this stretch of sea.

"There," Lugh said, pointing straight out from the cliff.

It was difficult to see much in the gathering dusk, but a large area of water had clearly been disturbed. Whitecaps rippled out from the spot where a creature's dark, scaly flesh sank beneath the waves. In a blink, it was gone.

"Did you see that?" I demanded.

"See what, Bry?" Lugh's brow furrowed as he studied the sea. Whatever had made the noise had either disappeared or blended too well with the shadowed, murky water.

"There's nothing out there." Lugh peered into my eyes, concerned. "Someone must have lost his catch."

"I don't think a broken net or a boat running aground would make that much noise." My hands shook as I clutched the custard.

Perhaps Lugh was right. Perhaps I'd imagined the creature. All the recent talk of death and disappearance was stirring up memories of the phantom I thought I'd seen when Grandad had died. The glistening black scales diving back into the deep moments ago had been nothing more than the trick of the cruel sea, just like the misty phantom.

I swallowed hard. "We should be going. Our families will be waiting."

"Thinking about your grandad?" Lugh made no move to pick up his baskets, slipping an arm around my shoulders instead.

Though his chest blocked my view, I couldn't help stealing glances at the sea. I half expected something to leap out of the water, soar up over the cliff, and grab me. "More about what made that sound."

Lugh pulled me closer. "It was just a storm going out to sea. The waves were probably made by dolphins. Everyone's on edge, between the best fishing spots running dry and that poor girl's death."

I set the custard down and leaned into his side. The scent of fresh-baked muffins wafted past. Lugh had visited the bakery with me earlier, and sweetness seemed to find him and cling like a second skin.

"I promise we're safe here, Bry." His fingers brushed my cheek. "You're still so pale."

"I'm fine," I lied, forcing myself to stand taller. "I just . . . realized how much I'll miss you when I move off this miserable rock." The moment I said it, I was struck by how true it was.

He dipped his head, drawing so close our lips almost touched. "Then don't go. No one's making you leave. And maybe"—his breathing quickened, and his heart thudded in his chest so hard it was drumming against mine—"maybe there are things worth staying for."

Then his mouth was on mine, hot, damp, salty. His chapped lip grazed my soft one, making me shiver, and I clasped my shaking hands behind his neck to keep him where I wanted him. Tangled up with me.

When we finally broke apart, Lugh was grinning. A moment later, when I caught my breath, so was I.

Then my gaze traveled back to the black water stretching toward the horizon, and my happiness ebbed away like the waves.

"We really should make sure everyone's all right."

I repeated Lugh's explanation about the crash to myself as we walked, but though his words should have reassured me, they only unsettled me further.

"Come on, Bry. You made it this far. You can't give up now!" Lugh called. He was standing on the beach under a cloudless sky, hands on his hips, feet buried in the white sand.

Despite catching a glimpse of something odd in the water the night before, despite my vow to Morag that I wouldn't set foot on the beach, Cat had persuaded me to accompany her and Lugh on their trip to the sands. They thought—and I reluctantly agreed—that it was the best place to search for whatever had made the crashing sound. Evidently, the strange noise had been so loud that many in town had heard it through their windows, and I wasn't going to sleep again until I proved to myself that it wasn't anything more than a wrecked ship.

"Just a few more steps and you're there," Cat said through gritted teeth, tugging on my hands.

I dug my heels into the soft dirt. "I'll watch from here. Besides, if something walks out of the water and grabs you, someone will need to run for help."

"Bri-dey." Cat puffed out her lower lip and exhaled. "Even if we don't find anything . . ." She paused, turning to the ocean, and then back to me. "I know you're curious. You want to find what that noise was as much as we do."

45

"Nothing's going to hurt you," Lugh added. "Not with us right beside you." He stretched his arms, beckoning me forward while Cat pulled again on my hands.

"Come *on*," Cat urged. "Nothing interesting *ever* happens in Port Coire. Ever. And now the one time something mysterious happens, you'd rather be home doing chores."

She had a point. Washing clothes for Mam sounded much more appealing than going anywhere near the treacherous sea.

But if there was even the slightest hint of danger here, I needed to expose it. I couldn't let my sisters wind up like the drowned girl or wake to find they'd vanished in the night like Nessa Daley. Mally, Liss, and Grayse were more precious to me than the largest pearl, than the heaps of gold rumored to be buried with sunken ships off the coast.

Taking a deep breath, I stepped onto the sand; the grains beneath my feet sent a ripple of shock through me. My friends clapped and cheered as I tried to stop my knees from knocking together. I lowered my gaze, hoping Cat wouldn't see me blush as we approached Lugh.

"Here we are," he said, drawing me from my thoughts as he placed a warm hand on my shoulder. He didn't seem to notice my frown. "Let's start the hunt!"

"For what?" I didn't want to pick my way between tide pools. With my luck, I'd fall in. No, I needed to stay as far from the water as possible.

"Just look for anything unusual," Cat suggested. She danced around me as she spoke, kicking up sand. "Where's your sense of adventure, Bry?"

I frowned harder. "Back on solid ground."

The mirth left Cat's face. "This is important, though," she said softly. "What if the sound we heard last night was someone's boat hitting the rocks? There could be another body, or someone too injured to shout for help."

"You're right." I grabbed Cat's hand, thinking of the mysterious girl's wet hair spread across the sand, and then of my sisters. But not even Cat's closeness could stop my legs from turning into jelly as we walked.

"I ran into Eveleen Kinry, from the tailor's shop, on my way to the bakery earlier," Cat murmured. "She insists it was a shipwreck. But she looked so troubled, I'm not sure she believed it herself. Some people think it was whales fighting."

"Mmm." I glanced over my shoulder. Lugh was crouching in a damp patch of sand, combing through a bed of shells. Not even his kisses could convince me to get that close to the water. "Maybe Eveleen saw something we didn't. Shame you didn't ask her what she really thinks it was."

"Nothing good, I'm certain." Cat knelt beside a large boulder. "Maybe there's blood on one of these." She narrowed her eyes, as if closer scrutiny would reveal a crimson river running down the stone. Then she glanced at me expectantly.

I crossed my arms. "Oh, no. I am not crawling around the rocks looking for bloodstains. Not even for you."

Dipping her hand in a tide pool, Cat murmured, "You'd think by now Mr. Gill would have—"

Lugh shouted, and we turned toward him.

"Found something?" Cat asked.

But it wasn't a cry of triumph. I ran down to the waterline, trying to ignore the fist that clenched around my lungs every time I caught sight of the crashing waves, leaving Cat to scramble after me.

Lugh sat just shy of the water, his face contorted as he clutched his right foot.

"What happened?" I demanded, dropping to my knees beside him. He groaned.

Pushing my hair out of my eyes, I peered at the sole of his foot. A large white shard, probably a shell fragment, was embedded deep in the center. I wasn't sure I could tug it free, but someone had to try. With a mostly steady hand, I reached for the giant splinter.

"Wh-what are you doing?" All color had left Lugh's face.

"Just taking a closer look," I answered. "I'll be quick." He nodded, and I yanked the shard of shell from his foot. It dropped into the sand as Lugh hissed and jerked away.

"Dammit, Bry! That stung." He craned his neck to inspect the blood oozing thickly from his sole, then met my eyes. "But thank you."

I started ripping a piece off the bottom of my skirt for him to use as a bandage.

"Don't ruin your—"

"This skirt's destined for the rubbish heap anyway. I wore it to Morag's." I handed him the scrap of fabric.

"What got you, Lugh?" Cat rushed toward us, frowning.

"Not sure. Piece of glass, maybe, or . . ." He trailed off as he scoured the area for the splinter. It was easy to find, smeared with red. "Looks like a shark's tooth, a big one." He rolled it between his fingers. "What do you think, Bry?"

The stained ivory sliver did resemble a tooth more than a shell, but it was straight as a sewing needle and unlike any shark tooth I'd ever seen. My stomach clenched as I wondered what sort of animal had such teeth.

"We should go before one of us steps on something worse." I climbed to my feet and offered Lugh a hand. "There's no sign of a shipwreck here, anyway." I remembered the dark scales I'd seen immediately after the crash—*because there wasn't one.* "We aren't going to find any trace of Nessa Daley here, either. Mr. Gill and the others have searched this beach over a hundred times already."

Lugh frowned and tossed the splinter into the waves. "You're right. But not because Nessa drowned. She's in Peel, and all this worry will blow over shortly."

As we hurried from the beach, Lugh limping and leaning on Cat and me for support, my thoughts turned to the ivory splinter. Whether it was a tooth or a claw or part of a shell, I was certain of a few things: there was something sinister happening in Port Coire, and no one—not Cat or Lugh or even love for my sisters—could force me onto that beach again.

CHAPTER FIVE

My foot slid out from under me as the pebble-strewn earth gave way. I flailed my arms, clawing at the air. The large tin pail I'd brought sailed out of my hands and bounced down the path to the beach.

I landed on my backside, staring up at the brilliant morning sky. "Stupid Morag." I wanted the satisfaction of cursing her while she couldn't hear it. "Stupid beach." I brushed dirt off my cloak and skirt. "Stupid eels."

I couldn't afford to lose the bucket. I refused to carry two dozen slimy snigs across town in my dress pockets. Trudging down the path between the cliffs, I took great care with each step. To my relief, the bucket had only tumbled a short distance.

The ocean flashed and sparkled under the sun in welcome, putting on a show for the girl on the island least likely to appreciate it. My bare feet met the mushy sand, making me cringe, and I picked my way around tide pools in search of the snigs.

If only Lugh and Cat could see me now.

As I walked along the shore, I fingered the horrible charm Morag had given me that morning.

"The throat bone of a Bollan wrasse," she'd said gruffly, putting the pendant around my neck with oddly trembling hands. "Also known as a Bollan Cross. It'll keep you from drowning." The fishbone vaguely resembled a row of human teeth, but I'd seen wrasses' impressive mouths enough times to know Morag wasn't lying.

If only I had the faintest idea of where to look for snigs, I wouldn't be on the beach long enough to need the bone's protection.

When I was quite small, and unafraid of the water, Grandad had shown me a nest of snigs. The silvery eels were no bigger than his fingers. But their nest had been out in water up to my knobby toddler knees, and there was no way I'd ever walk into the sea of my own free will now.

Inhaling the nausea-inducing scents of brine and stranded shellfish, I hitched up my skirt and knelt shakily beside a deep tide pool. Who knew what was waiting to bite or sting me in there? Still, my conscience demanded I put forth some effort.

I braced myself for the chill water, rolled up my sleeve, and plunged my hand into the pool. A gray-shelled creature about the size of a coin skittered out of reach.

Gasping, I withdrew my hand. What was I thinking, coming here? I was too scared to pick up a wriggling eel. I couldn't even stick my hand in a tide pool for a few seconds.

Rising unsteadily to my feet, I spotted a long piece of drift-wood resting in the sand nearby and grasped it, thinking I might be able to spear a few snigs on its sharper end—even if I lost the contents of my stomach in the process.

Cold sand oozed between my toes as I paced, scanning the area for kittiwakes. The white and gray seabirds preferred to eat snigs, so seeing their feathers would give me hope.

Nothing stirred but the breeze tugging my hair. Even the sun appeared to be a distant spectator, refusing to warm the sea and sky.

I trained my eyes on the ground, searching for anything I could bring to Morag to appease her: a perfect scallop shell, a jumble of sea glass, a smooth lump of lightning-struck sand. I didn't know what might put a smile on her wrinkled face, but gathering flotsam from the beach was worth the gamble for extra coin in my pocket.

A flash of emerald green caught my eye. I tossed my driftwood spear aside and grabbed it, expecting to feel the water-rounded sides of sea glass.

"*Mollaght er!*" I growled as a razor-sharp edge sliced into my thumb. Someone, probably a thoughtless tourist, had smashed a bottle and left it where anyone might stumble on the broken shards.

I wiped my stinging thumb on my cloak. Warm, sticky droplets trickled down my hand, but I'd earned cuts this painful from a tangle of briars plenty of times before. Picking up my driftwood, I scaled a hill of sand that didn't quite pass for a dune and stopped cold.

At the waterline lay a dark-haired young man, naked and horribly still. Despite the distance, there was no mistaking the crimson gashes on his stomach. Waves lapped at his feet as the tide moved in, and I pictured the dribble of water from the dead girl's mouth when the fishermen had turned her over.

This boy could be another victim. Of who or what, I wasn't yet certain.

Heart thumping wildly, I abandoned my pail and driftwood to dash across the sand.

"Please don't be dead," I choked out, sinking to my knees beside him. His fingernails were bloody and ragged, as though he'd fought hard against something. "Please, please, please don't be dead."

The wounds in his stomach weren't bleeding as I'd expected. I ran my thumb between the long gashes. His injuries had been made by something with massive claws or teeth. No Manx cat could make scratches that wide.

One of the boy's arms was draped across his middle, preventing me from fully seeing the worst of his injuries. I cupped his wrist and carefully lifted his arm with an unsteady hand. As I touched the deepest wound, my fingers tingled like someone had pricked them with a sewing needle. I jerked my hand back and swallowed hard to avoid being sick all over him, then flexed my fingers as the tingling subsided, taking deep breaths.

His skin was warm to the touch, perhaps feverish, but his chest rose and fell in a regular rhythm.

Suddenly, he gave a low groan and shifted on the sand.

My frantic heartbeat bolted along at an even faster pace. I imagined him hovering between the blissful ignorance of sleep and the fresh pain waking would bring. Mr. Gill would have to send for a doctor from Peel.

But who was this boy? I studied his angular face, yet nothing about his straight nose or strong jaw reminded me of anyone in town. His curly, dark hair—long enough for small whorls to graze his sharp jaw—could've marked him as the son of any number of Port Coire families. But I was certain he wasn't from these parts. I knew everyone my age in our town and the neighboring villages, and I'd never seen anyone so striking before. I would have remembered.

I glanced at his chest again, eager to reassure myself I hadn't just studied the face of a handsome corpse. After noting the continued cadence of his breath, I stared at his tanned skin and the muscles carved into his arms and chest.

It occurred to me that I should be running back to town for help, but I lingered at his side. Not wanting to see the mess of oozing claw marks again, I skimmed over them and followed the thin line of dark hair trailing down his lower stomach.

Growing up without any brothers, nothing I'd seen or heard before could have prepared me for that moment. I froze, my face blazing like I had a terrible sunburn, startled by the unexpected sight but unable to rip my gaze away.

"Where—where am I?" a rough voice asked in careful English.

I shrieked, scuttling backward across the sand like a nervous crab.

The naked lad looked around the beach, then at me. He tried to rise to sitting, but from the strain on his face, it didn't appear he could manage. He rolled onto his side, pushed up, and collapsed on the sand with a groan.

His dark blue eyes unsettled me. So did the rest of him. Heat crept up my neck, stinging my already hot face. With fumbling fingers, I unhooked the clasp of my cloak and threw it. The cloak landed on his legs, but not high enough to make him decent.

"What is it? Did—are you hurt, too?" He finally sat up, and pulled the cloak to his chest so the cloth covered his wounds . . . and other things. If he'd understood my gesture, maybe the gashes looked worse than they felt.

"*Moghrey m-mie.*" Why had I wished him a good morning when there was clearly nothing good about it?

He regarded me with a mixture of pain and confusion.

"*Shooill marym rish tammylt beg?*" I wished he wouldn't look at me. My face continued to radiate heat.

He kept staring. Either he didn't know Manx, or he didn't speak to half-wild girls.

"Sorry. Can you walk?" I reverted to English with great difficulty. "We should get off the beach. I'll find you a place to rest while someone brings a doctor. You might have a fever. Those cuts look infected."

"I think I'm able." He attempted a smile, but it twisted into a grimace. He glanced between me and the tide as it continued to creep in, then attempted to claw his way up the sand.

My stomach ached in sympathy at the thought of his gashes bleeding again, and I rushed to his side. "Let me help you."

His large, warm hands covered mine. I sank a few inches in the wet sand, knees buckling as he hauled himself off the ground. Somehow, I remained on my feet and he kept the cloak pinned to his body. He draped an arm around my shoulders and swayed.

I grabbed him around the waist to help him balance. And to keep the cloak snugly in place. "I'm Bridey." Warmth again spread across my skin, distracting me—at least mostly—from how near I was to the sea.

The stranger leaned on me as we carefully made our way down the beach, his breathing becoming more labored with each step. Once or twice, the heat of his gaze made my neck prickle. But each time I turned, he appeared to be watching the waves.

"What's your name?" I wanted to keep him alert. If he fainted, I wouldn't be able to carry him by myself.

"I don't know." He sounded more confused than he had earlier.

"Do you have family on the island?"

"What island?"

If I had woken up naked in a strange place, I would want to know immediately where I was. "You're in Port Coire. On the Isle of Man."

"Oh. No, I don't."

"Do you know who—or what—attacked you?"

He gave me a long look, then shook his head.

So much for conversation. Silence returned, heavier than before, as we passed the spot where I'd dropped my pail. I briefly considered claiming it, but another look at the stranger told me not to tarry.

Worrying at my lip, I considered where to take the naked, nameless lad. My first thought was the Gills'. Mr. Gill always knew what to do in a crisis, but Mrs. Gill would faint at the sight of a nude young man.

And then I realized I ought to bring him home. Mally had apprenticed as a midwife for over a year, and she knew how to clean cuts and scrapes. She'd done it for Grayse, Liss, and me countless times. And she'd been treating Mam's headaches as best she could for years.

"I'm going to take you to my house. My sister knows some medicine. She can make you comfortable until a doctor arrives."

He scowled. "No doctor."

It was a relief to hear him speaking. "That will be Mally's decision. I'm not going through the trouble of dragging you off this beach just to watch you die in our parlor."

He arched his brows. "It's my choice." Judging by his wheezing, he was growing weaker. "I said, no doctor."

"We'll see."

It might have been my imagination, but his next hiss of pain sounded more like an angry sigh.

We neared the tide pool in which I'd stuck my hand earlier. The sight of the path winding through the cliffs reminded me of how I'd fallen. "See there?" I pointed ahead. "It'll be a tough go, understand?"

He nodded, looking paler than he had minutes before.

"We can manage if we go slowly. You'll have to trust me, you, ah—you're sure you don't remember your name?"

"No." He must have seen the dismay on my face, as he added, "Call me whatever you'd like."

I shut my eyes. The black fin I'd seen in the harbor swam across my eyelids.

"Fynn." I opened my eyes. "It's all I can think of."

"Fynn," he repeated.

I took this as a sign of approval and guided him toward the path. "When we reach the top, keep my cloak around you as best you can. If we meet someone, you should at least look presentable."

Fynn nodded distractedly.

I tightened my grip on his waist and hoped my feet wouldn't fail me again. "Ready?"

While Mam and Mally tended Fynn's wounds, the rest of my sisters and I were sent to Mrs. Kissack's house, down the lane.

At dusk, Mally came to collect us, looking tired but pleased. I kept pace with her on the brisk walk home, the salty wind lifting our hair and skirts as it changed direction. "Is Fynn going to be all right? Did you send for a doctor?"

"Was he really naked?" Grayse added, eyes sparkling. She'd gleaned her information from Liss, who had eavesdropped from the bedroom when I brought Fynn home.

"Yes. No. And yes." Mally smiled over her shoulder at Grayse. "But he's wearing a pair of Da's trousers now."

"We've tended his fever and treated the infection," she continued. "Now he needs to rest and let his body heal. If anyone can convince him of that." She glanced sideways at me, her lips pursed. "I gave him something to help him sleep. He kept trying to pick off his bandages."

"Did he say what attacked him? Those gashes looked quite nasty." A gust of warm wind buffeted my face, bringing with it a smell worse than the decaying rubbish in Morag's cottage. The wind was suddenly too salty, too sharp, like a freshly gutted fish. I opened my mouth to ask if anyone else had noticed the change, but the odor vanished with my next breath.

"No. He didn't say much. He seemed grateful for what you did. You were brave today, Bry." Mally drew me against her side, our hips bumping together with every step. "You deserve a medal."

I only had to wait a few hours before everyone else turned in for the night. The day's excitement had made us all drowsy, but as soon as Mam's steps traveled down the hall to her bedroom, I slid out from beneath the covers and crept to the main room.

Fynn was asleep on the sofa, his head buried in the cushion as though he couldn't stand his surroundings. Whatever concoction Mally had given him must have been powerful. Da's trousers looked baggy belted around the lad's waist, while my cloak covered his chest and most of his bandaged stomach.

I perched on a bit of cushion near his head, fighting the impulse to wake him. He hadn't seemed too friendly on the walk home, but, then, he'd been hurting. I'd broken my arm rolling down a hill when I was Grayse's age, and I'd howled and raged for hours afterward. Gashes like Fynn's were bound to hurt even more.

I studied his dark curls and the tips of his ears, which were slender and sharper-looking than any I'd seen before. Gently pointed, like the leaves of an ash tree. Part of me wanted him to stay asleep so I could look at him for hours in the quiet, but another part wanted to wake him. To hear his voice again. To feel the unsettling swooping sensation that overtook me every time his eyes met mine.

Finally, here was someone new. Someone who was more than just a tourist, eager for a quick look around the island before taking the next boat to the mainland. Even if he was a tourist before, he was bound to stay a while now.

I wanted to keep vigil at his side, but my eyelids grew heavier by the minute. I didn't bother covering my mouth to hide a huge yawn.

I had only taken a few steps back toward my bed when a rustling made me pause. Fynn was tossing and turning, kicking at the edge of the sofa. I thought a story might soothe his slumber. That always helped when I didn't feel well.

I grabbed the paraffin lamp Mam kept near the door and lifted the glass chimney to light the wick. While I waited for the lamp to warm to full brightness, I carried it to the shelf that held Da's mess of maps.

Beneath crumpled papers documenting his best fishing grounds, a treasure waited: *Non-native Birds of the British Isles*. A tourist had left it on the dock one day, and Lugh had claimed it, wrapping it in white paper and giving it to me on my fourteenth birthday. He thought the gift was clever because of my nickname, Bridey-bird.

I considered it special because it was the only book I owned. The scent of its yellowing pages and the crinkle they made when turned were a constant reminder of why I needed to leave the island.

The lamp flared like a small sun, revealing the corner of *Nonnative Birds*. I picked it up and reclaimed my spot on the sofa, setting the lamp at my feet. If I angled the book toward the light, the words were fuzzy but readable.

I flipped to a random page and began in a low voice, "The Barnacle Goose was first introduced to Great Britain in . . ." I yawned, but Fynn had stopped shifting, so I continued on. "It is dis . . . dis-tin-guished by its white face and black plumage. . . ."

The black-and-white sketch of the goose blurred as my eyes drifted shut. I curled up, clutching the book to my chest, Fynn's hair tickling my feet. Somewhere in the distance—or perhaps on the fringes of the dream world—someone played a tune as soft as a lullaby. A small voice in the back of my mind wondered who would be fiddling at this hour, and urged me toward the nearest window, but sleep claimed me before I could turn thought into action.

CHAPTER SIX

"Bridey Reynylt Corkill!" Mam's sharp voice shattered my dreamless sleep.

Panic coursed through me as I opened my eyes. *Had someone else been attacked? Or disappeared?*

"What is it?" I sat upright, displacing Fynn's head from my lap in the process.

He continued to snore softly, content as a babe. How had he gotten so close without waking me?

Mam loomed over the sofa, an ominous crease between her brows. The paraffin lamp dangled from her hand, its wick charred. One of her feet tapped my book on the floor. "What on earth are you doing? Liss said you never came to bed last night!"

"I was reading to Fynn like you do when I'm sick, and fell asleep." I risked a glance at Fynn, whose eyes were still closed. It was a wonder he could sleep through all this commotion.

Mam's expression softened. "Oh. Of course you were reading, bird."

Her words had an odd lilt to them. Did I seem so innocent it was impossible to imagine me doing anything more with a lad in the wee hours than reading? Finding Fynn yesterday had certainly given me new ideas to contemplate, but I'd considered lads as something to be desired before now. There was Lugh, for one. The lad I hadn't thought of since Fynn's rescue.

Mam interrupted my thoughts. "You should change your dress and be off to Morag's."

Guilt twisted my insides in agreement. Though I wasn't supposed to work today, I ought to go see Morag and explain why I'd never finished my errand. Hopefully, she'd agree that saving a life was a reasonable excuse for not bringing her any snigs.

"And you best—"

"Ask if I can work extra to make up the time." I sighed heavily as Mam turned away.

My gaze traveled to Fynn, who shifted restlessly again. Maybe he'd had a nightmare about his attack. I wanted to reach out to him, to rest my fingers on his arm, perhaps, or to find a cool cloth to place on his forehead. One glance at Mam, though, told me I'd better leave the matter of Fynn's health to her.

Still, I refused to leave without answers. "What'll happen to him?"

Mam frowned. "He's not on death's door, if that's what you're thinking. They're nasty scratches, to be sure, but Mally's salve should keep the infection out."

"No, I mean, where will he stay? What if his wounds heal but he still can't remember who he is?" I didn't like the thought of returning from Morag's to find the sofa bare, and Fynn thrust onto a neighbor with a spare bed and no curious daughters.

Mam smiled and waved a hand dismissively. "He'll stay with us until he's sound in body, mind, and spirit. The Corkills don't turn their backs on anyone in need. And never mind the inconven—"

The front door swung open with a low groan, and Da stumbled inside, his lunch pail and fishing poles in hand.

"Peddyr, you're home early!" A crease formed between Mam's brows as she swept over to kiss his cheek. Da had been away at sea as usual, and we hadn't expected him back until suppertime.

"Something wrong with the boat?" I asked through a yawn.

"It's not that." Da didn't meet my eyes as he answered. "I saw some commotion on the beach, and the fellas and I decided to head in early in case there was trouble. It's not like we were catching much anyway. Danell Gill met us at the harbor."

"And . . . ?" Mam demanded.

Da brushed a hand over his beard. "Eveleen Kinry disappeared last night. Danell said her parents found her bedroom window open. They followed her footsteps to the cliffs, but if she jumped, there's no sign of a body."

Cold prickled along my arms as I thought of Grandad's cliff dive, of Nessa Daley, then of Eveleen. I'd barely known Nessa, but Eveleen had only been a year ahead of me in school—the few years of it I'd attended, anyway, before Mam got pregnant with Grayse and needed me home to help with the housework. Eveleen had skinned her knee outside my house once, and cried all afternoon while my mam held her. And we shared a birthday at the end of summer. She'd been so close to seventeen. Just like me.

"Suppose Eveleen went to join Nessa in Peel?" Mam sank into a chair, her face pale. "Girls get all sorts of wild ideas in their head at Eveleen's and Bridey's age."

"You don't think this has to do with what happened to the girl who drowned?" I glanced between my parents, unable to read their faces through a haze of tears. "You don't think she and Nessa and Eveleen were murdered by a madman or—or something?"

"Heavens, bird! What a thing to say." Mam's hand fluttered to her chest.

"And what about him?" I pointed at the sleeping Fynn. "Being attacked by a creature that tried to shred him to pieces!"

Mam didn't have an answer for me. Nor did Da, who looked bone-weary as he set down his gear and struck through another area on one of his maps. Another area where he couldn't find fish.

From somewhere overhead, a seabird gave a low, mournful call.

It began to drizzle as I reached the edge of the forested hill. Droplets pelted my face and hair, cold enough to freeze my blood, but not enough to numb the ache that had settled in my chest since learning of Eveleen's disappearance. Whatever had befallen her could very well be the same fate shared by Nessa and the waterlogged stranger.

Still, who would believe me if I suggested there was something dreadful in the water? Certainly no one in Port Coire, not the same people who'd refused to believe that something had called Grandad to the sea all those years before. Until I could identify the culprit and gather some sort of proof, I'd have to keep my mouth shut, or risk being called daft and laughed out of town. Or worse, coddled like an invalid by my own family.

Slicking back my hair, I tried to think of anything but the sea. Mam would be tending the fire now, unconcerned that her daughter was outside shivering. After all, she'd still sent me off to Morag's after the shock of the news about Eveleen had begun to fade. I envied my sisters, who could talk to Fynn when he woke. The only conversations I'd have all day would, no doubt, concern tea and witchcraft.

Several long strides later, I approached Morag's door. As I lifted a hand to knock, I tensed, anticipating the now-familiar odor that would hit me like a blow to the stomach. The drizzle became a downpour, and I flung open the door.

"It's Bridey!" The warm, sugary scent of baking mingled with the aroma of wood smoke, making my stomach rumble despite my mood.

Morag stood in her kitchen, a small alcove that lacked a door to separate it from the rest of the one-room dwelling. She gave no indication that she'd heard me, occupied with watching her stove.

"Would you like me to clean your kitchen?" Still, there was no reply. "I know you weren't expecting me today, but I wanted to repay you for the time I missed."

When she still didn't answer, I began my work. Cobwebs were never in short supply at the witch's cottage, it seemed, as if the spiders knew they were more welcome here than in town. I swept her hearth and scrubbed the floor, aired out her linens, and beat dust from her ratty curtains until there was more dirt clinging to me than there was to the cottage.

At last, as I picked up the sodden cloak I'd laid out to dry by the low-burning fire and fastened it around my shoulders, thinking of home, Morag limped toward me. Her expression was as vague as ever in the low light.

"Well?" she rasped.

I blinked. How was I meant to respond?

The silence between us grew. I removed my cloak again, not sure how long the witch planned to keep me standing there, when she said, "The snigs. You obviously didn't find any. So where's my bucket?"

I dropped my gaze to the floor. "I'm sorry. If you'd like, I can buy some snigs. And I'll pay with my earnings. Things took such a strange turn yesterday that I forgot about the time. It won't happen again."

After a moment's pause, I added, "Ma'am." I didn't want to offer her my excuse until I'd had more time to gauge her mood.

Morag narrowed her eyes, but then her face relaxed. "Never mind the snigs. They weren't important." She turned to the stove. "Fetch the kettle. It's nearly time to eat."

Relieved, I grabbed the kettle and poured steaming water into two mugs. "Were the snigs for one of your spells?"

Morag shuffled over, carrying a pan of what looked like cake. "Oh, no." She smiled, displaying all her gray teeth. "I meant to bake a pie. Since you didn't return with my snigs, I made blackberry instead." She offered me the hilt of a large knife. "Seeing as you've made this place spotless, you can take the first slice."

Pie. She had sent me to the beach—aware of my fear—so she could bake a pie? I clenched my teeth while trying to maintain a pleasant expression on my face.

"Go on." Morag waved a hand at my plate. "Try a bite."

My skin prickled with annoyance, though, just now, her expectant air as she held out the pie reminded me a bit of my gran. Grandad's death had undone her, and a fever claimed her just a year after his passing.

I forced a smile and cut a small slice. The witch hadn't attempted to poison me in the past week, so I slipped a forkful of berries past my lips. They burst open, oozing sweetness on my tongue.

"How is it?"

"Quite good." I took another bite. "It'd go well with milk. Or with an explanation of why you sent me to the beach for pie fixings when I'm afraid of the water." Startled by my own daring, I dropped my fork. It hit the table with a clatter.

"You were safe," Morag huffed, reaching for her tea. She glanced at the charm resting against my breastbone. "You still are, long as you keep that on."

"Oh. Right." I'd forgotten the hideous Bollan Cross, the fishbone around my neck. "You're certain you don't want it? Surely, you could put it on, and go to the beach yourself."

Morag pushed my mug across the table until it bumped my elbow. "It's yours. I insist. I'd like my bucket back, though."

I lifted the mug and took a sip of flowery tea. "I know. And I'll replace it, as I've said. I would've done so already, but I was busy saving a boy's life yesterday."

"You saved someone? Pray tell, from what?" Morag glowered at me, but beneath her sharp expression lurked . . . a glimmer of interest. "Tell me the story then, lass. For all I know, you're just making up excuses for not hunting snigs."

"The story?" I frowned into my tea. Perhaps living alone for so long accounted for the witch's abruptness, but she still made me as uncomfortable as wet clothes.

"Tell me how you saved the boy."

"I found him in the shallows while I was looking for snigs. At first, I thought he was dead. Something tore up his middle—a beast with giant claws, perhaps."

Morag's foot smacked against a table leg, making me jump.

"Are you all right?" I started to rise from my seat.

"Yes, yes. It's this old foot." She thumped a hand against her left shin. "Has a mind of its own some days."

Her skirt's hemline revealed a few inches of bare ankle and calf, the skin there scarred, white, and puckered where a wound hadn't healed properly. The deep indents around her ankle reminded me of the tooth-marks left on my forearm when Grayse had bitten me as a toddler, but Morag's looked more severe, as though they'd been made by a knife's tip.

"Have you seen a doctor?"

Morag shifted, pulling her foot from view. "Doubtless your mam's told you: staring's not polite."

I tore my gaze away and straightened in my chair. "I'm sorry. But I could fetch a doctor, if you like. Mally knows one in Peel who's quite gifted. I can't begin to imagine how much that hurts."

"It's not so bad. I make a balm to dull the aches on the worst days." Morag looked down, brushing crumbs off the table. "Now, would you like to head out in this storm to buy me a new bucket, or would you rather finish your tale?"

My face flushed, and I stumbled through an explanation of finding Fynn on the beach.

"And is he a local boy?" Morag's tone suggested she already knew the answer.

I shook my head and speared more berries on my fork, though I wasn't sure I could keep them down. Now that the pie had cooled, the room's foul odor was returning, despite my best efforts at cleaning. Or perhaps the stench was coming from me now.

"It's good of your mam to keep him while he mends." Morag's foot bumped the table again. "He ought to be grateful he's in such fine company. And you ought to be grateful the strangest thing the sea spat out yesterday was a boy in need of a bit of kindness."

"Beg your pardon?" I sat up straighter. Perhaps Morag knew something about the missing girls.

"You heard me. There are more frightening things in the sea than a boy with no memories. When you didn't return yesterday, I thought perhaps you'd encountered a sea ape. Or a *ceasg*. Or a *lusca*."

I blinked, wondering whether Morag was having a laugh at my expense. Her eyes gave away nothing, as usual. "What are those?"

Morag seemed to be attempting a smile, but it looked closer to a grimace. "They're living things, like you or me. A *lusca* is the biggest octopus in the world."

"I thought the biggest octopus was the kraken," I said quietly.

Da had told me the legend of the kraken once, a giant beast that dragged ships into the deep. When I had nightmares about it, he assured me it was pure nonsense, a tale made up by sailors to amuse children, though the ocean seemed vast enough to be hiding such a creature. I hoped whatever was lingering in the waters around Port Coire was something a fisherman could capture or kill.

"No. The kraken is only a story. But there are other creatures in the deep that have never been near land," Morag insisted, drawing me back to the present with her raspy voice. "Just because men haven't seen them doesn't make them any less real."

I faked a giggle, still unsure whether Morag was joking, or if she truly believed. Perhaps she thought she could scare me off with her stories so she might find an apprentice more willing to search the beach.

"I suppose *you've* seen them, though?" I frowned as I tried to read her expression.

"Maybe," she said coyly. "Or I've read about them." She pointed to a book resting on a rickety table. Gold letters, too faded to make out, adorned the book's dark cover. Even in the low light, its frayed pages were distinctly yellowed. "You're welcome to borrow that, if you think it would help you find what attacked your friend."

"I see." My skin prickled. Even with my sisters to protect, I wasn't ready to face whatever fresh nightmares were nestled in those tatty pages, and wasn't sure if I could trust the words inside a witch's book. "I do love reading, but I don't think that book is quite to my taste. It might frighten my sister."

"Your sister? The girl who came here with you? The pretty one?"

The words echoed in my mind, chasing away all thoughts of sea monsters. "She's quite lovely, yes. But I meant—"

"And have *you* ever looked in a mirror?" Morag leveled her gaze at me, but only for a moment.

I opened my mouth, but no words came out. Did she mean that if I used a mirror more often, I might be able to fix my unsightly qualities? My sandy freckles. The slight bend in my nose. My small ears. Or did she mean a mirror would show me how lovely I was? Whatever her intention, I was content with my looks—the good parts and the flaws.

"Would you care to tell me what happened to your leg?" I murmured, putting on a polite smile. Morag deserved a reminder of her own imperfections. Lugh would be proud of me for asking, besides. Still, my eyes darted to the door as the silence between us grew. I was asking for trouble, talking back to a witch.

"An accident. Long time ago," Morag said at last.

"What attacked you?"

"Nothing." She was as curt and gruff as ever.

"But what—"

"When I was a girl, my foot got caught in a hunter's trap. I tried to free it instead of waiting for help."

My irritation vanished. "That must've been terrifying."

When she said nothing more, I helped myself to another slice of pie and considered Morag's story. If she'd been injured as a child, how had she lived all these years alone? How could she afford to pay me or buy flour and milk? My stomach lurched as I guessed the age of the flour she'd used to make today's pie. It would have been from the last time Mam purchased supplies for her and hauled them up here, long before I began my apprenticeship.

"It *was* terrifying," Morag muttered at last. "But I had a good friend who made sure I would be well provided for."

"Who?"

"Your—that's none of your concern." The hard glint in Morag's eyes was enough to persuade me to pry no further. "Now, for your next task, I'll need you to find me some agrimony. Eight or ten stalks should do. They have—"

"Little yellow flowers. I know."

"Good." Morag slowly rose from her seat. "I need a handful of pennyroyal, as well. And mind you, don't eat any."

"I'm not a goat." I didn't want to know why she needed the poisonous plant. "Shall I start looking for it now?"

Morag's eyes widened. "In the rain? No, the herbs can wait for a drier day, and you shouldn't touch them with such filthy hands." She glanced pointedly at the ash under my fingernails from cleaning her hearth. "Go. Spend time with your guest."

The idea of running down the hill to see if Fynn had woken was tempting. But my family needed as much money as I could bring them. "Please, ma'am. I'd be happy to find the herbs today, if you're willing to pay extr—"

"I'm not a ma'am, I'm a Morag. And I was young once too, you know. I realize young people can't work *all* the time." She smiled, but on her, the expression was eerie and sad. "Of course," she snapped in her usual gruff tone, "I was never as clumsy as you. I never lost anyone's bucket."

I pushed my chair away from the table, my shoulders and back throbbing from the work I'd done.

"Go home." Morag shooed me toward the door, a wild gleam in her eye. "While there's still daylight, else the woods might swallow you up and never spit you back out!"

I called a farewell, and she slammed the door shut in answer. At least there was a certain familiarity to the routine developing between us.

A mild breeze greeted me as I left the forest behind. The rain had stopped. And though I skipped down the hill, my thoughts remained with Morag. Until I began calling, she'd been alone in her dark house with only piles of old rubbish for companionship. And, despite her choice to live far removed from the rest of Port Coire, there were rare moments when she struck me as lonely. But did she truly stay out of town because of her leg?

The shadow that sometimes crossed her face made me wonder if she remained in that cottage because she had something to hide behind her gruff words and spooky manner.

As I crossed the market, Lugh caught my eye, beckoning me toward the fountain. "Bridey! Finally!" he called, a grin lighting up his face. "I was starting to think you'd followed Nessa to Peel!"

I slowed my pace but didn't change course.

We'd hardly talked since our wonderful kiss. I'd had too much else occupying my time, but I wanted to try kissing him again soon. Maybe. Had the kiss really been wonderful? Surely if it had, it would have crossed my mind before now.

"There's a rumor you were involved in a daring rescue at the beach yesterday . . ." Lugh flashed me another dazzling smile. "I'd never have believed it! Tell me the tale before Cat gets hold of it and embellishes it with ridiculous detail."

I shook my head. "Not today."

Lugh's face fell slightly. "All right. But I've been thinking of you, Bridey." He gave me a look I couldn't quite read. "Haven't you been—?"

"Of course. All the time," I said, perhaps too quickly. Lugh frowned. "I really can't talk now, but come find me tomorrow, if you'd like, and I'll tell you all about the rescue." I started to smile in apology but must've hesitated a moment too long.

Lugh had already looked away, striking up a conversation with the nearest passers-by: two pretty dark-haired girls around our age.

I lingered at the edge of the market, wanting to explain why I couldn't join him, yet I couldn't put it into words. Something was pulling me toward home, reeling me in like a fish on one of Da's hooks.

CHAPTER SEVEN

After a day spent sorting herbs for Morag and hopelessly scouring the woods for traces of Eveleen and Nessa—Lugh never sought me out—I longed to sit by the hearth. But I hadn't even hung up my cloak when Mally pulled me into the kitchen. "Watch that for me, will you?" She pointed to the glowing stove, where a heavy pot of water was boiling. "I'm cleaning bandages for Fynn."

"Where's everyone else?" The house was quiet, save for Fynn's light snoring.

Mally lifted her dough-covered hands and shrugged. "Da's at sea, of course. Mam took supper to the Gills—they've both come down with a chill—and the girls went with her." She flashed her perfect smile. "It'll be just the two of us tonight. Mam made kippers, but . . ." Grabbing the bowl, she tipped it to reveal the ball of dough within. "I thought biscuits would do a better job of taking our minds off recent events." Her smile flickered.

Nessa Daley had been one of Mally's many friends.

"I knew you were my favorite older sister for a reason, Mal." I walked over to the bowl and swiped a finger in the dough— oatmeal with currants. It had been Grandad's favorite.

Mally leaned close. "I miss him, too." She glanced down at the counter. "I sometimes think that if Liss and Grayse had really gotten to know him, if they'd heard more of his stories like we did, they'd want to see the world with us."

"Remember his tale of traveling through England with a circus, shoveling horse muck for pocket money?"

"Or the time he traveled to Egypt with a shipping company just to see the pyramids?" Mally grinned.

I laughed. "That one wasn't true!"

"No," Mally gasped. "He swore it was! Remember—" She stopped short as the water bubbled over.

I grabbed a spare rag to wipe up the spill. "Have you stopped to think of how much trouble we're going through for a total stranger?"

Mally nodded. "Aye, but that lad out there could've died. His bandages need to be changed as often as we can manage." A familiar gleam entered her eyes. "He's rather handsome when he's not running his mouth, isn't he? If he were a few years older, and I wasn't so serious about Artur, I'd try to find out if he tastes as good as he looks."

"Mal," I groaned. "He could be anyone! He could have ten wives for all we know. Or be an expert thief."

"He's an odd one. I'll grant you that. The first time I tried putting balm on his wounds, he licked it off! Like he thought it was a treat! And he eats with his hands all the time," Mally giggled and tossed her dark gold hair over her shoulder. "But I'm still right, Bry. Admit it. He looks de-li-cious." She emphasized the words by tapping her finger against my nose, leaving traces of dough behind.

It was easy to forget Mally was twenty-one and not sixteen. If only she and I had been born a year apart, we could have planned our escape together.

Mally swept over to the stove. "Will you grab the tongs and pull out the bandages?"

"If I must."

"Don't tell me the witch's apprentice is squeamish over clean bandages." Mally failed to fight back a grin. "Fenella Kewish swore to me that you're learning to pickle toads and carve bat hearts while the rest of us are sweeping and doing the wash. She saw you gathering flowers near the hill today, and she reckons Morag's training you up to be the town's new witch."

Using the tongs, I yanked the bandages from the water and dropped them on a plate.

"Just because I know almost every plant on the Isle doesn't make me any closer to being a witch than Mrs. Gill is." I shrugged. "People here will believe anything. The wilder the tale, the better."

Had the rumors about Morag ever drifted up to her cottage? Did she care? A gossip like Fenella Kewish making up stories about me didn't give me pause, but if the town regarded me the way they did Morag . . . I'd move a lot farther away than up a hill.

Mally glided to the table. "Fenella's also the one who claimed to have spotted me kissing twelve lads last summer." She shook her head. "Some folks' lives are so dull. If they spent more time kissing, and less time worrying about everyone else—"

"You'd never get another moment alone with Artur because you'd be too busy delivering babies." I smirked as I slid into a chair.

"Artur!" Mally smacked a hand to her forehead. "I almost forgot. I promised to meet him tonight!"

"Where? It'll be dark soon."

Mally dabbed her face with a clean rag and combed her fingers through her hair. "That's between him and me." Her voice was light, teasing. "But listen, I need a favor."

79

Favors for Mally usually involved organizing her wardrobe or braiding her hair. Nothing too taxing. "Name it."

"I need you to change Fynn's bandages."

"You can't be serious."

"There are clean ones on the table by the sofa. It's simple enough." Mally whirled to the stove to check on the biscuits. "I'll explain while we eat."

Seeing Fynn naked as the day back on the beach had certainly been educational, but I couldn't change his bandages while he was awake and talking. "Can't it wait till you return, Mal? Please? I'm not skilled at caring for others the way you are. If there's anything else—"

"Just changing the bandages is all." Mally squeezed my shoulder. "You'll do fine. I've been keeping the wounds clean, and they don't smell. Unless . . ." She crouched by my chair, her lips curved with mischief. "You're scared to try."

"Don't be ridiculous!" I scowled at her. "I'm not scared. I'm the one who saved him, remember? I'm sure I'll manage."

When the biscuits came out of the oven, Mally hardly gave them a minute to cool before shoving one in her mouth. "Too hot!" she yelped. Her words were muffled by biscuit crumbs. She flung her apron over the back of a chair and breezed out of the kitchen.

The front door whooshed open and shut, leaving me alone with the ever-present murmur of the sea and Fynn.

The house wasn't often this quiet, and the more I noticed the stillness, the more the skin on the back of my neck prickled. For all I knew, there could be someone or something lingering outside our windows, or in the water far below. A creature with dark scales and fins, waiting for me to be alone so it could drag

me into the sea. Surely that's what it had wanted to do at the
harbor, before I shouted and Da frightened it away.

I didn't intend to give it a second chance. Snatching up the
biscuit pan, I strode into the main room.

Fynn's blue eyes followed my movements. His hair stuck up
in the back from being pressed against the stiff horsehair cushion. And he was shirtless, his chest lightly tanned, leading to a
narrow waist and the outline of bony hips.

He waited until I had placed the biscuits in front of him
before saying, "What's this? You aren't my usual nurse."

"How observant of you." Averting my gaze, I picked up the
fresh bandages, which were right where Mally had said they'd
be. He chuckled, and I fought the urge to join in, gesturing to
the biscuits instead. "Help yourself."

"I've already eaten. Your mother's kippers were excellent."
Fynn tried to push himself upright, but collapsed against the
cushion. "Besides, I'd rather talk to you."

I raised my brows. "Lucky me." Kneeling by the sofa, I took
hold of the bandages. "Don't bother sitting up. I imagine it'll be
easier on both of us for me to change these if you stay just as
you are."

"Thanks, but there's nothing wrong with these bandages."
Fynn peered down his torso. The cloth around his middle was
mostly white, but faint patches of pink showed through where
I remembered the worst of his injuries to be.

"Liar," I murmured.

He groaned. "I miss my usual nurse. *She* doesn't have such a
sour disposition."

I shifted closer for a better look and adopted a stern expression. "You need to follow Mally's instructions, or you'll wind

up a permanent resident on our sofa with wounds that won't close." More pink stained the bandages that disappeared into the waistband of Da's borrowed trousers. "You're quite the sight."

"As are you." Fynn extended a hand. The muscles in his stomach quivered as he strained to reach me. Not wanting him to re-open his ghastly injuries with the effort, I leaned toward him.

"What is it?"

He brushed his thumb across my nose, gentle and unhurried. My heart skipped like I'd just sprinted up the hill to Morag's cottage. "You have flour on your face." His fingers swiped across my cheek in long, slow strokes where Mally had tapped me with her fingers earlier. "Is that a Manx custom, wearing your food?"

Warmth crept into my cheeks. "If you're curious, you'll have to stay around long enough to learn our ways."

"I'm already learning. Just today, I learned how to use a fork."

Unsure if he was joking, I fought the urge to giggle and set aside the clean bandages to search for the salve Mally dabbed around his wounds. "If I were you," I added, turning my head to hide a smile, "I wouldn't tease the lass who's about to dress your wounds—unless you like your bandages wrapped too tightly to take a proper breath."

Fynn cocked his head, dark hair spilling into his eyes. "Should I have let you walk around with flour on your nose, then?"

Salve in hand, I crouched by the sofa again. "Hush. This will go quicker if you don't talk so much."

"But I still haven't thanked you for rescuing me." He rested a hand on my shoulder, and I froze. "It couldn't have been easy hauling me off the beach. You'd have had an easier time carrying a dolphin."

I glanced at the hand on my shoulder. "It was worth the struggle." My palms were slick. "Have you recalled what attacked you yet?"

Fynn's brows rose. "As I told your mother and your sister earlier—no."

"I hope you'll keep trying, though." Without thinking, I'd leaned closer to him. "Before you showed up, a girl drowned. And now two girls from town have gone missing. The littlest detail might help us catch the culprit before it's me or one of my sisters that goes over the cliffs and never comes home."

"I'll try to remember," he said softly. "It's the least I can do." He shivered suddenly from head to toe, but kept talking through his discomfort. "For my brave rescuer."

"Thank you." Blushing furiously, I unscrewed the jar of salve. "I should see to your bandages now, or we'll be at this all night."

"I don't have anywhere else to be."

I started removing his old bandages. Little by little, his wounds were revealed, the flesh around them deathly white from the combination of salve and wrappings. I peeled away the layer just below his waist and hesitated. Should I unfasten his pants to reach the last portion of the wrappings, or slide my hand down his stomach and remove them by feel? If I touched him below the waist, my face would glow brighter than the coals in the hearth.

I rested my hand on the sofa and cleared my throat. "Do you mind if I—?"

His hand suddenly covered mine. The contact made my skin tingle, but not in the way it had when I'd touched his wounds on the beach. This reminded me of the sensation that came with holding Lugh's hand lately.

Lugh, who hadn't come to see me since I'd abandoned him at the market yesterday. We hardly ever went this long without talking.

"I'll get the rest of these," Fynn murmured, drawing my gaze. I gave him a smile of thanks and was surprised by the reddish tint to his face. I lowered my eyes, pretending to study the salve until the last of the bandages dropped to the floor.

"You can look now." Fynn's trousers were buttoned, and he'd crossed his arms behind his head. "Let's have the foul stuff, then."

I arched a brow. "You mean Mally's homemade salve? The balm she spent hours making for you?"

Fynn's eyes shifted guiltily. "Yes, that."

"I understand you tried to eat some of it earlier."

"Won't make that mistake again," he muttered.

"But surely you know what balm is? With or without your memories?"

He didn't answer. He was probably exhausted. With a gentle touch, I smeared salve around his wounds. Mally had used the same mixture on my cuts and scrapes, and time never dulled the memory of its distinct burn.

Fynn sucked in a breath. "That feels about as good as gnawing off my own arm."

"I know." I paused with my fingers in the jar. Perhaps getting him to talk would distract from the sting. "Have you given any more thought to who you are? Where you're from, or your profession?" I considered what little I knew of him. "Maybe you were the captain of a ship, caught unaware by a storm that drowned your crew and destroyed your vessel."

Fynn managed a smile. "Do I look old enough to be a captain?" I shook my head. With the slight shadow on his jaw, he looked a few years older than me at most. "But maybe I worked on boats around the island."

I dipped my fingers in the salve jar again. "I don't think you're a native."

His smile broadened. "Prove it."

"Fine. If you live anywhere on the Isle, you'll be able to tell me this: what's the Manx symbol?"

Fynn barely thought for a moment before shrugging. "No idea. You've made your point."

"It's the Triskelion. It stands for life, death, and rebirth." I traced the symbol's three points in the air. "Hmm." I thought harder and drummed my sticky fingers against the sofa. "Your accent might give me a hint. Say something."

"I'm tired of being on this sofa, and I'd like to go for a walk on the beach." His voice was clear but his words were plain, devoid of the Isle's lilting brogue. I detected no trace of a Scottish burr or the crisp accent of the English.

"You're definitely an American," I declared, unable to suppress a giggle as I offered him my less sticky hand. "And the first one I've met. Tell me, what's it like there? Is there truly land available for anyone who wants a piece?"

He flashed a broad grin as he shook my hand. "That's right, I'm from America. You've solved the mystery. I have a bottomless bank account and fifty servants."

"Fifty!" I laughed as Fynn nodded emphatically.

Still, I didn't like the sound of his labored breathing. I quickly applied the salve to the last of his cuts, sneaking scandalous peeks at him as I worked. His tanned skin suggested he'd spent time in the sun, and his powerful arms could have rigged sails or wrangled cattle anywhere. When he remembered where he belonged, perhaps I could visit him there. That is, if he didn't mind the imposition from a near stranger.

"What about you?" Fynn asked, disrupting the stillness. "There's not much more to say about myself yet, unless you've already devised another life for me outside America." His smile reappeared.

"There's not much to tell." Picking up the clean bandages, I started binding his wounds.

"That can't be true." Fynn waved a hand at the hearth. "Grayse told me you chopped all that firewood. Is that how you earn a living?"

I ran the roll of bandages across his stomach, careful not to wrap them too tightly. "No. I've just started an apprenticeship outside town. It's mostly cleaning, but I need to do my best if I ever want to leave this rock."

"Where would you go?"

I paused to consider the question. "Any place without a sea view. Maybe Dublin. Paris. Boston. I have a second cousin in Kilkenny in Ireland, and I'm told it's miles from the ocean. Perhaps someday I'll see them all."

"I'd like to visit them all, too." Fynn's voice sounded fainter. Perhaps my clumsy nursing had exhausted him. "If it turns out I do have a fortune, I'll buy you a chestnut horse as payment for saving me. You can ride it across America."

I tied off the last section of bandages. "Wouldn't that be grand? My own horse." I joined Fynn on the sofa, my eyes on the scant distance between us. "For someone with no memory, you're quite fascinating."

Fynn's grin shifted to a grimace. "Good to hear. Now if I die of infection, at least I'll go happily. Oh, and Bridey?" He leaned in, radiating warmth. My breath caught in my throat as I inhaled the scent of the herbal salve beneath his bandages.

"What?"

A faint sheen of sweat coated his brow. "I need to lie down."

I blinked, jarred from a vision of him bringing his mouth closer to mine. A boy who I didn't really know. A boy who thought me brave . . .

As I leaped to my feet, the doorknob rattled. Mam, Liss, and Grayse tromped inside. Grayse was toying with the fishbone around her neck. I'd given her Morag's Bollan Cross and she refused to take it off.

I supposed it couldn't hurt. If Morag really was a witch, and that foul charm had any power, Grayse—and all of us, for that matter—would need its protection if anyone or anything wished us harm.

CHAPTER EIGHT

A week later, on a bright June morning, Mam sent me to buy a few skeins of yarn from Ina Cretney, who had almost as many children as her husband owned sheep.

Fynn had been pacing around the house for the past few days, and when I asked if he wanted to accompany me to the market, his eyes lit up. After Mally approved the outing, Fynn and I set off, passing one of Mr. Gill's search parties midway up the road. They roamed the cliffs above the sea constantly as they called Nessa's and Eveleen's names, but their eyes remained on the trees and hills, rather than the water. They'd never find anything that way.

The market at the center of town was a collection of stalls and weathered buildings gathered around a stone fountain of four leaping dolphins. The shops' roofs were ancient, and though their large windows were relatively new, the glass was already caked with grit.

The square was crowded, as it always was on such a fine day. The bustle of so many hats and skirts made my search for a glint of Mrs. Cretney's copper hair a challenge.

"Keep an eye out for a woman with a swarm of children tugging at her skirts," I muttered to Fynn, leading the way past a display of pies. There were few smiles among the shoppers today, even the ones with cakes and sweets in their hands. Even perpetually jolly Mr. Watterson, the cloth merchant, looked grim. Mothers kept their children close, when they were usually content to let them run about the square. Perhaps they were worried about the recent lack of fish. Or they'd finally realized that Nessa and Eveleen hadn't gone to Peel, and they weren't coming back.

"What's that?" Fynn asked with a puzzled look, pointing to a bright ribbon of taffy.

"Candy. Surely you remember candy," I said distractedly, gazing over the head of the child clutching the taffy with sticky fingers. I'd caught a glimpse of vivid red hair, and half hoped we were about to bump into Lugh, but the flash of red had vanished by the time I elbowed my way through the press of shoppers. If it really was him, and he was avoiding me, I could hardly blame him for it.

As we neared the fountain, someone called, "Bridey Reynylt Corkill!" in a perfect imitation of Mam.

I whirled around and met Cat's light brown eyes. Pressing a hand to my chest, I glared. "Don't do that!"

Giggles erupted from the tiny figure beside Cat. Her little sister, Alis, peered at us through a mop of black ringlets, displaying a jack-o'-lantern smile. She was missing more teeth than Grayse, despite being a year younger. In one hand, she clutched half a bonnag. The rest of the crumbly cake was probably in her stomach already.

"Where have you been lately?" Cat asked me, though she was slyly studying Fynn. "You must be the comeover everyone's talking about." She nudged me in the ribs and shot me an impatient glance.

Right. She expected an introduction. "Fynn, this is Catreena Stowell." I nodded to Cat, who grinned. "And her sister, Alis."

"You're from London, right?" Cat extended a hand and tossed her curls over her shoulder. "Came in with the latest boatload of tourists, hit your head, and fell into the water before our Bridey rescued you? That's what Mrs. Kissack's been telling everyone."

I frowned, marveling at how quickly news became gossip around here. I tried to catch Cat's eye as she waited for Fynn to take her hand, but she was watching him with interest. He gazed back at her with something like confusion. Finally, he raised a hand in return. But instead of shaking, he simply pressed his palm against hers, his eyes seeking mine as though hoping for a nod of approval.

"You're supposed to shake." Cat pursed her lips and dropped her hand to her side. "Honestly, they must not teach manners in London anymore!"

"I—I'm sorry." Fynn frowned. "I'm not from London. At least, I don't think I am." He launched into a brief explanation of his rescue, and how he'd lost his memory.

"So, Fynn." Cat beamed at me. "Has Bridey told you she's the best dancer on the island?"

Fynn flashed a grin. "She hadn't mentioned it. Tell me more."

"No, that's quite enough, thank you, Cat." I shook my head but couldn't keep from smiling. "What's happened?" I gestured around the crowded market. "Did a boatload of tourists arrive ahead of schedule? Or is Mrs. Kissack giving away sticky buns?"

"We were about to have a look," Cat answered as Alis attempted to finish her bonnag in one huge bite. "Austeyn Boyd and Brice Nelson say the dry spell in their fishing is over. They've caught some giant crabs."

Alis flung her arms wide, nearly smacking me in the stomach. "They're bigger than horses!"

Cat smiled patiently. "You don't know that. They haven't shown them to anyone yet, silly goose."

I tried to smile at Alis's antics, too, but my insides seemed to have turned to liquid as I tried not to think of what crabs the size of horses would look like.

"You know how Mr. Boyd loves to brag. He's just like his son," Cat continued, oblivious to my discomfort. She meant Thomase Boyd, one of the lads who used to court Mally. "He'll probably wait till the whole town's come out before he shows us the blasted things."

"Mmm." I scanned the crowd for a sight of the monstrous crabs, but to no avail. Instead, as I turned back to my friends, my eyes met Fynn's.

"Bridey." He glanced over his shoulder, then back to me, a faint frown crossing his lips. "Why is that woman glaring at us?"

I peered around. I'd been so set on finding out more about the fishermen and their catch that I hadn't noticed the tall woman quarreling with her two young sons. Her name eluded me, but I knew her face. She always sat in the front pew at church.

"I wanna toss a ha'penny in the fountain!" one boy cried.

"Just one? Please?" his brother added hopefully.

"Not today, boys." The woman paused to glare at us. "Not while *she's* here." She released one of her son's hands and made the sign of the cross in the air.

"Ay!" Cat shouted as the woman made to push through the crowd, then turned abruptly to see who called her. "Is there a reason you're being so rude to my friend?"

The woman drew herself up, frowning. "I don't consort with witches, Catreena Stowell. And neither should you!"

My face burned. The word witch rang in my ears, harsh and unforgiving. It was no wonder Morag avoided coming to town if this was the treatment she could expect to receive.

"You miserable old hag!" Cat called, putting an arm around me. "Bridey's no witch."

Fynn leaned in, his ruddy cheeks mirroring the heat in mine. "Witch?" he repeated in a low voice. "Why would that woman call you a—"

The clamor of the crowd rose suddenly.

"It's starting!" Cat grabbed Alis's hand. "It's starting! Hurry, you two, or you'll miss everything!" Without waiting for Fynn and me, she darted forward, pulling Alis with her.

"Tell Grayse to come play on Friday!" Alis called above the din.

"I will!" I shouted, but she had already vanished.

Folk were gathering by the rickety stand where fishmongers usually sat announcing their bargains. The top of Mr. Nelson's head, with its few obstinate white hairs, was visible at the front of the crowd.

Fynn and I exchanged a glance, and without warning, he took my hand. It was warm and calloused, and while holding Lugh's hand sent tingles up my arm, holding Fynn's made fireworks burst in my chest.

"Let's go see these mysterious crabs."

"All right." Sweat coated my palms. "But if I want to leave—"

"Say the word, and we'll go."

We approached the edge of the crowd, my knees wobbling. Fynn eyed the broad backs of two men as though he intended to push through.

I shook my head. "No. I'll not go any closer."

"Well then, neither will I." Fynn squeezed my hand, sending a pleasant shiver through me. I squeezed back, then lowered my eyes to avoid the spectacle.

"Look here!" Mr. Nelson cried. "See what I dredged up in my nets—there'll be a crab feast at my house tonight!"

The crowd fell silent, save for an infant's complaint. Then, several women oohed. A man gave a whoop of laughter, and the crowd burst into applause.

Mr. Boyd joined the boasting. "I almost nabbed this one with my largest scap net, but he broke through with his claw! Can you believe it? It nearly took my arm off."

"Incredible," one of the men near us muttered. "Simply fantastic."

His companion elbowed him and whistled. "Suppose I'll have to take up crabbing. Giants like those will fetch a pretty pound. . . ."

"Bridey." Fynn spoke close to my ear. "You can look. They're just big crabs. They don't have horns. They even look good enough to eat."

Slowly, I raised my head and studied what the fishermen displayed proudly.

The two crabs were like something from one of Mam's paintings. They made Mr. Boyd's and Mr. Nelson's heads appear tiny by comparison, like stars next to harvest moons. Each man's arms shook under the strain of holding a creature against his chest, and it was no wonder. The crabs were as wide through their bodies as I was tall. Sunlight glinted off their deep-set eyes and mottled red flesh.

The most horrifying part was their claws. A man could have used one of the enormous appendages as a club, and the blackish pincers looked capable of snapping limbs like twigs.

"Are those the things that attacked you?" I whispered to Fynn, my heart thudding dully in my ears. His wounds hadn't looked like pincer gouges, but with all that had happened recently, I didn't feel certain of anything.

"No. At least, I don't think so." Fynn eyed me with concern. "Are you all right?"

Unable to form words, I edged away from the crowd. A few folk cast curious glances in my direction, nudging their friends and tittering as I stumbled back. How could everyone gawp at those crabs like they were cause for celebration?

"That's it. We're going," Fynn declared.

We turned and started toward home. If it hadn't been for Fynn's wounds, I'd have broken into a full-on sprint.

We found Grayse in the hallway, standing against the wall, chattering happily to herself about something.

"Come see, Bry!" She reached for me, her wide eyes partially hidden by her unruly hair. Her dress was on backward, and when she tilted her chin up, faint smudges of black paint were visible on her chin and cheeks.

My heart sped up. "Where's Mam?"

"She's taking a nap for her headache. But she finished her new painting! Come! I want to show you the Bully!"

I would have much rather joined Fynn in the main room, but I agreed to follow Grayse to Mam's easel. "Look in on Mam, would you?" I called to Fynn. "See if she needs anything."

I returned my attention to Grayse. "Didn't Liss help you get dressed this morning? You know the collar goes in front, right?" We started down the hall together.

"Liss is out with some *boy*." Grayse gave a tiny grin. "And the collar goes whichever way I want."

"Oh, I see. My mistake." I grinned back, vowing to ask about the boy later. Liss never stepped out with anyone, and I could already hear Cat's amused speculation as to which lucky lad Liss was sneaking around with. But thoughts of my sister's secret paramour vanished as we turned a corner to see Mam's easel.

My mind refused to process the image on the canvas. First, there was the multitude of needlelike teeth. Three rows on top, and three on the bottom, shining in a serpent's gaping maw. Mam's wrist must have ached after painting the point of each malicious tooth.

"Bry?" Grayse looked up, chewing on her bottom lip.

"Give me a moment." I shifted my gaze to the bottom teeth smeared red. Not the vibrant hue of fresh blood, but deep burgundy like an old stain.

Gooseflesh flared on my arms. I wanted to understand what the creature in the painting was, for Mam's sake. I wanted to know how disturbing the dream had been that inspired this work, what vision had left her confined to her bed with another headache.

The serpentine head, painted inky black, took up most of the picture, with only a sliver of ocean visible around it. A livid yellow eye was dwarfed by the surrounding darkness, and a hint of a fat snake's body curved off the canvas. Then there were the jaws. Though the creature's mouth was gaping, an excess of skin around the corners led me to a dreadful realization: its mouth could open even wider.

"Don't be scared, Bry." Grayse sounded like Fynn at the market earlier. "The Bully's only paint."

"Go lay down with Mam, little fish," I said, fighting to keep my voice steady. Grayse hesitated, then nodded.

I walked back to the main room, legs shaking like they might collapse at any moment. Between the giant crabs, Fynn's injuries, and the recent disappearances, no one could deny that something strange was happening in the waters off Port Coire.

Perhaps the thing that lured Grandad into the sea—if, indeed, something had—was near the Isle once again. Yet the mysterious black fin I'd seen in the harbor, if that was the guilty creature, looked nothing like the filmy white figure that flickered in the waves as Grandad went under. Mostly, I was grateful I'd never seen anything so terrible as the creature on Mam's canvas.

I needed to run. To clear my head and put the town, the sea, and the serpent behind me.

Fynn's shouts trailed behind me. "Bridey, wait! Where are you going?"

I slipped outside and ran toward the distant green hills, desperate for escape.

The day kept getting worse. I wanted to cry or scream. I wanted to hurl Mam's new painting into the sea. I'd seen my fill of monsters, both real and imaginary.

What would Grandad have said about the horrible painting? He wouldn't have wished to hurt Mam's feelings, but I could picture him mouthing the word rubbish as soon as Mam left the room. Then he'd launch into the story of the time he went to Ireland and saw the mysterious art at Newgrange, an ancient tomb rumored to belong to old Irish kings. He said the beauty of the tomb's carvings was eclipsed only by the figures of the Irish women. This was before he met Gran, he always assured us, but she'd still cuff him on the arm with her shoe.

The memory almost made me smile. Almost.

I rounded the base of Morag's hill, breathing hard, and pushed myself onward. The rise behind hers was higher, more imposing. Dense woods lined the path to its treeless top, where I could pretend I was miles from the water.

The cool shade of the trees enveloped me. In the woods, the sigh of the wind was louder than the breath of the sea. A stoat hissed, half-hidden by the base of a large tree. Then, a twig snapped behind me, making me flinch, but I couldn't spot whatever had made the noise. Probably a nervous rabbit.

My anxiety faded as I climbed, replaced by numbness. By the time I walked out of the trees to the crest of the hilltop, the sun was sinking on the horizon. My throat was parched and my legs ached, yet I was grateful to be back in my favorite place.

A year after Grandad died, Da had taken me to Snaefell, the only real mountain on the Isle. Ever since, this hill had become my private mountain—Snaefell in miniature. Looking in one direction, all of Port Coire spread out below me, capped by a thick blue line where the sky met the sea. The other way offered a view of a different ocean, the endless green of hills and fields.

I flopped down in the scratchy grass, choking off a sigh of relief as the unmistakable sound of footsteps rushed toward me. Had Grayse followed me all the way here? I pushed myself to sitting.

"Little fish?"

I was answered by the ragged breathing of an injured boy.

For a moment, Fynn loomed over me, pale, sweating, and glassy-eyed. Then his knees buckled, and he collapsed beside me. He rolled onto his back and stared at the sky, chest heaving.

"Are you—?" I asked, but he held up a hand. The rapid rise and fall of his chest assured me he was alive, just as it had on the beach.

After what seemed like an hour, he turned to me. His eyes were clearer now. "I don't like hills. Or trees. If I hadn't been trying to catch you, I would've gotten lost in there."

"That's nothing to how I feel about the sea." I leveled my gaze at him. "What possessed you to follow me all this way? You could've reopened your wounds."

"You were upset." He slicked back his dark hair. "What happened back there? And at the market?"

"I . . ." My breath hitched as Fynn laid a hand over mine. Somehow, this lad I'd only known for a few weeks made me feel more alive than Lugh ever had. Thoughtful, caring Lugh, who I'd known my entire life. If I could trust Fynn with my fear after such a short time, I could trust him with anything. "I hate the ocean. And seeing those huge crabs just . . . overwhelmed me."

Fynn struggled to sit up. "What happened to make you hate—?"

I shook my head. "Rest. I can't talk about that just now."

He slumped on the grass. "All right. But back at the house—"

I thought, again, of Mam's new painting. The scales of her serpent had looked too much like the dark creature I'd glimpsed on the night Lugh and I heard the crash over the water. "No. I won't talk about that, either."

"You're impossible." A smile lit Fynn's face.

"Not *impossible*," I insisted. "I simply don't want to discuss the matter right now." I hurriedly cast about for a different topic. "Apparently Liss was out with some lad this morning. I never would have believed it."

"Oh, you mean Martyn Watterson?"

I blinked. Martyn was a husky boy, hopeless at catching fish, and even worse when it came to learning his da's business. "What do you know of it?"

"Liss's sweetheart. He seems like an idiot to me, but I'm sure she has her reasons." Fynn took one look at my wide eyes and grinned. "She's been helping him with his reading when she knows none of you will be home. He came to the door one morning, and I answered it. She begged me not to tell anyone, and in exchange . . ." Fynn's amused expression vanished. "I asked her to tell me more about you."

My throat went dry. "You should've asked me." I paused. "But you just told Liss's secret."

"Well, you don't seem like someone who would betray her sister's secrets. So my mistake ends here." Fynn smiled, not a trace of remorse in his gaze. "I hope you can persuade Liss to forgive me. As your friend Catreena wisely pointed out"—he paused to grin, inviting me to share in his joke—"they don't teach manners in London anymore."

"I'll try." I bowed my head to hide a smile. "But I won't promise."

An hour ago, I would have believed nothing good could come of this horrific day. Now, my perfect sister was flawed after all, and I was on my hill with Fynn, high above the dark worries intent on plaguing me.

As I watched the sun set, gilding the edges of Fynn's damp curls, I noticed him staring hard at a spot above my left ear. I raised a hand to my hair. "What is it? Is there a bee?" My carelessness had gotten me stung once too often.

"There's no bee."

I waited for him to say more, but he continued to stare. "What is it, then?"

"The sun in your hair," he murmured, frowning slightly, "turns it pink, like a seashell. I've never seen anything so perfect."

My cheeks flamed red. "Your wounds must be making you delusional." With a glance at the fiery sky, I added, "We should be going. Mam doesn't like any of us staying out past dark anymore."

Fynn laced his fingers through mine and I followed him toward the darkening forest. Despite the nearness of the ocean, the wind suddenly smelled clean and sweet, without a hint of brine.

The trees welcomed us into their shadows, reminding me of the things I needed to collect for Morag. "Let me know if you see any agrimony, would you? Tiny yellow flowers. But only if they're close to the path. We really should be home."

Fynn grimaced. "Is that for supper?"

"No! I need to find it for Morag." I smiled. "You must have heard me mention my work before. You likely had a job yourself. Or maybe where you're from, sleeping on other people's sofas is a respectable profession?"

Fynn's laughter sent warmth up my spine. "I'm not familiar with work that involves gathering flowers."

"I'm apprenticed to a witch. At least that's what most folk around here would say. Really, I'm helping a cranky old woman with her errands. She's been a recluse since before I was born, and with good reason. You saw the way some people were behaving at the market." I scanned the sides of the path for yellow petals as we hurried along. "They fear her without knowing her. And now me too, apparently."

"She'd better treat you well for all the trouble she's causing you."

"She's not as terrifying as she first seemed." I pushed aside an overgrown thorn bush to peer beneath it. "I've only been helping her a few weeks, though, and it's quite a job keeping her cottage clean. I'm starting to suspect her only magic is making huge messes just to give me something to do."

The woods grew darker. A prickling between my shoulders urged me to quicken my steps, dragging Fynn along.

"Why so rushed?" He tugged on my hand, trying to slow my pace.

I turned, shivering slightly. "This isn't a good spot to linger. There are . . . things . . . out here after dark I'd rather not meet."

Fynn gazed off into the trees, then back to me, and looked puzzled. "What things?" He stood a little taller. "Whatever they are, I'm not afraid." He nudged my shoulder. "I have the Isle's best witch by my side, after all."

For a moment, I couldn't speak. When he said *witch*, it wasn't the same way the woman in the market square did. From his lips, it sounded like a badge of honor. How could he have such confidence in a girl he hardly knew? I didn't understand it. But I was certain of this much: I more than liked it.

"*Mooinjer veggey*—the Little Fellas—roam these parts at night on the way to their revels," I whispered at last. "Or so Mam says. I've never seen them, though, and I've been out here past dark a time or two."

"What are Little Fellas?"

"You've never heard of them? They're like ghosts, but they come from a place all their own. That's why some call them the 'Middle World Men.' Our mams leave cakes out for them each night."

A hint of a smile shadowed the corners of Fynn's mouth. "Even yours?"

"Of course. Haven't you noticed the bowl of milk and slice of bonnag near the front door?"

"No." Fynn's smile grew, stretching from ear to ear. "Little Fellas. What an odd notion. Do they actually eat the cakes?"

"I don't know. There's always a new one in the bowl by the time I wake. My grandad used to tell me how he met one of the Little Fellas when he was a lad. A wisp of a man who only stood as high as Grandad's knee."

Fynn grinned, peering between the trees curiously. "Whether it's true or not, it's an interesting story."

"He'd gladly tell you a thousand of them. My favorite is the one about the Golden Pig. Grandad always said that if you ate a whole barley cake and a slice of bacon, and washed it down with well water, you'd see the Pig. It's supposed to bring good fortune."

Fynn shook his head, but a smile stretched across his face. "Where's your grandad now? I'd like to meet him. And his lucky pig."

"He passed away when I was nine."

Fynn squeezed my hand. "I'm so sorry."

"It was a long time ago. In any case, it's not wise to speak of Them." I shivered.

Still, the threat of encountering the Little Fellas was a more appealing one than meeting whatever scaly thing lurked in the water. To me, fairies were spooky pieces of Mam's stories, while Fynn's hand in mine was warm, solid, *real*. But if the giant crabs and the mysterious pearl I'd found were proof of impossible things, then perhaps the Little Fellas were hiding in the trees at that very moment, laughing as we hurried through the dark.

CHAPTER NINE

I usually lingered in my weekly bath, but tonight I had to hurry. At any moment Liss and Fynn, who everyone in town now knew as "the injured tourist staying with us for a spell," would be back from the market with ingredients for supper. Mam had promised us something special, since her headache was mostly gone and Da was returning home from an especially long stretch at sea.

A worn silk screen afforded me privacy as I pulled off the blue dress I'd worn yesterday. Seeing the grass stains on the front made me smile, calling to mind the way Fynn had watched the last of the daylight warming my hair. We were so close, he could have kissed me then. Something must have held him back. And while part of me wanted him to, a little voice in the back of my mind whispered that he might suddenly remember where he belonged and leave in the night without a word of farewell.

Somewhere in the wide world, he had another life better suited for him than what we could offer here. Surely he had adoring parents and siblings. And perhaps there was a lass, clever and beautiful, who was even now tearfully praying to every god she could name, begging for his safe return.

I shook my head to banish the thought. The coals hissed in an almost hypnotic way, and the sweet fragrance emanating from the hearth made my eyelids heavy.

I was about to climb in the washtub when the sight of the bathwater made me pause. My skin prickled with a reminder of the Bully lurking in the main room.

Peering around the edge of the screen, I searched for Mam's latest painting: the giant mouth with teeth like a straight razor. All I saw was Grayse on the sofa with her dolls.

"Where's the Bully, Grayse?"

"I wish you girls would stop calling it that!" Mam's voice rang out from the kitchen, accompanied by the thunk of her rolling pin hitting the counter.

"We wouldn't call it names if it wasn't so horrible," I muttered, soft enough for only Grayse to hear. "When will you let Mally take it to market, Mam?"

"I don't know, sweetheart. I can't imagine who would buy such a thing."

Was Mam afraid of the image, too? And if she didn't think anyone would pay for it, there was little hope of us being rid of it. Who enjoyed the things others deemed grotesque or unworthy?

The answer came to me in the form of sea-foam eyes and strong tea.

"May I give the painting to Morag? She might enjoy it." Having the horrible picture watching over me as I worked seemed a better fate than attempting to sleep with it skulking in the next room.

After a lengthy pause, Mam said, "I'll consider it."

It wasn't as good as a promise, but for now, it would have to do.

Da stumbled in later than expected, reeking of brine and sea foam, and Mam ushered me off to slip on my nicest dress.

Standing before my cloudy mirror, I was attempting to pin my hair at the nape of my neck when a rush of cool air slithered over my arms. No doubt Grayse had left the window open again. I hurried to close it, and was adjusting my grip on the sticky wooden frame when a sweet melody reached my ears. I leaned closer to the window, peering out into the syrupy blackness where clouds scudded over the moon.

There was no one in sight. The hulking outlines of the cliffs were barely discernible, and the sea beyond them crouched under the cloak of evening, invisible to human eyes. But the soft song continued, and with it, my desire to find the musician swelled. I pushed the window open farther and sat on the narrow ledge.

"Bridey, what are you doing?" A tall shadow darkened the floor, startling me from my makeshift seat.

"Does Mam need help with supper?" Shaking my foggy head to clear it, I closed the window with a firm shove and latched it for good measure.

"I just thought you might like to know what we'll be having tonight." Fynn leaned against the doorframe, a wicker basket dangling from his right hand.

"Probably a heap of fresh Queenies, still in their shells. As you know, I don't eat anything from the sea." I'd drifted toward the doorway without realizing it, the bewildering music still echoing through my thoughts.

"Actually, we bought lamb and potatoes." Fynn angled his head down, bringing his mouth much closer to mine. His breath warmed my cheek each time he exhaled, drawing me firmly into the present moment.

"That sounds marvelous," I managed, trying to control my racing heart. "Thank you—for accompanying Liss."

If I tilted my chin up, our lips would meet. I reached for his arm, and heat rose from his skin through the thin fabric of Da's shirt. I tightened my grip, my fingers pressing against hard muscle.

He made a slight motion toward me, dropping the basket, but hesitated. I nodded, and his arms wrapped around my waist, drawing me into his warmth. I raised my face to his, ready for the crush of his lips against mine, wanting to share more than these nervous breaths.

"Who wants to play Happy Families?" Grayse asked brightly.

For a moment, Fynn's lower lip grazed mine, sending a jolt from my head to my toes. Then Grayse's presence shocked us both, and our chins banged together.

I resisted the urge to peek at Fynn, or to rub the stinging spot on my chin where his stubbly skin had scratched mine.

"Now's not a good time, Grayse." My face and neck were on fire. But as I looked at my littlest sister smiling and clutching an orange box to her chest, my anger faded.

"Look, Grayse," Fynn began. "We were just—"

"Having a secret. I know." Grayse put a finger to her lips.

Relief washed over me. "Thanks, little fish." I kissed the top of her head before finally glancing at Fynn and was pleased to note that the back of his neck was flushed.

"What's that?" Fynn pointed to Grayse's box.

"Happy Families," Grayse said, with the air of a parent explaining something to a small child. "It's a game. Every card in the box has a funny person on it, and you have to ask the other players if they have the cards you need." Grayse gave Fynn a sympathetic look. "There must not be *anything* fun where you're from."

"Maybe not." Fynn smiled. "But I'll still play with you."

Grayse squealed with delight, then focused her pleading gaze on me. "Will you play too, Bry?"

I pressed my lips together. What I really wanted was a few minutes alone to collect myself and finish putting up my hair.

"*Please?*" Grayse added.

"Please, Bridey," Fynn echoed, and his low tone sent a pleasant shiver up my back. His lips turned up with a teasing smile. "Play Happy Families with me."

I tried to answer, but my mouth had gone dry. "Give me a moment. I'll meet you in the other room."

Grayse hurried off, shaking the box, but Fynn lingered near the door. In the moment I'd looked away from him, his expression had turned cooler, distant. Like he'd just had an unwelcome flash of memory, or the interruption had bothered him more than he cared to let on in front of Grayse.

"Off you go," I said, smiling shyly before shutting the door, and granting myself a moment's privacy to splash water on my blotchy face.

In the main room, my sisters, Fynn, and Da formed a circle by the hearth. Grayse shuffled a stack of cards while Da sipped tea and pored over one of his older maps. Liss moved over to create a space and patted the floor beside her. My leg brushed Fynn's as I sat, which did nothing to soothe the lingering redness in my cheeks.

"Fynn," Da said, setting down his map. "Where might I find giant crabs like the ones Boyd and Nelson caught?"

Fynn stared at Da. "I'm sorry, sir?"

"I understand you don't remember anything before your accident, but I know what you are. I've figured it out just by watching you these last few weeks."

Fynn went utterly still beside me. "You do, sir?"

"'Course!" Da slurred. "You're a fisherman! With your build, and your excellent eye for fish—I saw the herrin' you selected for my wife at the market—there's no doubt. The sea's in your blood, my lad."

Fynn's rigid posture relaxed. "You're right, sir. There's salt in my veins." Softer, he added, "So much I can almost taste it."

Da attempted to clap Fynn on the shoulder, but cuffed him on the ear by mistake. "Why don't you join me at sea, son? I could use the extra help finding *anything* out there."

Fynn grinned. "I'd like that, sir."

"Then it's settled!" Da leaned back and took another swig from his bottle.

The distant sounds of Mam and Mally making supper drifted into the room. Maybe I could persuade Mally to tell Fynn he wasn't well enough to leave yet. After all, it was more than likely his attacker was still out there.

After supper, Grayse begged everyone to play another round of Happy Families. Da had more maps to mull over, but once the table had been cleared, Liss, Mally, and Mam followed Grayse to the main room.

"Coming, Bry?" Liss called.

"Maybe later." I stacked our plates in the sink and cast a sideways glance at the table, but Fynn had wandered off. Listening to the chatter in the other room, I started scrubbing dishes.

As I worked, I gazed out the window over the sink, my thoughts drifting like the waves. White foam sprayed up from the rocks as usual, but—what was that shape hovering over the dark water? It was tall and broad-chested like a man, yet filmy—incandescent. I blinked, trying to get the image to sharpen into focus, but when I searched for the figure again, it had disappeared. Had I just seen a ghost? Grandad's ghost? Or worse, the apparition that had called him out of this life and into the next? If this was what had lured Eveleen and Nessa from their homes, it was a wonder they hadn't died of fright on the spot.

Blood rushing in my ears, I pressed my nose to the chill glass pane and held my breath. Nothing remotely human reappeared. Perhaps my tired eyes were conjuring images in the sea spray, though I thought not. But if I shouted for Mam and Da now, they'd stick me in bed and have Mr. Gill phone a doctor. Even if they tried looking out into the nighttime sea, with my luck, whatever I'd seen wouldn't show itself again.

Covered in gooseflesh, I abandoned my dish washing and went in search of Fynn. He stood on the far side of the main room, studying one of Mam's older paintings—a likeness of me as a toddler. Mam had captured me playing in the ocean on a calm day, my hair like a small white-capped wave as I bobbed among the blue.

"I'd love to see such a beautiful image now," Fynn murmured. "Whatever happened to make you hate the sea so, it must have been dreadful. You don't seem to be afraid of many things."

"I wasn't always afraid. And nothing happened to me." I spoke around a lump in my throat. I longed to tell Fynn what I'd just seen, but the thought of him questioning my sanity overwhelmed all desire to mention it. "I just know there are some things best left alone, and the sea is one of them. I'm surprised you don't agree, after washing up half-dead."

Without thinking, I rested my hand on the top of Mam's horrific new painting. Someone had turned it to face the wall.

"Is that your mother's latest masterpiece?"

It was odd, the way he said *mother* instead of *mam*, but his neat, careful pronunciation intrigued me. "It's rubbish, really. Nothing interesting." I hoped the disdain in my voice would be enough to keep Fynn from wanting a peek.

He gripped the edge of the canvas. "I'll just have a quick look."

As he turned the painting toward us, the color drained from his face. Silently, he studied every inch of the serpent and its blood-stained teeth, which were longer and sharper than I remembered. Fynn slowly exhaled.

"Fynn, what is it?" When I'd waited long enough for an answer, I laid a hand on his shoulder. "Do you need to lie down?"

His cobalt eyes met mine. "I'm fine, thanks."

I slid my hand over his back in soothing circles. "No you're not. What's the matter?"

"The painting startled me."

There had been a slight hesitation before he spoke, and I wondered if he was being entirely truthful. My hand stilled on his back. "If you're lying to me, Fynn, I swear I'll find out some—"

"I'm sorry." He leaned forward, so close we could have attempted another kiss. "I confess, it more than startled me. I wasn't expecting to see anything so . . ." He stared at the creature. "Foul."

I reached for his hand. Again, I considered telling him what I'd glimpsed out the kitchen window. But it was late and dark, and the misty figure wasn't the first such thing I'd imagined in the waves. It could easily have been sea spray, blown into a strange shape by the wind, and made into a man by my nervous mind.

The other possibility was too much to contemplate at this hour.

"Where did your mother see that creature?" Fynn turned the canvas to face the wall with unnecessary force.

"She didn't. She paints a lot of unusual things from her dreams. See?" I pointed to one of her mermaids, then to the inky-black water horse swimming beneath a boat, and yawned widely. "If you're sure you're all right, I think I'll be off to bed."

"Good night, Bridey. Sleep well." Fynn brushed his thumb over the top of my hand. My skin was still tingling as I fell asleep.

Something crushed my lower leg, jarring me awake. I groaned as Liss climbed over me. Rubbing my leg, I listened for Grayse's rhythmic breathing. By some miracle, she slumbered on.

I silently cursed Liss as I squinted into the dark. There was no starlight to help me make sense of why she was heading for the door at such a late hour. She always took care not to wake me when she got up to use the outhouse. Was she sick?

"Liss," I whispered. "Wait for me."

I slid out of the warm blankets, the fog of sleep releasing its hold. It seemed I'd closed my eyes only moments before to revisit my near-kiss with Fynn.

The bedroom door creaked open.

"Liss, *wait!*" There was no time to find my slippers. I crossed the cold floor in pursuit of my sister.

Liss waited for me in the hallway. Even in the shadows, her frown was visible.

"What on earth are you doing?"

"Going to have a look outside. I heard shouting." Liss shivered and rubbed her arms, though the air in the house was mild. "If you want to come, be quiet. There's no sense waking Grayse."

As we neared the front of the house, the voices grew louder. Fynn stood in the doorway.

Over his shoulder, out in the night, a procession formed. Paraffin lanterns—twenty or thirty in all—bobbed like a parade of fireflies. But the sounds accompanying the light show would have better suited for a funeral.

"Alis!" a man shouted over a woman's wailing. "Alistrina!"

A wave of dread coursed through me.

"Who's Alis again?" Fynn turned, not bothering to close the door. He seemed to have been aware of our presence despite our silence. "That name sounds familiar."

I shook my head and pressed my lips together, but Liss answered, "Catreena's little sister. What's happening?"

"She's gone missing." The faint glow of the search party's lanterns painted Fynn in grim light. "They're heading toward the cliffs." He stepped aside to allow us a better view, and sure enough, the lights were drifting downhill.

Whatever was plaguing our town couldn't be preying on yet another girl. Especially not one as small as Alis. She'd invited Grayse to play dolls just the other day, looking so bright and full of life as she demolished an entire bonnag at the market.

Pushing past Liss and Fynn, I rummaged for a cloak to cover my nightgown. I couldn't help Alis if she had gone over the cliffs, but I could find Cat and hold her hand through the terrible ordeal.

"I'm coming with you." Fynn handed me Mam's cloak, evidently realizing what I was about to do.

"Me, too," Liss said firmly.

"None of you," Mam commanded from the hallway, "are going anywhere." She shut the door firmly, then put her hands on her hips. Her eyes were owlishly wide, and she surveyed the three of us with a look that could have cut through steel.

I didn't dare move when her temper was so near to boiling over.

"It has clearly escaped your notice, so I'll inform you for your own good. It's *dangerous* out there. Girls, back to bed. Your da will join the search. Fynn, you're a grown man, so whether or not you go is your choice. But if you decide to risk your neck after I've just finished healing you, I'll reopen every one of your wounds myself."

We stared, openmouthed, at Mam.

"*Now!*" Her eyes flashed a warning.

Liss and I darted to our room and crawled back beneath the covers.

Though I was certain I wouldn't be able to close my eyes for a moment, I lapsed into a restless sleep sometime before dawn.

CHAPTER TEN

The next morning, Grayse was the only person in the house who attacked her bread and jam with any enthusiasm. The rest of us sat around the table, drowsily picking at a stack of toast.

"When's Da coming back?" Grayse pushed aside her empty plate and twisted the Bollan Cross around her neck, smearing it with blackberry goo from her sticky fingers. "He said he'd take me to the bakery today!"

Fynn, Liss, and I exchanged glances, waiting for Mam to break the silence.

Across the table, she rubbed her forehead and heaved a sigh. "I don't think he'll be able to take you anywhere today, little fish. I'm sorry."

Grayse puffed out her lower lip, always a warning sign.

"Mally," Mam said quickly. "Why don't you and Grayse make shortbread? There's a bag of caraway seeds in the top cupboard, behind last year's preserves."

Mally led a pouting Grayse over to the cupboards. Mam finished her tea and followed them.

"That's her fourth cup." Liss frowned. "Just watching her is giving me jitters."

"It's her fifth, actually," I corrected, toying with my mug. I needed to occupy my restless hands. Thinking of chopping firewood, I slid out of my chair, but something warm grabbed my right hand and held tight. Fynn's mouth curved in a faint smile.

The ache in my stomach was replaced by a hot, fluttering feeling. Still, I glanced at the door every few seconds. I imagined Da bursting in with news of Alis's rescue—a story of how she'd only snuck out to look for shooting stars, or to build sand castles in the moonlight.

Perhaps, I thought as I watched Mam gulp more tea, I should encourage all the girls in town to wear Bollan Crosses like the one I'd given Grayse. I doubted Morag's eerie fishbone charms could really prevent anyone from drowning, but at least then I'd be *doing* something, not just sitting here. Already Alis was likely out of the search party's reach, lying among the coral where no one but crabs and fish would discover her. Like Eveleen and Nessa.

Mam returned to the table, another cup of tea in hand. She took her seat as the door banged open and Da trudged inside. Mam's hand trembled, sloshing tea over the side of her mug. "Peddyr, is Alis—?"

"She's gone. We found some small footprints near the cliffs, but that's all. We searched everywhere." Da grimaced. "Either the Little Fellas are angry, and they've put a curse on the town, or a madman is preying on our daughters."

Stunned silence followed his words.

"In all my years, I've never . . ." Da bowed his head. "As I was leaving, her mam found her cardigan in their yard."

Mam took Da's arm. "Come now, you and the others did all you could . . ."

"Maybe we ought to leave out bigger cakes, so the Little Fellas won't take our girls," Da muttered darkly. "It might help to show Them more respect."

I stared at my parents. Da—strong, practical, fair-minded Da—wanted to appease the fairies. Nothing was right anymore.

"Peddyr, that's enough! I don't want to hear any more talk of unnatural things." Despite her words, Mam's face was as pale as Da's. "Let me fix you some strong tea."

The moment Mam steered Da into the kitchen, I rushed to the door with Fynn close behind. Given how miserable I felt, Cat was surely feeling far worse. She'd stood up for me in the market, and now it was my turn to support her.

"Where are you going?" Liss called.

"Cat's house," I answered as Fynn pushed open the door.

A light rain began as we came within sight of the low sand-stone building. The sensation of Fynn's large hand joined with mine was quickly becoming familiar.

Even more familiar was the red-haired figure standing near Cat's door. He tipped his head back and closed his eyes, seeming to welcome the cold drizzle rolling down his face.

"Morning, Lugh." I tugged on Fynn's hand to slow our approach. "Has there—has there been any more news about the search for Alis?" The words sounded hollow, but I'd suddenly been transported back to the night of our kiss. The obvious was all I could think to ask, especially with Fynn still holding tight to my hand.

"Oh!" Lugh shook the water from his shaggy hair and blinked. "Morning, Bry." He smiled faintly, but it faded when he looked at my hand clasped with Fynn's. His gaze shifted to the lad beside me, all traces of his smile vanishing. "You must be Bry's new friend. The comeover all the lasses are sighing about."

"I go by Fynn. I'm sure Bridey's mentioned that." He narrowed his eyes but extended his free hand to Lugh.

Lugh flexed his fingers at his sides, staring at Fynn's hand until he lowered it. "Actually, Bridey hasn't told me anything about you. You're the reason I've barely seen her lately, I assume." He moved closer, bringing his face inches from mine. "Tell me, have you forgotten everything that happened before *he* came around?"

I dropped Fynn's hand like it might burn me.

"Of course not!" I stared at the curve of Lugh's jaw, unable to raise my eyes higher. "Don't be ridiculous." I dropped my gaze to the mud.

"If you need a reminder," Lugh said quietly, his breath warming my cheek, "I'd be happy to give you one. . . ."

"Nothing's wrong with my memory!" Heat rushed up my neck. Lugh had never given me trouble before, and I wasn't sure how to respond. He wouldn't meet my eyes.

"I just wish things could go back to the way they were. Before—"

"Stop upsetting Bridey." Fynn clenched his fists. "If you can't control what comes out of your mouth, I'd be glad to help with that."

Lugh rounded on Fynn, his eyes flashing. "What makes you so special, anyway? Do you know her favorite color? Or what she fears? What's the first thing she wants to do when she leaves the Isle?"

"I never said I was special." Fynn raised a fist, and I stepped between them. "Bridey can clasp hands with whoever she damn well pleases."

"You want to throw punches?" Lugh glowered at Fynn from around me, taking a step back and spreading his arms wide. "Go on. Hit me. Can't hurt worse than I do already."

"Stop it, both of you! This is not the time. Think of Cat and her family!"

I drew a deep breath, prepared to elaborate on how childish they were being when another voice cried, "Easy, lads!"

Several of Cat's relatives pressed against the nearest window, vying for a better look at the scene in the front yard. One of Cat's uncles flung open the door and barked, "That's enough, you two!"

Glancing from Fynn to Lugh, I wasn't sure whose face was redder. "Listen, Lugh——"

"Don't." He swallowed hard. "I can't talk to you right now, Bry. Cat needs me. I shouldn't even be out here." He spun on his heel and hurried inside. The curious faces in the window began to disperse.

"I don't like him," Fynn snarled, his breath tickling my ear.

"Don't say that. He was just being an idiot." An ache settled in my chest. Part of me wanted to follow Lugh, to throw my arms around him and say something that would wipe the hurt from his eyes. But I didn't know the right words.

Cat's uncle had shut the door, but he left it unlocked and Fynn held it open for me. Smiling at the little bow he gave me, I tried to leave the memory of Fynn and Lugh's shouting outside with the rain.

Given the number of visitors crammed inside the cottage, finding Cat or her mam in their main room was a daunting task. It seemed all of Cat's relatives, even the ones who lived outside town, had arrived to lend their support.

The way they sniffled and embraced one another, it was as though everyone believed Alis was dead. I thought so, too, but a part of me still hoped we were wrong—that Nessa and Eveleen would stroll down the road tomorrow with Alis in tow.

Fynn stood behind me, shaking water from his hair and wringing it from his shirtsleeves. I squeezed his hand before wandering off in search of my friend. But the only raven hair among the folk gathered in the kitchen belonged to Cat's mam.

She stood apart from the crowd, looking pale but dry-eyed as she spoke with Ms. Elena, the elderly mam of Liss's mistress at the tavern, and the oldest woman in Port Coire. Perhaps on the entire Isle.

I hesitated in the hallway, listening for a pause in the murmur of their voices.

". . . remember the *glashtyn* killings? I suppose you're too young to recall that awful year," Ms. Elena rasped. Her hearing had been failing for years, which usually made her the loudest one in any room, but now she took great pains to speak just above a whisper.

"A few drowned back when I was a lass, most of them young girls, but some men, too. I didn't have any sisters, but I worried for myself. I watched the water every time I was to be on my way, even to a neighbor's house. And no one was away from home after dark."

"What's this glass-thing?" Cat's mam asked quietly. I detected a hint of wariness in her voice.

"A monster from the sea, a rare beast capable of coming on land. I never saw it, but one of my friends swore a *glashtyn* was responsible for the drownings. Killing young women is their specialty. She said it had a large black fin, rounded at the top—"

"Surely you mean one of the Little Fellas, not a"—Cat's mam dropped her voice even lower—"a *sea monster*. There's no such thing."

My pulse sped up as I crept closer to the edge of the wall. Ms. Elena seemed to be describing the same fin I'd seen in the harbor.

"No, I mean a monster. A beast as unnatural and wicked as the Devil himself." Ms. Elena sighed. "I wouldn't be telling you this if you weren't the daughter of my dearest friend, as no one ever believes me. They all think I'm daft." Her voice shook slightly. "Now, the night before one of my cousins drowned, I saw something in the water, too. It looked like the ghost of a man floating above the waves. It disappeared when I blinked, but I can still see it just as clearly today as if it stood now before me."

I resisted the urge to throw my arms around Ms. Elena. Her story reminded me of the figure I'd seen above the waves just before Alis had gone missing. Finally, someone else was admitting to seeing strange things in the water off Port Coire.

I took a step toward them as Ms. Elena gave a delicate cough. "Then there were more drownings almost eight years ago, when Alured Corkill and two of the Nelson girls died. You remember that, of course."

Alured Corkill. Grandad. Hearing his name froze me to the spot.

"I remember those drownings, aye," Cat's mam said softly. "But I don't see what that has to do with what's happening now. Mr. Corkill and those poor girls didn't leave their windows open and vanish into the night, did they?"

"No, but they were lost to the sea all the same." Ms. Elena cleared her throat. "Alured Corkill and the Nelson girls' deaths were the work of the *glashtyn*, mark my words, or whatever it was I saw that night before my cousin drowned. But everyone just said, 'Oh, Elena's finally losing her mind.' And now the monster's come to burden us again." She added, a little louder, "I hope someone's listening now."

My mind raced with strange beasts of the sea. Until I'd heard Ms. Elena's stories, some small, stubborn part of me had been clinging to the hope that the dangers facing us were familiar ones: men, sharks, storms.

Yet Ms. Elena had seen the unexplainable, just like I had. If I could find the strength to go looking, perhaps there was still a chance of catching this killer, be it *glashtyn* or other beast, before it lured anyone else into the deep.

"What should we do about the glass-tin, then, assuming it exists?" Cat's mam asked, so softly I could barely make out the words. She didn't sound convinced, but she wasn't calling Ms. Elena daft, either.

"Pray. Latch our windows, lock our doors, and keep a closer eye on our girls. Hopefully, the *glashtyn* will go away when it finds no more victims here."

Cat's mam sniffed. "It's already taken more than enough from me, this monster, if it's real as you say. My husband has contacted our Parish Captain, and I'm certain he'll investigate. Whether this is the work of beast or man, the authorities will stop it."

"I've never heard," Ms. Elena said slowly, "of a man slaying such a beast. But you must do whatever brings you peace, of course."

Gathering my courage, I turned the corner. Ms. Elena's eyes widened. "I heard everything," I whispered, glancing between the two women. "And I saw something in the water last night, probably an hour before Alis disappeared. Out our back window—"

"Bridey!" Cat's mam seemed to wake from a daze, and put a trembling arm around my shoulders. "It's so good of you to come."

"I left the house as soon as Da told me about . . ." I swallowed hard. "About Alis." I flicked my gaze back to Ms. Elena as she began hobbling away into the kitchen. "Ms. Elena, wait! I think I saw the *glashtyn*, too."

"Keep your voice down!" Ms. Elena paused, arching her wispy white brows. "If you really believe, you'll listen to an old woman and lock your doors and windows." She narrowed her eyes, scrutinizing me. "You're just the beast's type, I'd say. Don't be the next victim, Bridey Corkill."

She turned away as a red-haired woman touched her arm and murmured something to her.

In the silence, Cat's mam huddled against me, as though she needed my support to keep standing. "I hope Elena's wrong," she said. "But I don't know what to believe anymore. I'd never have thought, for instance, that Alis would leave her bed in the middle of the night, and fall from . . ." She swayed slightly, and I held her up while she took deep breaths.

As we slowly made our way to the nearest chair, I searched the crowd again, but there was still no sign of my friend. Once I'd found someone to fetch Mrs. Stowell a cup of strong tea, I asked, "Where's Cat?"

The words brought fresh tears to her eyes. "I'm afraid she's asked for privacy."

"But she'll want to see *me*."

Mrs. Stowell motioned toward the back of the house, and I made my way toward Cat's room. Yet when I twisted the knob of her closed door, it wouldn't budge.

Resting my forehead against the smooth wood, I called, "Cat, it's Bridey! Let me in!"

I was answered with a wave of sobs.

"*Please*, Cat! Tell me how I might help." If one of my sisters vanished, I would certainly want Cat by my side through the ordeal. Still, she did not answer. I waited, listening to the rain pound the roof.

"I'm going to Morag's now, if you won't let me in. I need to do something more than standing here."

If I lingered in this hallway much longer, I might see Lugh again, might get a deeper look at the hurt in his eyes. Hurt I'd put there. I didn't know if I could stand the sight.

The time had come to find out if Morag truly believed in the sea monsters she'd described to me, and if she did, what powers she might have to stop them. Maybe I couldn't bring comfort to Lugh or the Stowells, but I could try to prevent the killer in the sea from tearing another family apart.

"I don't care what you do! I don't care about anything right now, unless someone has a way to bring Alis back." A pillow thumped against the door. "Just go."

"I'll make things better," I whispered to her closed door. "You'll see."

The trouble was, I didn't quite believe the words myself.

Chapter Eleven

No one smiled or waved as I crossed the nearly deserted market square on my way to Morag's. The few folk not at Cat's house or mulling things over by the comfort of their own hearths went about their business with bowed heads, some casting anxious glances over their shoulder as they tended their gardens or swept their steps.

"Poor little Alis. The search party hasn't found a thing, and not for lack of trying," Mr. Cretney remarked to his wife as they repaired a broken shutter.

"But who could be behind all these disappearances? Not any of my neighbors, surely!" Mrs. Cretney dropped a handful of nails as I hurried past. "Do you think the old witch has finally figured out how to work a curse on this town?"

I pressed my lips together and looked away.

"I haven't a clue, dear," said Mr. Cretney.

I pointed toward the cliffs, though I doubted either of them would understand that no signs of Alis or Eveleen or Nessa had been found because they'd been taken somewhere unreachable. Nothing kept secrets like the sea.

Ms. Elena's words drifted back. *Don't be a victim, Bridey Corkill.* I didn't intend to be. With any luck, Morag would know something to aid in my search for the town's monster, whatever it was.

As I ran to the witch's house, the bright sky and twittering birds seemed to mock me. The sky should have looked thunderous, the birds silent out of respect for our sorrow.

"Morag!" I leaned against the weathered wood of the cottage, panting. "Mor—"

The door swung open, and I made a wild grab for the frame to keep my balance. Morag raised her brows as she put a gnarled hand on my shoulder to steady me. In her other hand a spoon dripped with sticky-sweet batter.

"I wasn't expecting you today, Apprentice Bridey," she grumbled, stepping aside to let me in. "Though I should know by now that you rarely turn up when you're expected."

"There's something terrible happening in town." I took a few deep breaths and sank gratefully into a chair at Morag's table.

"Is there?" Morag hobbled to the kitchen and began fixing tea.

"Remember the two girls who went missing?" I hesitated, wondering how to explain about Alis without my eyes leaking worse than Morag's rusty water pump. "Another vanished last night." I dug my nails into my palms to stop myself from losing my nerve. "And around that time, I saw something in the water that looked like a ghost. And I've seen other things, too. Something dark and scaly, the night of the big crash."

Morag kept her back to me as she poured the tea. Boiling water shot over the side of the first mug.

"How does any of that concern me?" she asked at last.

"I thought you could tell me about monsters. Being a witch and all. You swore to me they exist."

"And you laughed," Morag said shortly. "I didn't think you believed me."

"I thought you were teasing me." I bowed my head. "I'm sorry. But I'm not laughing now, and I need your help. Do you have a spell to get rid of them?"

Morag finally turned, a grim but determined light in her eyes. "I'm sorry to disappoint you, lass, but the only magic I possess is in herbs and charms." She shuffled to a stack of rubbish and picked up the battered book she'd shown me before. "Here. This will tell you far more than I can." She thrust the book into my arms. It was heavy as a toddler, and the motion sent a wave of dust and mold into my face. "Keep it for as long as you need."

"But—" I sneezed, and set the book on the table to examine its tatty cover. "By the time I read all this nonsense, who knows how many more of my friends will have disappeared?" Morag still wouldn't look at me. "A little girl went missing last night. She was seven. *Seven.* She liked cake and horses and spending time with my sister."

"I'm sorry," Morag grunted, returning to her kitchen. She started mopping the spilled water. "But I can't help you, and even if I could, why would I bother aiding a town that mocked and abandoned me?" Her eyes flashed. "Take that book and go now."

"If you know anything, please—"

"There are monsters in the sea, that's the extent of my knowledge. All I will do"—Morag paused, breathing hard—"all I *can* do, if it will get you to drop the matter, is make more Bollan Crosses so none of your wretched friends drown."

I scowled at her. "Morag, please! Whatever I saw last night, I think it's the same thing I thought I saw when Grandad jumped."

"Go now," Morag repeated, gentler this time. Still, there was something behind the words. Not a threat, but maybe tears. "Go. Now. And never ask me again about any of this."

"Fine," I huffed. It was plain there was nothing I could do or say to convince her. I reluctantly grabbed the heavy tome off the table and sprinted out the door, not slowing until I came within sight of home.

Fynn was reclining on the sofa when I stormed into the house. It seemed everyone else was still at the Stowells'.

"You left early?"

"Same as you," Fynn said groggily, sitting up. "I was tired of all the questions about why no one was looking for me, and how a tourist could be clumsy enough to fall off a boat on the calm ride here. What's that?" He pointed at Morag's book.

"Just a stupid, useless old thing." I tossed it into a corner, where it landed with a bang. "Morag isn't going to be of any help." Only my tremendous love of books stopped me from kicking the moldy tome. "How can she not care if every one of us walks off the cliffs in the night?"

Strong hands fell on my shoulders, holding me captive in the shadows. I turned to Fynn, and a wild fluttering replaced my rage.

"Relax, Bridey. I won't let anything happen to you—any of you."

"You can't promise that." The tears I'd been holding back since leaving Morag's cottage threatened to stream down my cheeks, but I fought them back, blinking hard. I wouldn't cry on her account. "You could be a businessman from London, for all you know. How can you fight whatever beast is behind this? Your last encounter with the sea ended poorly."

"Fighting isn't always about being strongest." Fynn squeezed my shoulders. "Winning demands cleverness and strength of will, as you well know."

"But what if there are things out there you're not prepared for?"

Something about the way Fynn looked at me made me want to tell him all my secrets. It felt . . . dangerous. I'd never shared so much of myself with anyone. And yet, I couldn't resist. Steeling myself against the painful possibilities of his reaction, I whispered, "Suppose I'd overheard someone say they think there's a sea monster in Port Coire?"

In the mouth-dry, hands-shaking moment of silence that followed, I snuck a peek at Fynn. His posture was rigid, but he hadn't scoffed or turned away. He watched me steadily. "Does that sound . . . mad to you?"

"A sea monster?" His voice was higher than usual. "Why would someone say such a thing?"

My stomach sank. "Lugh would have listened," I muttered as I started to turn away. "He would have at least considered the possibility." Though Lugh had never once said he believed my story about Grandad. He'd protected me from the stares and whispers of others, but he never thought there was anything in the water.

"I believe you," Fynn declared, locking eyes with me. "After being attacked and seeing those giant crabs in the market, I'd say those who don't believe in the possibility of monsters are the mad ones."

"You do?" I touched his arm, which felt warm and solid as ever. This was no dream. "You swear it? Just like that?"

"Just like that."

"Thank you." I wished I could give him something more than whispered words of gratitude, but short of bringing him the moon, I doubted there was any way to repay him for the trust that meant everything to me.

"There's no point in trying to warn my parents. I've tried in the past," I added a moment later, my head still spinning. Fynn nodded. Breathing a little easier, I asked, "Have you ever heard of a *glashtyn?*"

His fingers dug into my skin. "No."

"Ouch! Are you trying to leave a mark?"

He dropped his hands to his sides. "I'm sorry. I've never heard that word."

"Never mind. I'm—" I took a deep breath. "I'm just trying to find answers. I'm scared of who we'll lose next. Alis is gone. What if it's one of my sisters next time? Or Cat?"

"You can't think like that." Fynn rested a hand on my back. "Being afraid for them won't help them."

"You're right." I raised my eyes to his. "I want to find the monster that's making people disappear, and stop it. But it's in the sea, and I haven't swum in years. I don't know if I remember how. If something drags me below, I'm doomed. I want to protect my sisters, but I can't even save myself."

"Come for a swim with me in the shallows. Tomorrow morning." Fynn's eyes gleamed with an unearthly light. "All the disappearances have happened at night, so we should be safe in daylight." I shook my head, already uneasy, but he pressed his point. "Once you're in the water, the motions of swimming will come back to you."

"You don't understand. I *can't!*"

He gave me a puzzled look. "Help me, then. Tell me why an islander like you can't swim."

Fynn didn't breathe a word as I explained about Grandad. "You're stronger than you think, Bridey," he said at last. "You *can* swim, no matter what painful memories are haunting you. And I'll be right there with you to scare off any unwanted creatures. We'll guard each other."

I hesitated. Fynn seemed so sure of everything, even without his memories. If I went to the beach again, I'd surely embarrass myself horribly in front of the boy I wanted to impress most. But my desire not to be a victim, as Ms. Elena put it, was stronger.

The time had come to get my feet wet again.

"Tomorrow," he added, watching me with a frown. "Or the offer's gone."

I narrowed my eyes at him and sighed. "You strike a hard bargain." I extended my hand to shake. "But first, we need to find our monster."

Fynn's hand gripped mine, warm and steady. But not even his nearness could distract me just then. I hurried to retrieve Morag's book from exile.

Holding my nose to avoid the musty smell, I sank to the floor and cracked the cover. The tome had probably made a dent in her savings.

Fynn sat down across from me, frowning. "Morag said that book's an index of *every* sea creature?"

I nodded, skimming the words on the first page. *Beasts of the Deep*. This wasn't so different from my beloved *Non-Native Birds of the British Isles*.

Each page concerned a specific sea creature. Information was printed in blocky writing. Multiple sketches of each beast adorned the margins of the text.

I flipped past the *Bishop-Fish*—a fish with the face of a wizened man and a head shaped like a bishop's cap "last seen in Germany, in the year 1531." I briefly glanced at *Giglioli's Whale*, which looked like an ordinary whale except for its double dorsal fin and sickle-shaped flippers.

"Don't you want to have a look?"

Fynn was gazing around the room at Mam's paintings. "I can't read." He shrugged. "Either I never learned, or it's the—"

"Memory loss," I finished for him, as I continued to turn the book's tattered pages. Its entries didn't appear to be in any clear order. Zaratans—sea turtles so enormous they were often mistaken for small islands—preceded grindylows, creatures that drowned people, though they looked nothing like the monsters I'd seen. The drawings of skeletal women with stringy black hair and razor-sharp teeth made me shudder.

Next was the entry for the lusca, supposedly the world's largest octopus. I remembered this one well from my talk with Morag.

The next beast resembled a horse, except for its dolphin tail and the fins along its spine. The word above the horse-creature's head caught my eye: glashtyn.

I studied the drawing again. This was one of the creatures Ms. Elena had described to Cat's mam, though it looked nothing like the phantom made of sea foam I'd now glimpsed twice. It was a closer match to the water-horse in Mam's recent painting.

Shivering, I hoped none of Mam's other outlandish creatures would appear in this book. I turned more pages, black-and-white sketches blurring together, but the Bully, her most recent painting, mercifully never appeared.

Fynn drummed his fingers against the floor as I worked, and the rhythm reminded me of a sea chanty Da often sang.

At last, after passing over an illustration of a hairy whale and an entry devoted to evil green water spirits called the fuath, my misty phantom appeared: a wispy man in elegant but outdated clothing, hovering on the page beside his name as he played a fiddle. Fossegrim.

"Foe-say-grim," I said aloud. "This is it! This is what I saw!"

Fynn leaned forward, running his fingers over the images and words with a longing I recalled from when I was small. Maybe I could teach him to read.

"'*Fossegrim*, male water spirits native to Scandinavia, are known for their love of music,'" I read aloud. "'Their fiddle tunes call men, women, and children alike to the nearest body of water, where the souls drown as they try to reach the source of his haunting song.'"

A chill ran through me. And then a memory stirred. "I thought—" I paused, licking my dry lips. "I thought I heard music when Grandad jumped off that cliff. Everyone told me I'd imagined it, but . . ."

"It seems you've found his killer." Fynn narrowed his eyes at the drawing of the *fossegrim*. "We won't let him escape justice a second time."

I nodded, lost in the thought that there could be more than one creature stalking our shores. After all, the *fossegrim* didn't have a curious fin like the one I'd seen in the harbor—the *glash-tyn* did. And then there was the scaly thing I'd glimpsed the night Lugh and I heard a crash over the water, a river of dark flesh that disappeared in a blink.

Gooseflesh covered me from head to toe the longer I stared at the *fossegrim*. "All right," I said slowly. "The *fossegrim* took Grandad. Does that mean everything else in this book is a"—I gulped—"a vicious killer?"

"Just because you've never seen these creatures doesn't mean they're all *monsters*." Fynn's eyes never left my face. "Maybe they're like people. Some are wicked, some are fair. Some look out for their neighbors, and others only care for themselves."

I thought back to the sketch of the *grindylow* women with their gaunt faces and pointed teeth, and something tightened in my chest. "If they're really anything like people, they all have the potential to do harm."

"Perhaps you're right." Fynn dropped his gaze to the book.

"'*Fossegrim* prefer colder waters, but as scavengers drawn to places where other beasts are feeding, they have been found throughout the northern hemisphere. Legend has it they sometimes play to attract a human bride. An instance of this was first documented in Oslo, in the year 1297 . . .'"

I winced. "Do you think that thing wanted Alis, or one of the others, as a *bride?*"

Fynn blanched. "It's possible."

"But Alis was so young!"

Perhaps my missing friends had refused to be this monster's wife, so it dragged them to a watery grave. My stomach lurched.

I shut the book with a snap. "How can we keep everyone safe?" I'd collected enough material from its pages to plague me with nightmares well into my sixties. "I've tried warning this town before. They won't listen."

Fynn shrugged. "Short of telling them to stuff cotton in their ears, I don't know. But as soon as I'm able, I'm going to find the *fossegrim* and I'll kill it."

"You can't!" I grabbed Fynn's hands. "You need to heal. I'll not lose you over your ridiculous urge to act the hero."

"Don't worry. I won't go tonight." Laying a hand against his stomach, he confessed, "My wounds are aching again. And besides, I promised to prove to you that you still know how to swim. Tomorrow."

Somehow, his words and his smile only made me more nervous.

Chapter Twelve

A sunny day greeted me, complete with swooping gulls and the familiar *whoosh* of a breeze gusting past the house. Shrugging off a hazy nightmare that had something to do with black water, I walked into the main room to find Mam at her easel.

"Where's everyone else?" I'd remembered my vow to go to the beach today just moments after waking, and it filled me with unease. "Fynn?"

Mam didn't look up from her canvas. "He's down at the harbor with your da, working on the boat."

"How long will they be at sea?" The thought filled me with an even more intense dread than I usually felt every time Da went off to his job.

"Oh, they couldn't go out today. They have to patch a hole in the old bucket." In my almost seventeen years, Mam's way of referring to Da's boat never changed.

My heart resumed its regular rhythm. "Right."

Mam stopped swiping her brush across the canvas to study me. "Fynn asked that you meet him by the cliffs after lunch." Resuming her work, she said casually, "I used to meet your da out there."

A knot formed in my stomach as I steeled myself for the impending lecture. Several minutes passed as Mam worked in silence.

I was curious to see the new painting that had her so occupied, and moved behind her.

I took in a creature with the head and body of a horse, powerful fins, and a dolphin-like tail. Its deep blue eyes held the wisdom of the ancients, yet there was a wicked gleam there, too. Its powerful forelegs were poised to strike another familiar creature, the serpent, with its terrible fanged mouth open in a snarl. The dark water around them suggested that they were leagues below the ocean's surface fighting over something that looked suspiciously like a girl in a working dress. A girl I'd seen before. Her hair and the shape of her face stirred a fuzzy memory that slowly became clearer the longer I looked.

She had washed up on the beach by the cliffs. Her eyes had been milky then, not the lively blue-gray Mam had captured. But the waist-length dark hair and heart-shaped face were the same.

Mam hadn't been present when they found the girl's body.

"What made you paint that girl? And the Bully again?"

Mam lowered her brush. "A dream, bird. It was about two very hungry creatures that dragged a girl into the water, and neither wanted to share their meal." She sighed and for a moment her face showed the strain of lost sleep. "Sounds horrible when I try to explain, doesn't it? Though . . ."

She hesitated, glancing between me and the painting. I leaned closer, nodding in encouragement. "My dreams have been stranger than usual lately. Darker, more vivid." She rubbed her temples. "Perhaps I need to stop eating pie before bed, but I've been so worried lately."

"You and everyone else." I pointed to the canvas with a trembling finger. "That's the girl I saw on the beach. The one who drowned weeks ago. What if . . . what if some of the things you see in your dreams are *real*?"

Mam laughed, dropping her paintbrush. "Oh, Bridey. If she looks like that poor girl, it's only a coincidence. As you said, I never saw her." Mam retrieved her paintbrush, then bustled toward the kitchen. "Come. I'll make eggs and toast before you meet Fynn. This should go without saying, but I expect you to conduct yourself properly, young lady . . ."

I nodded absently, staring at the painting. I'd never thought of Mam's dreams as anything more than fanciful imaginings until I'd opened Morag's book.

But if sea monsters existed, perhaps the beings in Mam's paintings did, too.

The sight of Fynn standing at the top of the beach path chased away all thoughts of Mam's painting. He waved as I approached, and a strong gust of wind swept back the unkempt dark hair from his face.

"There's a barber who lives three houses down from us. I could introduce you. Right now, if you wished. And Mrs. Kissack probably has some fresh scones waiting at the bakery for us . . ."

He frowned. "Don't tell me you've changed your mind. After we shook hands the proper way, and all."

Something in his gaze made me eager not to disappoint him. I pulled open my cloak, offering a glimpse of Mally's blue bathing dress underneath.

Fynn ran a hand over his hair, making it stand on end, and grinned wolfishly. "You're certainly dressed for a day at sea. Shall we, then?"

I followed him down the narrow path, each step costing extra effort, as though there were weights bound to my legs. "I dreamed of the ocean last night." The words tumbled from my lips before our feet touched the sand.

"Dream, or nightmare?"

"Nightmare. As always." It had been the usual dream about Grandad, only this time, I was the one who dived off the cliff at the end.

I hesitated at the edge of the beach, trying to focus on each breath, the rhythm of inhaling and exhaling, instead of the soft grains beneath my feet. Yet I couldn't entirely ignore the tide creeping in, devouring more of the shore with each passing minute. Or the kittiwakes floating on the sun-drenched surface of the water, some with their bottoms in the air, bobbing for tiny silver fish.

Even the sight of waves fizzling out made my knees weak. It was difficult not to think of the Bully, Mam's oily serpent, and of the *fossegrim*. Of Nessa, Eveleen, and Alis gasping for air as the misty phantom held them underwater.

Halfway to the waves, I discarded my cloak. Fynn did the same, revealing his bare chest—and his scars. The marks had dulled to jagged pink lines for the most part, though they still needed time to fully heal. I sucked in a breath as his trousers dropped to the sand. He wore Da's oldest—and smallest—pair of striped swim trunks, which by some miracle clung to his narrow waist.

My cheeks and neck warmed.

I grabbed Fynn's hand in preparation for the salty plunge. We walked to the waterline, my pace slowing as we drew ever closer, and I flinched as chill sea foam finally tickled my toes. "I wish the water wasn't so cold," I gritted out with the little air left in my chest.

"It won't feel so bad once you've been in a while."

"If I don't bash my head against a rock first and die." I couldn't help gazing toward the horizon, looking for a filmy figure hovering above the water.

Fynn's fingers closed over my shoulder. "You won't be anywhere near the rocks. We're going straight out, so you can get used to the feeling of being in the water. Then we'll come back to the shallows so you can practice swimming." He pointed past the cliffs, to the distant spot where the sea turned from blue-green to deepest navy.

"We're going out of the cove?" I gasped.

"I'll be holding you the entire time. No monster could ever steal you from my grasp and live to tell the tale." Fynn winked, and though he sounded sure of himself, as usual, I didn't understand how he could make such a rash promise. Or how, after seeing the same images in Morag's book as I had, he could look upon the sea with such eager eyes.

Turning, he strode swiftly into the churning surf, leaving me standing amidst popping foam and broken seashells.

"Be careful!" I yelled after him. I paced the wet sand, kicking sharp pieces of shell out of my path. One minute, Fynn was up to his waist in the dazzling water, and the next, he'd disappeared.

"Fynn!" I shouted, my throat burning. "Fynn!"

"Over here!" He resurfaced, with water rolling off his chest and a piece of kelp adorning his hair like a crown, like a young Neptune rising from the waves. In that moment, he was like nothing I'd seen before, filling me with wonder despite the blood rushing in my ears.

Then he waved, breaking the spell. I put my hands on my hips, but it was a minute before I could scold him. "That wasn't funny!"

He swam with ease around the rocks in the cove, his arms darting in and out of the blue while his legs created white fountains where they struck the water. I'd never seen a body slide and twist through the sea with such grace. Perhaps Fynn had been a fish in another life.

A wave carried him back to shore. He rolled across the sand laughing, the healing skin on his stomach straining with each breath. He narrowed his eyes against the sun. "Now it's your turn."

Taking my hand, he led me slowly but deliberately into the surf. To my fate.

The wet sand sucked at my feet with each step like the beach wished to anchor me there forever. I clutched Fynn's arm for support as the crashing waves reached my ankles, making my skin crawl. The tickle of sea foam was gentle, but the nearby slap of water on the rocks seemed to say, *Don't trust me. I can be as soft or harsh as I please.*

My knees shook, and soon the shaking spread throughout my whole body. I tried to focus on my breathing, but I couldn't count the seconds I was drawing in a breath when the water pooling around my feet seemed to be coaxing me forward, gently tugging my ankles each time a wave retreated. Trying to pick me up and take me with it, as though to the sea, I was nothing more than a piece of flotsam to be easily swallowed.

His brow furrowed. "Tell me if you need to turn back."

As the water crept up my calves, all I could do was nod. I needed to turn back. I should never have attempted this. Fynn's fingers curled around mine, but not even that was enough to help me take another step into salty, murky water where I might tread on the squishy tentacles of a *lusca* or the rubbery fins of a *glashtyn*.

As I turned toward shore, a ribbon of slime caressed my foot and wrapped itself around my ankle. The *grindylows'* long hair and bony, grasping fingers flashed to mind, and I gasped for breath.

Jerking my foot back, I fled the shallows with Fynn shouting after me. I ran until I reached dry sand, then finally let my legs collapse from under me. I lay there, trembling, as Fynn dashed to my side.

"I've slain the monster for you." He tossed a ball of kelp onto the sand.

When my shaking subsided enough for me to sit up, I jabbed the tangle with my index finger. "T'eh myr tromlhie dou."

"I don't speak Manx, Bridey," Fynn said gently.

I buried my face in my hands. "All this—the water, the things that grab at me with no warning—it's as though I'm trapped in a nightmare." I took a shaky breath. "I wouldn't have to learn how to swim or try to fight a sea monster if everyone in town would just listen for once. But I know what they'd say if I told them about the *fossegrim*. They'd call me mad. Just like you will now, thanks to my display out there."

Fynn leaned close. "I'd never call you that."

"No? I'm shaking because of a wet plant!" I turned to him, not quite meeting his eyes. "Did you feel the least bit afraid when you swam out there earlier? I mean, something out there sliced you open."

He shook his head. "No. But fear can be a good thing. You can't have courage without it. And it makes you alert. You notice things others don't—like the *fossegrim*. You stand a better chance of helping this town than either Mr. Gill or the authorities."

I tried to smile, but we were still on the beach, and much too close to the sea. "Are you afraid of anything?" I asked. Fynn nodded, but kept his silence. "What, then?"

"You." As I blinked at him, he hastily added, "The way I feel about you. It . . . confuses me sometimes. That's why I'm glad we're out here." He took my hand and squeezed it. "Doing this together. I think it'll help me clear my head."

"Does your confusion have anything to do with Lugh? Because we're—"

"No. But we can talk about it later. Right now, it's time you made peace with the sea." Fynn scooped me into his arms and stood, holding me dizzyingly close. I put my arms around his back and felt his heart beating as hard as mine.

Brave, calm, self-assured Fynn was *nervous*.

A wave thumped me on the back as we moved forward, and droplets sprayed my face. I took a calming breath and inhaled his familiar scent—brine and lavender water and damp earth. The smell of the air after a rainstorm. Fynn.

As we passed the breaking waves and glided into deeper water, a feeling of weightlessness overtook me: my body remembering childhood explorations of the sea. A small voice whispered that if I let go of Fynn, I could float here forever, no different than a feather or a leaf.

"Look around you." Fynn's voice startled me, much louder than the slight hiss of the waves.

I tilted my head, studying the sky. Fat white clouds drifted along while a lone bird circled the sun. There was hardly any wind to speak of. The water moved in gentle ripples, nothing like the dark oceans in Mam's recent paintings.

Bracing myself, I dropped my gaze, expecting to glimpse a dark shape slithering beneath us. But there was only the flowing skirt of my bathing dress, and Fynn's legs kicking as he treaded water.

"This isn't as horrible as I'd imagined."

Suddenly, it struck me just how alone we were, and that made me as nervous as what might be hiding below. I tried to focus on the boy in front of me, the boy who believed me so effortlessly, and all the things I wanted to say to him. "Fynn, I—"

I've never felt this way about anyone. Promise me that, whatever happens—whatever you remember about your past—you'll stay with me until we can leave this dismal little town and carve out a life for ourselves together.

Ridiculous.

As I raised my eyes to Fynn's, his hand slid to the back of my neck, and he pulled me closer until our lips touched. Startled by the sudden warmth spreading down my body, I gasped against his mouth. He made a low noise, almost like a growl, but the sound was swallowed by another, firmer press of his lips to mine. I ran my hands along his back, feeling the tensed cords of muscle working to keep us afloat.

"You still confuse me." There was a haunted look in his eyes, one of sorrow and longing and something almost feral.

"How is that possible?" I demanded. "I'm here, aren't I?"

"That's just it. You're here, and you taste so good, yet all I want to do is . . ." His tongue grazed my bottom lip, teasing my lips apart. I wasn't sure how I knew what he wanted, but I did. He ran his tongue over my teeth, tasting of salt and dark sugar—maybe treacle.

How had I ever been cold out here?

Fynn's fingers knotted in my salt-crusted hair and tugged, easing my head back to expose my throat. His lips left mine, leaving a kiss on my chin before moving to my neck. I closed my eyes, shutting out the sea, the sun, dulling my senses to everything but him.

Though I was floating in the seawater, I'd never felt so safe—until the roar of the waves broke through. I clutched Fynn's shoulders, the warmth of the past moments quickly replaced by dread. Fynn smiled against my throat before the heat of his lips moved away.

"It would seem the current has found us. Are you ready to head to shore? We'll ride the waves in. Hold tight."

I squeezed his shoulders harder. His assurances didn't stop me from wanting to vomit as the current, like a giant shepherd's crook catching errant sheep, jerked us toward the breaking waves.

I struggled for breath as we rose with a swell, and nearly fainted when the large wave threw us into a mixture of soft sand and swirling sea foam.

"Bridey? Are you all right?" Fynn had landed a few feet away and slid across the sand toward me.

If I could walk into the sea, I could do anything. So this time, I kissed him. And though I bumped my nose against his in my haste, he didn't seem to mind. His hands found my waist, pinning me in place.

Keeping my movements slow and deliberate, I ran my hands over the scars of the wounds that had brought him to Port Coire. His injuries seemed to belong to a more distant past. Together on the beach we were fierce, out of reach of the water's threat. We'd faced down the ocean and emerged whole, with only sand in our hair to show for it.

I slid a hand farther down his stomach, and he made a low noise in his throat. "Did I hurt——?"

A shrill gull's cry drowned out my question. Fynn and I leaped apart. And as the clouds parted to reveal the sun, I realized how much of the afternoon was already gone.

"Maybe we should go." As I followed Fynn onto drier sand, a putrid odor, like spoiled milk, wafted under my nose. "Do you smell that?" I called above the crashing of waves.

He turned, scenting the wind like a hound, and made a face. "Something must've died." He studied the water for a long moment before shrugging. "Probably a seal."

"Still, I think it's time we return home. Dusk will be here before long, and there's the *fossegrim* to consider."

"Dusk is a few hours off yet." Without warning, Fynn flopped down in the last stretch of sand before the path, taking me with him. "We still have time." He leaned in, like he wanted another kiss, but I put a hand on his chest and pushed him away.

"Promise me you won't suddenly remember how much you loved your old life and leave me to rot alone in Port Coire."

"I don't have any proof to offer you," Fynn said quietly, "other than my word: I intend to stay."

"Then come with me to Morag's. We didn't exactly leave things on a friendly note yesterday, but perhaps she knows a spell to restore memories."

"You couldn't just take my word?"

I shook my head. "*Please*, Fynn."

He frowned.

"If she can't help, I'll simply have to make my peace with the things I may never know about your past, just as I'm trying to make peace with the sea. Then I can kiss you again." Lowering my eyes, I added, "I *really* want to kiss you again."

"All right. I'll go with you." He slipped an arm around my waist and pulled me close.

I rested my head on his shoulder, watching the shifting tide. I thought of the last time I'd stood on this beach with Cat and Lugh, and shivered as I realized the three of us might never be together like that again. With Alis gone, with the way I'd hurt Lugh, our bonds had been forever altered. And there could be no reversing it.

I closed my eyes and listened to the wind, hoping it would carry away this constant ache of missing my friends, an ache that didn't soften even with Fynn so near.

We stayed in the shadows of the cliffs until the sky turned a rich marigold. There was still plenty of time to walk home before the *fossegrim* could make its appearance. Sand fell from the skirt of my bathing dress with every step, and my throat ached from talking.

When the first row of houses came into view, I considered what we'd say if Mam had recovered from her latest headache enough to notice our bedraggled appearance. "Be careful not to let Mam ask you too many questions," I advised. "She can smell a lie on a person like a shark scents blood. And—"

I forgot the rest of the words as sweet strains of music filled my ears. I paused, glancing toward the sunset sea. The melody seemed to be coming from across the water. Was someone practicing their fiddle on the beach?

"Bridey," Fynn murmured.

His words washed over me as the fiddle's melody ensnared my attention, my thoughts, and my heart. I longed to sit beside whoever made such beautiful music.

I walked to the edge of the cliff, shrugging off Fynn's touch. The drop would be steep, but I would take the fall if it brought me closer to the maddeningly perfect music. My feet jerked forward as if pulled by invisible strings.

Come, come. Come to me. I've been waiting so long. Words swirled through my mind, chanted by an unfamiliar voice. Though devoid of rhythm, somehow I knew they belonged with the fiddle's haunting tune.

"I can't." And yet, was there a reason not to go to the fiddler? Did I have a family? I couldn't recall their names or faces . . . The fiddle sighed so sweetly. I forgot my name along with the rest. There was nothing keeping me here.

Just a few more steps, then I'd be falling free.

The music would catch me.

I twirled about, and my body felt so light, I realized I wouldn't fall. I would fly. I was a seabird. I would soar with the melody until I landed in the fiddler's arms.

My love, my life, you'll make a beautiful—

"Bridey!" Fynn shouted. He wrapped his arms around my waist and yanked me away from the very edge, spinning me around until I no longer faced the sea. "Put your fingers in your ears!"

He grabbed my wrists and forced my hands up, pressing them hard against my ears.

As the dulcet tones of the fiddle faded, my desire to leap into the ocean vanished. A wave of cold horror spread from my head to my toes as I realized what I had been about to do.

Fynn lifted me over his shoulder with a grunt and ran toward town.

I glanced back in time to see a white figure hovering over the water. Its broad shoulders reminded me of a man, but no living being glowed like that. He appeared to be standing on the water's surface, just past the waves, drawing a bow across a small stringed instrument as white as his skin and elegant clothing. This had to be the figure I'd seen from the window. The same spirit that took Grandad. The *fossegrim*.

"Turn back!" I demanded as Fynn kept running. "Turn back. We have to fight it!"

Fynn shook his head, refusing to stop until the shadows of houses blanketed us. He set me gently down and doubled over, panting.

"Why didn't you turn back?" I collapsed in the grass, comforted by the firmness of the ground.

"We're not ready," Fynn said with a groan. "For one thing, how can we fight it if we have to keep our hands over our ears? And for another, we don't know if it can be killed like an ordinary beast." He turned, glancing toward the sea. A red stain blossomed along his side. "I thought the monster only came out after dusk. I never would have asked you to stay out for so long if I'd known this might happen." He made a fist. "On second thought, I should go see if a good beating will finish that thing off right now. I almost lost you."

"But you didn't. And we need to get you home." I reached for his hand with my shaking one, and he stilled, his eyes widening with pain as his rush of adrenaline finally ebbed away. In the process of saving my life, he'd reopened his nasty wounds.

Chapter Thirteen

Fynn draped an arm around my shoulders, allowing me to carry some of his weight, just as he'd done when I found him on the beach. Dusk fell around us as we struggled toward home, another ten or twelve houses up the lane.

More red stained his shirt with each passing moment, and it didn't take us long to attract the attention of the few curious neighbors who weren't yet snug in their homes.

"What happened to him?" Mrs. Kissack called, her words echoed by Mrs. Kinry. The two women stood in the Kinrys' yard, no doubt having a suppertime visit. I wished they would stop gawking and offer to help.

"I'll tell someone to send for a doctor," a young lad across the lane offered, dashing away before I could stammer out a thank you.

"What happened?" Mrs. Kissack demanded again shrilly, her hand fluttering at her throat. "Who attacked you? Speak, lad!" She glanced from pale, shaky Fynn to me with wide eyes. "Bridey?"

My head and heart pounded. I'd almost leapt off a cliff, enchanted by a monster's melody. Between the unabashed stares of Mrs. Kissack and her friend, and Fynn bleeding and gasping beside me, I was too shaken to carefully weigh my words.

"There was something in the sea—the beast that took my grandad. It almost got me, too."

Someone gave a derisive cough, and my skin prickled. I longed to bury my words forever like the sea swallows a lost ship.

Mrs. Kissack threw me a pitying look I knew too well—the one she usually reserved for the very old and very daft. "You might want to reconsider your story before the doctor shows up, dear. He'll need the *facts* to determine proper treatment."

As if proving her right—though I knew he couldn't help it—Fynn groaned, leaning harder on me, like his legs might soon give out.

"She's madder than the witch on the hill," Mrs. Kinry murmured from behind her handkerchief. "Mad as her grandfather who jumped off that cliff."

"It's not her fault!" Mrs. Kissack snapped at her friend as Fynn and I resumed our struggle toward home. These neighbors of ours wouldn't be any help. "It seems Morag Maddrell has addled her brains. It's exactly what I knew would happen if she kept the witch's company. I told her mother as much just the other day, when I saw her at . . ."

I started humming, trying to block out their voices as I guided Fynn farther away. "We'll be home soon," I whispered.

"We should pray for her!" Mrs. Kinry's booming voice chased us up the lane.

"I made a mistake." Memories of the town's merciless stares and whispers flooded my mind, echoes of the last time I'd tried to tell what had happened to Grandad. If I hadn't been so shaken, I never would have let those words pass my lips today. "A terrible mistake."

Fynn grunted to show he'd heard. His half-lidded eyes and the sweat beading on his forehead made me all the more desperate to get him safely home.

Mam met me at the door, taking the burden of Fynn's weight and shouting for Mally.

Time seemed to slow, as though I were moving through a dream. I fetched clean rags, then put water on to boil in the kitchen.

Fynn had saved my life today, yet I was powerless to help him in return. I leaned against the sink, taking deep breaths, trying to fight off the shakiness that hadn't left me since I was nearly lured over the cliffs. The salt air blowing through the open window cooled my flushed face as I listened to Fynn's ragged breaths from the next room, but the murmur of the sea trickling in with the breeze sounded too much like laughter.

I slammed the window shut.

There was nothing to do now but pace the kitchen, fetch supplies for Mally when she called for them, and hope the lad who'd run off to send for help was as good as his word. Even so, it would take hours to find a doctor and bring him here.

"I think the bleeding's stopped again." Mally's voice was faint and uncertain.

Wringing my hands, I tracked the moon's journey across the sky, trying to ignore the feeling of a massive fist squeezing my chest every time Fynn made the slightest noise. My stubborn eyelids were growing heavy, but until I knew he was out of danger, I would fight the haze of sleep and keep my vigil with the moon and stars.

Someone pounded on the door.

"It's nearly four in the morning!" Mam hissed. "Took the doctor long enough."

I poked my head into the main room in time to watch her open the door. I blinked, wondering if I'd fallen asleep at the kitchen table and was only dreaming this moment, but the vision before me didn't change. Instead of the tall, gray-haired doctor from Peel who usually came to us, Lugh was framed by the doorway, his fiery hair ablaze from the light of torches at his back. Behind him were several men, including his stern-faced father and Mr. Gill.

Lugh's da opened his mouth to speak, but Lugh was faster. "My mam is missing. She took supper to my aunt, and she was supposed to come straight home after, but she never did." In the torchlight, Lugh looked ill, his face hollow like it had been after last winter's fever. "We checked with my aunt, and my mam never even made it there . . ."

"I'm so sorry," Mam said at once, putting a consoling hand on Lugh's shoulder. For a moment, I thought he would shrug her away, but he merely flinched, accepting the warmth of her touch. "Peddyr is at sea now. He can join the search party as soon as he's ashore—"

"That's not why we're here," Lugh interrupted, his voice strained. He locked eyes with me for the briefest moment, sending a shiver up my back as I glimpsed his haunted look, then dropped his gaze to the ground. "Thomase Boyd says he saw . . ." He paused, then squared his shoulders. "He saw Fynn sneaking around near my aunt's house earlier. Around dusk, right when Mam would have been arriving there."

I shook my head, my mouth too dry to speak. That was impossible.

"That's right," another voice said. Mally's former suitor, Thomase, pushed through the small knot of men to stand beside Lugh. "And there's another thing, too. My da and Mr. Nelson never came home from sea today. They promised to be back by suppertime. That comeover on your sofa—" Thomase clenched his fists and took a step across the threshold, scanning the room for Fynn—"has a lot to answer for."

"No, he doesn't."

The words rang out with force. Mally and I had spoken at the same time.

"Fynn was with *me* at dusk." My face grew hotter as I added, "He was with me all day! Ask Mrs. Kissack or Mrs. Kinry. Plenty of people saw us. We were hurrying home. Fynn's wounds—"

"Stop, Bridey," Mally cut in, crossing her arms and looking daggers at Thomase. "We don't have to defend ourselves, or Fynn, to these idiots."

My gaze flitted over the faces of the other men in the search party. Mr. Gill had a supportive hand on Thomase's back, as though he was so quick to believe the worst about Fynn—no surprise from him. Some of the other men had faraway looks, like they weren't sure who to believe.

Lugh caught my eye again, mouthing an apology, but I wasn't of a mind to accept it. I trusted Fynn, and that meant Lugh should, too. Believing Fynn could have anything to do with the disappearances was as bad as accusing *me*.

"Bridey," Lugh murmured, but I focused all my attention on Mally and stuffed my hands in the crooks of my arms to hide how they were shaking.

"If you keep making false accusations, I'll make sure you're laughed out of town, Thomase Boyd." Mally shook her head, still bristling. "Honestly. I don't know what I ever saw in you. Now off with you. Go! Help Lugh find his mam instead of wasting time pointing fingers where they don't belong. Or someone might break them!"

Mam stepped in front of Mally, blocking Thomase from taking another step inside. "That poor lad on our sofa is injured. There's no way he attacked anyone. Good night to you all!" She started to shut the door in their faces, but before she closed it all the way, she called softly to Lugh, "I hope they find your mam soon, dear. I pray they do."

After latching the door, she leaned against it, rubbing her temples.

Fynn shifted restlessly, and Mally hurried to his side.

I crept quietly into my bedroom, where Liss and Grayse had somehow managed to sleep soundly through our nighttime visitors' raised voices. Climbing under the warm quilts, I snuggled against Grayse's back.

But as I lay there, my mind churning over my brush with the fossegrim and Thomase Boyd's insane accusations, the gray light of predawn slowly filled the room. Sleep wouldn't be coming any time soon, and I had much more important things to do than rest.

I had to stop the fossegrim before it claimed another soul.

Hopping out of the bed it seemed I'd only just crawled into, I pulled on yesterday's rumpled clothes and snuck into the main room. Mam and Mally had finally gone to bed, and not even Fynn stirred as I stuck my feet in my boots. He was surely in a deep sleep from one of Mally's tonics.

But when I crossed to the door, a familiar voice whispered, "And where are you headed at this unseemly hour, Ms. Corkill?"

I turned to the sofa in time to see Fynn crack an eyelid and grin. I smiled back. It was a good sign that he felt well enough to make jokes.

"Morag's. Tell Mam where I went, would you?"

"What's the rush? Morag probably isn't awake yet." Fynn's voice was gravelly with sleep. "Come. Rest with me a while. It'll help me heal faster."

My feet itched to close the distance between us, especially as the memory of our time at sea drifted back. But Lugh's face flashed to mind, so gaunt in the torchlight, and I shook my head. "If there's any hope of finding Lugh's mam alive, I need to see Morag now. She gave me that book of sea monsters and claimed it would help me, but it didn't say how to kill the fossegrim."

As I had lain in bed, I'd thought of how Morag spilled boiling water when I mentioned the disappearances. "She definitely knows something she isn't telling, and I intend to get the truth from her today."

Fynn arched a brow, looking curious as a housecat. "And how do you plan to do that?"

I dashed to the serpent canvas, which no one had moved since Fynn turned it against the wall, and lifted it into my arms. "With a bribe, of course. She'll love this awful old thing." It was still wrapped in a sheet, thick enough to hide the Bully's face, and I liked it that way. I hurried to the door.

"Bridey," Fynn choked out. It sounded like he was struggling to sit up. "Wait."

Once again, I paused and turned back to him. "I want you to stay a while because . . ." His face was pale and pinched, though somehow, I sensed, not with pain. "Because I wanted to say good-bye. In case I'm not here when you get back."

I nearly dropped the painting as my arms went limp. "What? Why wouldn't you be here? You're hurt." I swallowed hard. "And I thought you had good reasons to stay in Port Coire. At least for a while yet."

"I heard everything those men said last night. I don't belong here . . ." Fynn's words were difficult to make out over the rush of blood in my ears. "I'm putting your family at odds with the town by staying. That seems a poor way to repay your kindness. And as for you . . ." His eyes glistened as he swallowed and said in a low voice, "After yesterday, I realized just how much I care about you, and—"

"And showing how much you care means taking off just because a stupid lad like Thomase Boyd told a petty lie?" I wanted to cry and shout. My voice shook with the effort of not waking Mam. "You and I know what's really luring people away!"

Fynn winced, but his mouth was set in a firm line. "This isn't just because of what anyone said. Caring about you means I want what's best for you. And while you can't see it now, and there's no way you could understand, being around me isn't—"

"No? I'm not capable of understanding whatever foolishness is running through your head?" I clutched the painting with white knuckles. "Well, hopefully you understand this: You don't get to decide what's best for me, no matter how much you claim to care. I do. And what's best for me is you staying here. If you really feel anything for me at all, you'll do just that. If not, then perhaps it is best you leave. See how far you get with your wounds half-mended, and good luck."

I spun on my heel, hoping I'd been quick enough to hide how my heart was breaking. I needed fresh air. I needed Fynn to be here when I got back. I needed to get rid of this blasted sea monster.

"Bridey, I'm doing this for your—"

"I'm going now." I nudged the door open but called back over my shoulder, "I'll see you when I return."

I hope.

I didn't let a single tear fall until home was far behind me. Lugging the painting to Morag's was, at least, a distraction from the awful turn the morning had taken.

A few houses up the lane, a blonde woman in a long gray skirt kneeled in her garden, though it was barely sunup. She hummed as she trimmed clusters of flowering yarrow, a gentle melody, yet the sight of her twisted my stomach in knots.

"Morning, Mrs. Kissack." I hesitantly waved to the baker, wondering if she'd told anyone about the things I'd babbled to her and her friend the day before. I was afraid to ask.

She stopped humming and glanced up. For a woman who made cakes and sweets, she looked rather fierce. "Bridey." With a stiff jerk of her head, she returned to her plants.

I crossed into the market square, where a few of the usual merchants were setting up shop for the day. Most of the fishermen's baskets, which usually displayed their catches, were woefully empty despite Mr. Boyd and Mr. Nelson's giant crab discovery. I tasted the bitterness of the town's worry on my tongue each time I gulped a mouthful of briny air. I couldn't wait to reach the shelter of Morag's hill.

As I rushed past the pottery stall, Thomase Boyd fell into step beside me.

"Hello, Bridey. Seen any krakens lately?" Thomase drawled, seemingly oblivious to the fact that I was in a hurry.

My stomach dropped. Mrs. Kissack and her friend had already been busy telling people how daft I was, then. I'd never buy another scone from her after this.

"See any monsters on your way here?"

I tried to act like I hadn't heard Thomase, though my burning face gave me away.

"My da and Mr. Nelson's empty boat turned up in the harbor at first light," he murmured, soft enough for only me to hear. "And here I thought your friend was only after our women. Tell him from me, if he so much as glances at my mam and sister, I'll make sure it's the last thing he ever does."

I paused, tempted to smack Thomase in the face with the covered painting. "I don't think you have anything to worry about," I gritted out. Of course, that wasn't true, not unless I found a way to fight the fossegrim.

"What does that mean?" When I didn't answer, he added, "You'd best stop watching the sea and watch your back instead, Bridey Corkill, or you'll be his next victim. And what a painful loss that would be."

Thinking of Fynn and his sudden urge to leave after kissing me just yesterday, my blood ran hot. "Listen here, Thomase. Why don't you go bother someone else? I'm in the mood to hit something this morning, and your face is awfully close. And a wide target."

"I know what I saw yesterday," he growled. "Mr. Gill believes me, and so should you. It was the comeover. Lie to yourself if you must, but Gill won't be the last person I convince. You can't hide the truth."

I quickened my step. "You're mad."

Thomase laughed. "I'm the mad one? I've heard you like working for the old witch. Think you're special, don't you? Well, you and that hag are the daft ones, and your friend is no better." He jabbed the air with his index finger, calling out as I dashed away, "Trust me, folk would be glad to see the back of you disappearing over a cliff!"

"This town is lucky to have me," I said, my words carrying on the wind. They might not have realized it, too busy giving me sideways glances and sniggering behind my back, but I was trying to save them all.

"The search party found her footprints!" Thomase's voice was so faint, I could just make out the words. "Leading right to the water . . ."

Out of sight of the market at last, I paused in the shade of a tree at the base of the hill. My heart ached for Lugh, yet my mind kept circling back to Fynn. Back to the kiss that almost made me love the taste of saltwater. Back to the boy who thought me brave. Had he ever felt anything for me, or had he only meant to use me to pass the time until his memories returned? Surely he'd recalled something if he was suddenly so keen to leave me and this town behind. My hands curled tighter around the edges of the painting as I realized what hurt the most: he hadn't even asked me to go with him. I might've said yes, once I knew my family was safe.

But they weren't yet. That was up to me and, perhaps, Morag.

Fixing the faces of my missing friends and neighbors in my mind, I knocked on the warped cottage door.

Seconds stretched into minutes as I waited for Morag to answer. I pressed my ear to the wood, hoping to catch the sound of a foot dragging across the floor or the hiss of a kettle. But there was only the sigh of the wind through the trees.

"Morag?" I called. "You can't keep avoiding me like this!" I knocked again.

And again.

I called and knocked until my knuckles were red, and my voice hoarse. "I'll just leave your gift out here, then, where it might be ruined!" I trusted that my voice would carry through the rotting wood.

Once more, I pressed my ear to the wall and listened for a familiar scraping sound, but none came. Still, I stood and waited.

The thought of staying here all day was tempting, when I didn't know what I'd find at home—Fynn, or no Fynn. I shivered, struck by an echo of the pain I'd feel in the absence of the boy who might be stealing my heart.

But judging by the stretching shadows, I'd been here long enough to make Mam nervous, even if Fynn had remembered to tell her where I'd gone.

"Fine." I raised my hands in surrender. "I'm leaving now. But I won't stop coming here until you've told me what you know about sea monsters, Morag!" I kicked a small stone, sending it hurtling into the trees. "I know you don't care about the folk I've lost, but the disappearances won't stop until we kill the monster that's stealing our friends! Maybe you'll care when it's someone you love, like—" I broke off, drawing a breath.

Who did Morag love? Surely she cared about someone besides her miserable old self. No one wanted to be alone all the time, no matter how much they argued to the contrary. My gaze fell on Mam's painting, and the answer came to me.

"Like my mam!" I shouted. "You could lose my mam if this monster isn't stopped. I'm going to try to fight it on my own, but if my mam gets taken in the meantime, you'll know who's to blame."

I ran until I was clear of the trees. Towering thunderheads obscured the sun, threatening a late afternoon storm. Of course, it was possible that Morag might not know how to hunt a fossegrim. That I might have to figure it out myself, with or without Fynn. But the more she avoided me, the more I was sure she had something to hide. Otherwise, as usual, she'd be ignoring me while I swept her hearth and made tea.

Anger bubbled inside me as I followed a different path home, careful to avoid the market and the stares I was sure to receive there. I had been starting to like Morag, and now I had to wonder whether she knew something that could've saved Grandad all those years ago.

"You win for today," I muttered, though I knew she couldn't hear me. "But I won't be giving up easily."

Not when my sisters, and my town, depended on me.

As I came within sight of home, I hesitated. If Fynn was truly gone, I didn't think I could stand the sight of the empty sofa. And if he wasn't, if he'd made me worry all morning for nothing, I might not be able to keep myself from hitting a wounded lad.

I opened the door, bracing for the silence and the sting of Fynn's absence. But I was greeted by a burst of noise—Da's deep laughter and Mam's off-key singing filled the house. I hadn't heard the like of it for weeks, maybe months, and the sound made my pulse quicken.

An unplanned celebration was unusual, even by our family's standards. Even when fish and tourists were plentiful.

"There you are, Bridey!" Mally stood in the center of the room, beaming at everyone gathered: Mam and Da, Liss, Grayse, and a reedy lad with red hair—Artur. And tucked into one corner of the sofa, beside Grayse—Fynn.

My heart leapt. I barely had a moment to look a question at him, and for him to carefully avoid my gaze, looking miserable, before Mally turned her radiant smile on me.

"Come, dear sister!" She drew me into a floral-scented hug and squeezed my sides so hard I coughed. "Artur and I are going to be married! He proposed last night, after—well, I'll tell you that part when we're alone."

The crushing losses of my friends and neighbors had pushed the possibility of Mally's engagement to the back of my mind. I hugged her around the middle, trying to feel a shiver of happiness, but images of Nessa Daley gathering flowers and Alis's jack-o'-lantern smile prevented me from offering more than a weak grin. "That's wonderful, Mal. When's the wedding?"

An excited squeal followed my words. "We're going to have a feast!" Grayse cheered from the sofa, nearly walloping Fynn in the stomach in her excitement. "Capons and geese and hogs and breads and puddings . . ."

"The wedding's on Thursday. Can you believe it?" Mally's voice was as bright as Grayse's, but something in her eyes told me she would be missing Nessa and Lugh's mam helping her with the wedding preparations.

I looked to Mam. A wedding so soon was absurd. But she nodded, seeming to be at peace with the idea. I shifted my gaze back to Mally. "How will you put a wedding together in three days? It takes months to write to relatives, and arrange the music, and—"

"There won't be time to invite a whole scutch of people from out of town," Mally interrupted. "Artur's uncle offered him a job in London, and our boat leaves a week from today." She kissed the top of my head, her haunted eyes at odds with her radiant smile. "I'm going to miss you, Bry."

"No, you won't." Mally frowned, and I hurried to add, "You'll be too busy seeing the sights in England with me when I visit every other month."

"Oh, good!" Softer, she added, "And be safe in the meantime, all right?"

"I will." I embraced her again, holding on longer this time. "Now, what can I do to help?"

"Let's discuss the preparations over tea, shall we?" Mally's smile finally reached her eyes. "Perhaps Fynn and Artur can talk in the meantime. I'm sure they can find something in common."

For the first time in my life, I was jealous of Artur. I needed to talk to Fynn, to find out what had changed his mind about leaving, or if he was simply putting off breaking my heart for another day. I wouldn't beg him to stay, but I at least needed to know what memory prompted him to abandon us. Me.

Still, it wasn't every day my eldest sister got engaged. Faking a smile, I followed Mally to the kitchen, listening to her prattle on about seating arrangements and music while I worried about having a wedding with the fossegrim lying in wait for a girl to call his bride. I couldn't think of a greater beauty than Mally. What if the fossegrim found her lovely face too much of a temptation, and rose out of the water to claim her?

Mally couldn't have chosen a worse time for a wedding.

CHAPTER fOURTEEN

Gasping for breath, I threw back my blankets and sat up as a dawn glow seeped through the window. A quick glance at my younger sisters assured me they were still asleep. How had my thrashing not awakened them?

Several gulps of air helped me shrug off the haze of exhaustion, but when I tried to recall the dream that had made me panic, I remembered only stinging water filling my nose and lungs. It made my chest feel so heavy that, even now, a weight remained pressed against my heart.

Out in the hallway, a floorboard popped. Perhaps Fynn was awake. I hadn't had a chance to talk with him alone last night on account of the celebration, and I was eager for a chance to ask what had changed his mind about leaving.

I hurriedly dressed, but by the time I emerged in a skirt and blouse, the house was silent. Da's boots and fishing gear were gone, and Fynn was curled up on the sofa, completely covered by a spare wool blanket.

Deciding not to wake him just yet, I glanced at Mam's easel. A canvas sat there, shimmering wetly, and a piece of paper rested on her chair: *Going to pick up some Samson for my head, then over to M.M.'s for a visit. Will be back around noon. Love, Mam.*

I scrunched my eyebrows, staring at the note. The only M.M. I knew was Morag Maddrell. Why would Mam pay her a visit when there was so much to do before the wedding? Did she think, for even a second, that Morag would want to help plan a celebratory feast, much less attend one?

I laid the note back on the chair. If she'd gone to purchase Samson at the tavern before visiting Morag, her latest dream must have given her another headache. Still, the dark brew of treacle and hops was bound to dull the pain, at least for a few hours.

Curious to see what vision had seized Mam this time, I glanced at her new canvas. But I regretted the decision as soon as I laid eyes on it. The scene was set close to shore—a blue-eyed, raven-haired girl besieged by a serpent. Under a sky the color of a cast-iron pan, a gale tossed the girl's tiny boat and whipped her long braids out behind her. The serpent gnawed the girl's leg while she jabbed its saucerlike eye with a harpoon tip.

Shivering, I turned away, but something about the girl's raven braids and sea-foam eyes made me look again. They were Morag's eyes. And though I'd only seen her in braids the color of dull silver, their clumsy styling was familiar.

I edged toward the sofa, gripping its sturdy back for support. The serpent in the painting was clamped down on the girl's left foot, the same foot Morag claimed to have caught in a hunter's trap.

I laughed, a mirthless sound. Staring at the serpent's teeth, I remembered something.

The night Lugh and I heard the big crash, which seemed so long ago now, I'd seen a massive dark shape dip below the ocean's surface. And the next day, while hunting for shipwreck debris, something long and sharp and white had pierced Lugh's foot.

It must have been a serpent tooth.

Heart hammering against my ribcage, I hurried to the bookcase and cracked open Morag's book. The serpent had to have an entry. I must have missed it while searching for the *fossegrim*.

I flipped the delicate pages at lightning speed, collecting only paper cuts for my trouble.

No luck. Near the back of the book, however, someone had carefully ripped out the last sheet. Perhaps Morag couldn't stand to be near the serpent after it attacked her, even in paper form. Remembering the sharpness of the tooth I'd held, I could understand why.

Casting the useless book aside, I went to wake Fynn. I had to tell someone about Morag and the serpent. Perhaps he could help me decide if it was yet another beast we needed to worry ourselves about. But when I returned to the sofa and gently peeled back the blanket, there was no Fynn. Just a couple of lumpy pillows beaten into the vague shape of a boy.

What if he'd gone hunting for the *fossegrim* without me, despite his promise? Or worse—what if staying to celebrate Mally's engagement last night was his way of saying a silent farewell to us all?

I rushed outside. "Fynn!" Stumbling toward the road, I called for him over and over.

Mrs. Gill stopped sweeping her front step to glare. "Young lady, are you aware that everyone can hear you? I thought even you'd have the decency to keep your tongue after the wild things you've been saying of late." She shook her head. "If there are sea monsters in Port Coire, then I'm the queen of Spain."

Ignoring her, I forced myself to take deep breaths. If Fynn was leaving, there were many paths he might've taken. The harbor, where the tourists' ferries ran to places like Dublin and Liverpool, seemed a good place to start.

But as I stood there, breathing deeply, I was hit, again, with the stench of spoiled milk. Fynn had assured me before that it was nothing more than a dead seal, yet the carcass would surely have been picked clean by now. No, the putrid scent had to be coming from something far worse.

I turned, directing my shout toward the sea. "Fynn, can you hear me?"

Mrs. Gill dropped her broom with a noise between a sigh and a growl. When she frowned, she bore a striking resemblance to a six-horned Loaghtan sheep. Muttering under her breath about my mam and the dangers of being *litcheragh*, she banged her door shut.

I spun on my heel, pausing long enough to scowl after her and call, "My mam's not lazy!" before hurrying to find Fynn.

He wasn't at the harbor. Nor was he on any of the cliffs we'd visited together. It wasn't until I was trudging homeward, bone-tired and defeated, that I spotted a familiar pair of Da's old boots dangling from a tree branch.

I grabbed the biggest rock I could find and hurled it into the tree.

"Watch it!"

I crossed my arms, not at all satisfied with Fynn's reaction. "What in Manannán's name are you doing up there?"

Fynn dropped down from his perch. His clothes were rumpled, his hair unkempt, and there were deep shadows beneath his eyes. "I could see all of Port Coire from up there." He shrugged. "I was just saying good-bye."

"Why?" I bit down hard on my trembling lip. I refused to cry.

He lifted a hand, then quickly dropped it as I stepped back. His eyes shone with concern as he studied my face. "You're so pale. Did you see the *fossegrim* again, or—?"

"My mam's done another painting of that foul serpent. Not that you'd care."

The boy in front of me worried me far more than the serpent, though. It could be dead by now, for all I knew.

"Tell me," I said, glaring at Fynn, "why are you leaving?" I hated the whine in my voice. "And why didn't you ask me to come with you? Have you remembered a past that's calling you home?"

"Bridey. Stop." He brushed a lock of my hair away from my eyes, conjuring memories of our kiss at sea. The taste of treacle, the heat of his tongue, the pull of his fingers in the tangle of my hair. I wanted to feel and taste those things again.

"I promise you, I remember nothing of my life on land before you rescued me." He shot me a pained look. "But where I'm going, you can't possibly follow."

"I don't understand," I whispered. "You came here, completely disrupted my life, and won my—" I took a deep breath and met his eyes. "Won my trust. And my heart. And now, you're fleeing on a whim you won't explain?" I stood taller. "Well, I won't accept it! You'll have to give me a better excuse than 'I'm going somewhere you can't follow.' I'm every bit as capable as you."

Slowly, his frown turned into something I'd seen on his face before. Sorrow, mixed with longing. "I know you are. But—"

"Has this summer meant nothing to you?"

"Don't be ridiculous." Sweat beaded on Fynn's brow. "You mean *everything* to me. Only it won't matter if . . ." He hesitated, his eyes searching mine. "I want to stay here with you, if you decide that's what you want. It was my mistake not to let you choose. I see that now."

I nodded. "You've got that much right. But whatever do you mean? What won't matter?"

"There's something I need to show you." Fynn's expression was grim. "Before you decide how you feel about me—"

"It's rather late for that." I grabbed his hands, determined to hold on now that I'd found him again. "Out with it."

"You're sure you want the truth?"

I nodded. "Positive."

"Then meet me on the beach in an hour." He paused, clearing his throat. "You don't have to get in the water, and we won't stay long enough to make anyone worry or put ourselves in danger again. Just come. And know that I've fallen for you, too."

I wanted to shout, to dance, to sing. Warmth spread all the way to the tips of my toes as I repeated his words. "You—"

"You say you won't kiss me again until the witch brings back my memories, but there's nothing to bring back. I know who I am, and I know who I want."

He leaned in and kissed me with a ferocity that made my heart swell, but even his closeness didn't silence the questions running through my head. What did he mean, he had no memories to bring back? And why couldn't he show me whatever it was right here, instead of on the blasted beach?

We shared a second, longer kiss. Then he rushed off without another word.

"Fynn! Wait! You'll hurt yourself again!"

The boughs of the trees hissed softly as he passed them; he didn't look back.

When he was no more than a speck in the distance, I touched my swollen lips and stared at the spot where he'd been, far more confused than I was before I found him.

Fynn paced the sand in Da's swim trunks, bare-chested but for his bandages, a lone figure on the deserted beach crunching sharp pieces of shell under his feet. He was mouthing words to himself, alternating wild gestures with running a hand through his hair.

I paused to observe my surroundings. He looked like he might startle if I approached too quickly. The tide pools on either side of me brimmed with new water brought in by the encroaching surf, and the bright day laid all the pools' secrets bare. If only the sun could illuminate whatever Fynn was hiding from me as easily.

I crouched in the sand where a red-orange starfish clung to a rock. Within hours, the sun would bake it dry and steal its life. Taking a deep breath, I gingerly grabbed one of its five legs and pried it loose. The star put up little resistance and dropped into my waiting hand.

Cradling the small creature, I strode past Fynn and waded into the shallows. That would get his attention. Sea foam swirled around my ankles, but I summoned all my courage to ignore it and returned the star to the sea. "Good luck, little one." The orange creature disappeared beneath a wave.

"Since when do you care about anything from the sea?" Fynn placed a hand on my shoulder, sending heat through my arm.

"Since it brought me a boy, I suppose." I backed away from the waves, expecting Fynn to follow. But when I reached drier sand, he was still standing right where I'd left him.

"I'm going to show you now." He raised his voice as he stepped into the crashing surf. "I know you'll be frightened, but I don't want any more secrets between us."

A hot prickling started at the nape of my neck and spread across my skin. "Fynn, if this is dangerous, you don't have to do it. Mally stitched your wounds up again, and you could undo all her work—do you really want to be in that much pain?"

He waded out farther, the water lapping at his knees. "My heart is yours, Bridey Corkill. I hope you'll forgive me for what I didn't say before." He turned abruptly and dove into the waves. His dark hair looked bold against the whitecaps.

My knees threatened to buckle as I searched the horizon for signs of the *fossegrim*, or something just as sinister, waiting to devour the boy I so adored.

Fynn's head bobbed near a group of large rocks, then disappeared. The moments stretched in agonizing silence broken only by the cries of gulls and the rumble of waves.

I shouted Fynn's name until I was hoarse. The edges of my vision dimmed, tunneling toward the spot where he'd vanished beneath the waves. How long could a person breathe underwater? Something had surely grabbed him.

I rushed into the surf, hitching up my skirt. Chilly water surged around my knees as the black fin I'd seen so many weeks ago in the harbor glided toward shore. Shuddering, I stumbled back, coating myself in sea foam. I trained my gaze on the beach, knowing my panic made me easy prey.

Halfway across the beach, I tripped on a mound of shells, and landed facedown in the sand. I spat out a mouthful of grit, taking heaving breaths as I scrambled to push myself up.

Something crashed near the water, louder than the meeting of water and rock—a snort from some foul creature's mouth, followed by the muffled smack of feet against wet sand.

I turned as a hulking black horse lumbered out of the waves, shaking white foam off its sleek coat. Blinking, I pinched my arm.

The horse was still there, half-submerged in the waves and staring at me with luminous, dark blue eyes. This ghastly creature looked nothing like the chestnut horses I'd met on my aunt's farm. Its ears were twice the length of a normal horse's, thinner and pointed. The creature's forelegs ended not in hooves, but in webbed flippers. More webbing covered the bends of its legs, and gills lined its neck. White scars shone on the creature's belly, and a large, round fin rose from its back.

The *glashtyn* from Morag's book and Mam's paintings.

I tried to scream, but only a croak came from my throat. The beast tossed its curly, black mane and slapped a flipper against the sand, displeased by my broken sound. The waves receded, revealing the creature's dolphin-like tail.

Even though I knew it couldn't rush to attack me, I staggered back and nearly fell again as the creature gave a strangled cry, more like a man's gasp than a horse's whinny. It appeared to be shrinking, muscles rippling and twisting into another form. Flippers became fingers, the giant tail divided to form legs, and the mane became a mess of familiar dark curls.

I shut my eyes, took a deep breath, and slowly exhaled. I'd finally done what the good folk of Port Coire assumed I had so long ago: lost my mind. When I dared to glance at the beast again, it was no longer standing there. Shivering in its place was Fynn, naked as the day I found him, wide-eyed and dripping.

"*Monster,*" I stammered.

He shook the water out of his hair. Da's bathing suit must have been ruined during his transformation. He started toward me, worry creasing his forehead.

But for every step he took, I scrambled back. He'd been lying to me this whole time. I didn't want him anywhere near me.

"Bridey," he said quietly. "I'm still the same person you—"

"You *lied* to me! You're not who I thought you were at all!" Fynn winced, but the hurt look on his face was nothing compared to the agony he was causing me now. "You're no better than the *fossegrim*." I bit my chapped lip, suppressing a sob.

"I'm a *glashtyn*, but I'm no monster." He stopped advancing. Sea-dweller or not, at least he had enough sense to leave me be. Blood leaked sluggishly from his deepest wound, and to my dismay, seeing his pain still caused my stomach to clench in sympathy. "The serpent your mother keeps painting—it tried to kill me the day I washed up on this beach."

Glashtyn. Ms. Elena had told Cat's mam that the *glashtyn* liked to drown girls. And Fynn had pretended he didn't know the word when I'd asked about it.

My head spun. "You drowned that poor girl who washed up on the beach, didn't you? And Nessa? Eveleen? Alis? Lugh's mam? You were just blaming the *fossegrim* for *your* murders! Where are their bodies? Why didn't you take me, too? Oh, God." Tears spattered the front of my blouse as I thought back to our day at sea. How swiftly and surely he'd picked me up and carried me into the waves.

He could have been planning to steal me then, like the others.

Fynn clutched at his chest. "I didn't drown anyone! I don't know why the *fossegrim* came here when I did. I'd never even seen one before it attacked us. But the serpent fought me, and I nearly died. It was fair fortune that I landed here with you, and not on some other shore." He swallowed, then reached out an imploring hand. "You saved my life. Truly. And my heart is yours, if you want—"

"Don't you dare say you love me." A shrill laugh escaped my lips. "It seems we know nothing of each other." The voice echoing in my ears didn't sound like my own. "And don't come near my family. Go back where you belong! I never want to see you again."

"Bridey, I only showed you because I didn't want to keep any secrets . . . You asked to know! You wanted the truth!" Fynn's words were lost to the wind as I raced up the path between the cliffs, glancing over my shoulder only to make sure he wasn't following.

I sprinted through town by way of my neighbors' yards, dodging the vague shapes of chickens, cats, and washtubs. I paused once, by a stone blur that vaguely resembled the Gills' house, to grab a yellowed garment hanging from a line. After dabbing my streaming eyes and nose with someone's night-gown, I hurried across a field into the sheltering shade of the forest's silver birch and rowans.

The climb seemed to take twice as long as usual, perhaps because I kept turning to peer down the hill. Fynn had trailed me here before; he could find it again. But not even a rabbit stirred in the brush.

My shoulders slumped. There were so many things I wanted to ask him, once my anger had faded. Why the serpent attacked him, and was he was even capable of loving a human? His false-hoods stung worse than the dreadful moment of watching him surface from the waves as a beast from a book of monsters.

I emerged from the trees with my stomach rumbling. I skirted the edge of the woods and began to search for anything edible among the bracken. A sweet perfume tickled my nose, and I chased the scent to dark raspberries dangling from thorny canes, begging to be picked.

Something rustled the leaves. I froze, looking toward the path, but it was only a bird taking flight.

As my sobs slowed, I rested at the crown of the hill. The short, scrubby grass was warm from roasting under the sun, a wonderful contrast to the icy sea water.

I gazed at the clear sky as I ate the raspberries, recalling every detail of Fynn's shift from terrifying sea monster to handsome lad. He was a brave, funny, kind boy who cared for me, who had believed me about the threat in the water when no one else would. And he was a *glashtyn* with flippers, sharp teeth and a tail. A sea monster.

A giggle escaped my lips.

I had named him Fynn. Not a Manx name, like Braddan or Colyn or Rory. Fynn.

Another giggle bubbled from me, followed by a peal of unrestrained laughter that would have surely confirmed the town's suspicions about my delicate mental state, had I been overheard. I laughed until my sides threatened to burst, but all too soon, tendrils of worry took root in my chest again.

If Fynn was a creature who murdered innocent girls, why hadn't he dragged me to the depths during our swim lesson? With no one around to bear witness, it would have been so easy. But there was no doubt that the *fossegrim* had lured Grandad off the cliffs, and that it had tried to do the same to me. Maybe

Fynn really did care for me. Still, there was no proof that he hadn't preyed on my friends and neighbors.

Whatever his intentions, I needed answers, not his half-truths.

And I knew of only one place where I would find them.

Chapter Fifteen

Raised voices carried on the wind as I drew closer to Morag's cottage. Who from the village would visit her? Perhaps someone had come to harass her on a dare, as I'd once done with my friends when we were younger.

"I wish you'd stay longer, Mureal," Morag said, an unfamiliar tender note in her voice. "Are you sure you should walk home now? You don't look well, dear."

I recalled the note Mam left by her easel. Of course, she was still here visiting. But I wanted to see Morag alone. I ducked behind the nearest tree and stole a glance at the cottage.

Mam and Morag stood together in the doorway, Mam's willowy figure looming over Morag's hunched one. "I'll be fine, moir," Mam said, wrapping her arms around Morag's bony shoulders. "But what about you? You reek of whiskey."

I retreated deeper into the shade of my tree, wondering whether I'd heard correctly. If Mam had said *moir*, not Morag, then she'd called the old woman *mother*. Mam's parents died before I was born, so it was natural that she would seek the company of someone older. But Morag? Shaking off my surprise, which seemed trivial in light of what I'd just learned about Fynn, I focused on their conversation.

"It's just a headache," Mam protested. "I've had these hundreds of times since I was a girl. And I bought some Samson—"

"Bah!" Morag spat in the dirt. "That stuff's more likely to give you a toothache than cure your head. Wait here, Mureal. I have something that might help."

I dared to peek at the cottage again, just as Morag returned with a sachet in hand.

"What is it?" Mam asked, accepting the little bag.

"Varvine, dandelion root, and precious mugwort." Morag's voice grew softer. "To be taken twice a day, understand? That should keep the worst of your dreams at bay, and without them, your head should feel much clearer."

Mam nodded. "Thank you, moir. For everything. Having a lass Bridey's age about the cottage this summer can't be easy—"

"Nonsense! Though I admit, I haven't seen much of her lately. And it's my own fault. I needed some quiet."

Mam clutched the sachet to her chest. "Just send word when you'd like her. And I'll come again soon." As Mam turned to leave, I pressed myself flat against the tree and held my breath, hoping she wouldn't look beyond the path.

The swish of her skirt and the soft padding of her bare feet grew closer, then faded as she made her way down the hill.

Morag shuffled back to her cottage. I rushed to the door, but she had already shut it, so I pounded on the wood. "Morag, we need to speak!" I banged again, this time for the sheer satisfaction of rattling her wall. "It's about Fynn, and . . ." I hesitated, but there wasn't time to waste with the *fossegrim* still on the loose and perhaps more monsters near our shore. "I know what really happened to your foot!"

The door whined as it swung inward, and Morag reappeared, blinking at me. "All right then. No need to bust down the door. You've come to ask me more questions about monsters, then?" She shook her head. "There's no stopping you, I see that now."

I opened my mouth, searching for a way to put all my troubles into words. Fynn. The *fossegrim*. The serpent. The tale of Morag's foot being caught in a hunter's trap was rubbish, and I wanted to hear the true story from her lips. I'd had my fill of being lied to.

Morag's gaze slid past me, searching the trees. "You look like you've seen one of the Little Fellas. Have you . . . ?".

My lip trembled, and within seconds, Morag's face became a blur. "Fynn—our house guest—he's a *glashtyn*. He showed me." I mopped my wet cheeks with my sleeve. "We had a terrible fight."

Rubbing her temples, Morag studied me for a long moment before speaking again. "And he didn't try to drown you?"

I shook my head.

Morag swayed, and I wrinkled my nose. Mam was right. The old woman did smell of whiskey. "Hmm. It's in a *glashtyn's* nature to drown girls. But I've heard of stranger things than a creature being put off its supper."

"He cares for me. He wouldn't hurt me." The words left my lips with the swiftness of conviction, though I wasn't sure I believed them. I wanted Morag to tell me I was right, that it was possible for *glashtyns* to love human girls instead of drowning them.

But she merely arched her brows. On someone else's face, the expression would have been comical, but her eyes were too unnerving to make me laugh. "Seems to me he already has. Hurting is what true loves do best."

I thought of the things I'd shouted at Fynn, and tears again filled my eyes.

"Inside with you!" Morag snapped, drawing me from my muddled thoughts. "If you carry on watering the ground like that, I'll have weeds cropping up all over the yard. And then you'll have to pull them."

Caught between another sob and a bubble of laughter, I hiccupped. "No, thank you. But I know your foot wasn't stuck in a hunter's trap, and we have much to discuss about monsters. As you said, there's no stopping me." I attempted a grin.

"If you want to hear about my foot, come inside. I have a tea to calm your nerves." Morag stepped aside, gesturing to the dim interior of the cottage. "You don't want to confront the boy while you've got a face like a boiled lobster."

"Excuse me?" I rubbed my cheeks.

"You heard me, lobster-girl. Come in. If he cares a whit about you, he won't have gone anywhere."

I didn't want to admit she had a point, so I followed her inside.

She puttered around, clinking dirty dishes as she searched for mugs. I looked about, hoping to see what Morag had done with Mam's painting. Either stacks of tattered cloth and old furniture had swallowed it, or it was gone. "Where's the gift I brought you? The awful painting from Mam."

"I burned it."

"Oh. I can't say I blame you." It seemed a shame to have burned Mam's work, but I knew Morag's reasons.

She frowned as she poured our tea, splashing something deep amber into hers. After a moment's hesitation, she added a generous splash of the amber liquid to mine as well. "There you are." She pushed a mug toward me, then took a deep drink from hers. "I never thought I'd have to tell this story again."

There was a hollow ring to her voice, and for the first time I noticed the purple smudges under her eyes. "Take your time," I said softly.

Morag frowned but launched into her story. "When I was a girl, perhaps a year or two older than you are now, I went to catch fish for supper. The sky had been dark all day, so I thought the storm would continue to hold off, but I was wrong." She paused, biting her lower lip. "The rain started. I made for shore, but a giant serpent reared out of the sea. It sank its teeth into my leg and tried to drag me from my boat, but I had a spear—"

"And you jabbed the serpent in the eye," I finished.

It was exactly as Mam had painted it.

Morag's face paled. "Tell me how you know that." Her voice came out a whisper. "Oh, of course. Your mother. She didn't mention that particular dream to me."

"It was her newest painting." I gazed into my steaming mug, picturing the fear in the younger Morag's light eyes. They looked much the same now.

Morag met my gaze and took a deep breath before continuing. "It would seem you know the truth of her dreams, then."

My hands clenched around my mug, but I ignored the sting of the hot porcelain against my palms.

I thought of the selkies and mermaids wrapped in garlands of pearls. Gooseflesh rose on my arms and legs. "Why haven't you warned the town? Think of the lives you could've saved!"

Morag's reply was almost too soft to hear. "Don't you think I've tried? Why do you think they mock me so?"

I bit my lip, knowing all too well how that felt. "One of us has to tell Mam about her dreams, at least!"

"No, girl. It's much kinder not to."

"What do you mean?"

"Mureal isn't strong like us." Morag smiled sadly. "Strong like you, rather." She bowed her head and sighed. "She has an ability few possess, a bond with the sea not unlike the connection some have with the spirit world. But it makes her delicate. To learn that her visions are more than dreams would surely undo her. You, on the other hand, won't fall to pieces just because there's a *grindylow* in the harbor or a *fossegrim* on the beach. You have a great ability to acknowledge the hidden and carry on living."

I shook my head. Morag made it sound as though I were the type who could see the boy she'd kissed turn into a sea monster, shrug, and go fix supper. Silence settled over the cottage, thick and stale as the air around us.

Finally, I cleared my throat. "Why did the serpent attack you? Is there more than one? Does it eat people, or just kill for pleasure?"

A muscle jumped in Morag's cheek, but she continued staring into her tea. "This is why I didn't wish to talk about the monsters with you. I gave you the book. That should be enough to satisfy your curiosity." She drained the rest of her mug before settling her unfocused gaze on me. "I don't have the answers you seek and I can't help you. All I know about the serpent is that its bite will make you plead for a swift death."

"Then, can you tell me how to find and kill a *fossegrim*?"

"I don't know. I've never gone looking for one." Morag's foot knocked rhythmically against the table leg.

I gritted my teeth. I was wasting time here, time I could have spent searching for Fynn. If Morag couldn't answer my next question, I would leave. "Tell me about *glashtyns*, then. Are they dangerous? What do they do, besides drowning lasses?"

"*Glashtyns* are rare creatures native to the waters around the Isle," Morag said flatly. It sounded as though she was quoting her monster book. "They aren't related to horses, despite their looks. When they come on land, they take the form of dark-haired boys with blue eyes. They like to hunt fish when they aren't smuggling girls into the sea, but drowning lasses is their favorite sport."

Morag continued to level her probing gaze at me, and I stared back. "What interests me about *your* glashtyn is why he hasn't tried to drown *you*."

"I'd like to know that, too. Could it be . . . because he cares for—?"

"No. A predator doesn't love its victims. Your friend didn't just abandon his desire to hunt women, no more than a stoat can stop hunting rabbits. Not without help, anyway."

"What do you mean?"

Morag reached for her mug again, and blinked upon finding it empty. "If he feels anything for you, it's because something changed him, took away his compulsion to kill. Was there anything unusual about him on the day you met, aside from his injuries?"

Heat crept up my neck as I recalled that first meeting with Fynn. "He was naked. Not a scrap on him."

"There's nothing abnormal about that. I eat my breakfast in the nude. *Think*, girl!"

I looked down at my hands in my lap, trying to focus on the details of Fynn's rescue instead of dwelling on the image Morag's words had conjured. That day, I had kneeled beside

Fynn's motionless form, so petrified I hadn't even thought to check his breathing. I ran my fingers between his wounds, probing for the heat of infection, and—

"When I touched his cuts, it felt like I'd stuck my hand in a beehive."

Morag cracked a rare smile. "Now we're getting somewhere. Was there anything on your hand when this happened?"

I shook my head. "Nothing. My fingers just tingled for a minute."

Morag pursed her lips, tracing a groove in the table with her index finger.

Dropping my gaze to my hands, I examined a bright pink welt on the right one. A thorn from the raspberry bramble must have nicked me when I was foraging earlier. I hadn't injured that hand since the day I met Fynn, when the shard of glass had sliced my thumb. The wound had still been fresh when I touched him.

I thrust my right hand across the table, and Morag frowned as though I'd offered her a piece of rotten fish. "This is the hand that felt strange when I touched Fynn. I slashed my thumb on a broken bottle."

Morag's eyes went from whiskey dreaming to alert in a flash. "And were you still bleeding when you found him?"

"Probably a little."

"That might explain it." Morag rose and paced around the table. "Somehow, your blood gave him a bit of humanity. Allowed him to control his urges."

My cheeks grew warm.

"Oh, don't look at me like that, girl! I mean his *predatory* urges. What makes a bird catch a fish, and so on." She resumed her pacing, her bad foot dragging behind her. "He's been freed from the instinct to kill. I'm certain he would thank you for such a gift, but he's probably just as ignorant about what happened as you are."

I cradled my hand against my chest. "You're saying a drop of my blood allowed him to choose whether or not to drown me? That it's still allowing him to choose?"

"Aye. All it took was a touch. The mingling of your blood." Her eyes shone. "That's magic, a kind few ever possess."

"Nonsense."

"Not nonsense. Magic." Morag continued to circle the table, making my head spin.

"But . . ." My stomach twisted as I considered a terrible possibility. "Does that mean Fynn's feelings for me are some sort of magic, too?"

"Of course not. Matters of the heart can't be affected by enchantments." With a sigh, Morag finally resumed her seat. "Young people. The only magic they know is the sort they find in each other's eyes."

There was a definite note of bitterness in her tone, but I'd pried into her life enough for one day.

I pictured Fynn's cobalt eyes, always narrowed when we walked through town, but bright and inquisitive when we were alone. No matter what he was, my fingers ached to touch him again, to memorize every ripple of muscle, every bump and imperfection.

"Drink your tea now." Morag motioned to my untouched cup. "And rest assured, the boy won't hurt you. You've tamed the beast. But there are plenty of other sinister creatures in the water, as we both know."

I pushed my chair in and folded my arms over my chest, making it clear I didn't intend to linger over tea today. "I'm sorry, I can't stay. I've got to find Fynn before the *fossegrim* does."

Lifting my cup, I took a huge gulp and coughed. I'd never tried whiskey before, and Mam would've had a fit if she knew, but it was surprisingly good. The liquor burned through my blood in a dizzying, heady way that felt like courage.

As I took a step toward the door, Morag muttered, "Wait." She tapped her fingers against her cheek and fell silent. I was about to take another step when she said, "To put out the serpent's eye, I used the tip of a spear. Steel. Perhaps if someone could get close enough to pierce the *fossegrim's* heart with steel, it would finish him, or at least wound him."

"And to kill the serpent, if it should rear its ugly head?"

"I don't think that monster has a heart." She laid a hand against her chest. "It'd have to be poison. The question is, which one would do the trick?"

"Why don't you try, then? It attacked you. If it's near the Isle, assuming it's still alive after it tangled with Fynn, it's a threat to our fishermen."

"Fishermen? Blazes, girl, it can swallow boats whole when it's hungry. But I can't be the one to poison it." Morag shook her head violently. "It's still here, mark my words. Slithering around the Isle, waiting for me." The lines in her face looked deeper, etched in shadow, like she'd somehow aged twenty years since I'd seen her last. "It's come back here to take my life as payment for its eye, and it won't leave until it gets what it wants." She raised her chin a fraction. "I don't intend to let it finish the job."

"Right. Well, if you'll excuse me, I need to go find Fynn before the *fossegrim* takes another victim." As I strode to the door, my gaze fell on a tangle of string and bone. I stopped and brushed my fingers over the pile. "You've made more Bollan Crosses."

"Some. I have enough twine, but I've only a handful of wrasse bones. I need more." Morag's eyes dimmed for a moment, like a wisp of cloud passing over the sun. "Take those and give them to your mam and sisters."

I stuffed the crosses in my skirt pockets, ten in all. I paused, then pulled one out and slipped it over my head. I didn't feel any different with it on, but Morag was so insistent that they worked, it couldn't hurt.

She leaned across the table to grab my almost-full mug. Liquid sloshed over the sides as she drew it toward her mouth. "And I'll make a poison for the serpent in case there's a soul alive who's brave enough to kill it. I'd never forgive myself if anything happened to you or your mam." She eyed the fishbone charm now dangling from my neck with approval. "Be careful, and watch the water always. I don't want to lose my best apprentice."

Despite the leaden feeling in my stomach, I nodded. "I'm your only apprentice."

"True, true."

"Mally's wedding is tomorrow, but I'll be back to work after. You should come if your foot isn't bothering you." I waited for her reply, but none came. "If you're not doing anything important, like making serpent poison or . . ." I hoped she might glance up, at least for a second, but she had returned to studying the dregs of my tea. "I'll save you a place at the family table."

Hoping Fynn hadn't taken me at my word and dived where I could not follow, I opened the door to the golden afternoon.

Morag's trembling, whispered thank you followed me.

Chapter Sixteen

There was a chill to the wind as I started down the hill. I rubbed my arms and peered at the horizon. Great columns of clouds, fluffy as churned butter, yellow-white as cream, glided toward town. The clouds' black bottoms warned of a spectacular storm to come in the evening. As I rushed homeward, I said a silent prayer for Da to hurry back from the day's fishing.

I crossed a strawberry field that had long since gone wild, green and gold grasses swishing against my skirt. From a distance, the town looked deserted, but I narrowed my eyes and scanned the shadows for dark hair and the faded blue of Da's old shirt.

Where could Fynn be? Still on the beach, wrestling with whether to leave? Sitting up in a tree again, where it would take hours to find him?

I darted through the dwindling afternoon market. Aside from two women stuffing skeins of colorful yarn into baskets, the square appeared to be empty. Most of the pie-sellers and fishmongers had gone home early, no doubt to guard their families as dusk fell.

I waved to the two women, though neither returned my gesture, then hurried toward Ms. Katleen's tavern. It had been Ms. Elena's until three years prior, when Ms. Katleen inherited the place from her mam.

With the sun slipping from the sky, fishermen would already be filling the tables, their voices loud, their cups overflowing.

A fisherman seemed the most likely to have seen Fynn, either sitting on the beach or slicing through the waves.

I was steps from the tavern doors when fingers closed over my wrist.

"Let go of me!" As I attempted to twist free, I met Lugh's dark green eyes and gasped. The hand gripping my wrist released me.

"I'm sorry." His voice softened, and he held up his hands—surrendering to what, I wasn't sure. Like Morag, he seemed older than when I'd last seen him, though there were no lines creasing his face. It was in the set of his shoulders and an unfamiliar hardness in his eyes. "I didn't mean to startle you, Bridey. I just wanted to see you, and you're a tough lass to find lately. If you aren't running errands for the witch, you're off somewhere with the comeover. You never stand still anymore."

"That's not fair," I said, biting my lip. "I've tried to visit since your mam went missing. All you had to do was open the door."

Lugh turned, bringing his face close to mine until our noses touched. "You're right. I didn't want to see anyone. You understand." When I nodded, he swallowed. "But you're not exactly the girl I used to know, and I miss her. I thought—I thought you had felt the same way about me."

I lowered my gaze, feigning interest in a discarded handkerchief being pushed across the ground by the wind. He had a point. Before Fynn's arrival, when I'd thought of embraces, lips locked, hearts racing, I'd thought of Lugh. But not anymore.

"He's stolen my heart," I blurted. "I'm so sorry." Heat crept into my face as I watched the handkerchief twirl. "I used to think about us, too. Rather a lot. But I can't change how I feel. If Fynn had never come here . . ."

194

Lugh touched my cheek. "You don't understand, Bry. It's all right if you don't want to be my girl, but that doesn't mean you can stop being my friend." His eyes glistened. "Cat misses you, too. She hasn't been right since Alis disappeared." He shook his head. "You still matter to your friends, no matter what the rest of this stupid town thinks. I only hope you can say the same of us."

I tried to form words, but my throat resisted. Instead, I threw my arms around him. Lugh stiffened, but after a moment, his hands pressed against my back.

"I'll be a better friend. Just give me time." My insides writhed like I'd downed a bucket full of Morag's beloved snigs. "Everything's been so strange lately."

Lugh's sigh gusted through my hair. "I know. Nothing's felt right since that girl washed up on the beach. I keep hoping my mam and the others will turn up one afternoon with a grand excuse for where they've been, but I know they won't."

"What do you mean?"

"They're gone. Dead. I can just feel it."

"Oh, Lugh." I laid my head on his shoulder, like I'd done countless times since we were small, and willed myself not to cry for his sake. "I miss them, too."

"You don't know the worst of it," he murmured into my hair.

"Don't I?" I thought of the fossegrim's song, of the way my feet had nearly marched me over the cliffs. Of Fynn's stubborn wounds, and of the serpent's razor teeth. To kill the fossegrim, I'd have to find a spear and let it try to lure me to my death again. I couldn't let Fynn fight it while he was still injured.

That is, if he hadn't already sped out of Port Coire, and my life, for good.

"She was with child."

Lugh's words jarred me from my thoughts. "Your mam was—?"

"Aye. That's why she'd gone to my aunt's for supper. To share the good news."

I pressed my trembling hands to the sides of his face. His eyes held the same haunted look shared by everyone in town these days. "I promise you, I'll make things right. I'm going to find out what happened to your mam, and to the others, and make sure the guilty party never harms another soul."

Lugh frowned. "How can you promise that? Bridey, do you know something about the disappearances? Who's behind them?"

"Nothing you would believe."

"If you're planning to do something daft—"

"No more questions," I said quietly, stepping back and nodding toward the tavern. "Just trust me. And I'd best hurry. I'm trying to find Fynn. But will I see you and Cat at the wedding?" I shook my head. "Mally picked a terrible time to fall in love."

"That she did. But I wouldn't miss the wedding for anything." Lugh squeezed my shoulder. "And I'll try to make things right with him. With Fynn. If you trust him, so do I."

I smiled. "Thank you." I wished I had something more to offer Lugh, something stronger than comforting words. My hand brushed over the Bollan Crosses bulging in my pocket. "Here, I want you to have this. Give one to Cat, too, would you?" I untangled strands from the mess and handed them to Lugh.

He studied them, frowning. "How many of these awful things are you carrying around?"

I adjusted the sleeves of my blouse. "Seven, now."

"Is this some new English fad?" Lugh turned a cross over in his hands. "They don't seem to be very well-made."

"No, they're no fad. But they just might keep you from drowning if you find yourself someplace where swimming for your life won't save you."

Lugh narrowed his eyes. "Does this have anything to do with your story about your grandad? Because, Bry, it's past time to—"

"Look, if you care for me as much as you say you do, you'll wear it. Please. I can't lose you, too." As I turned and ran the short distance to the tavern, Lugh called a farewell. I waved over my shoulder. "Be safe! Don't go near the water! And I'll see you at the wedding."

Taking a deep breath, I pushed open the heavy tavern doors.

The fug in Ms. Katleen's was even thicker than the humid, storm-charged air outside. The stench of dark ale, mildew, and salt crawled down my throat, banishing all desire for food. If I closed my eyes, I could pretend I was back in Morag's cottage.

Why Liss liked working here was a mystery.

Pressing against the wall, I scanned the faces of the patrons, no easy task in the dim lighting and swirls of bluish smoke. Unlike the deserted market, the tavern was crammed with bodies. It seemed everyone was keen to drown their sorrows lately, even some of the most devout churchgoers who hadn't, to my knowledge, touched a drop in years.

Near the front windows, a woman buttered bread while her husband smoked. Several older fishermen lounged at a table, gulping steaming bowls of soup and looking as though they had nowhere else to be. Their wives had all left them in one way or another by now.

Younger men sat at the bar, frowning over the rims of their mugs. They didn't have to point or curse as I passed—the gleam in their eyes said it all: *strange girl, witch child, madwoman.*

I squared my shoulders and moved deeper into the room, past a man who chomped on a pipe as he made eyes at shapely Ms. Katleen. Seated in the darkest corner at the back of the room, his face half in shadow, was Fynn, staring into a glass of ale, prodding the foam above the dark liquid. He didn't look up until I dropped into the chair opposite him.

My stomach flipped as his eyes met mine. He offered me a half-smile, and in that moment, every word I had wanted to shout at him vanished. I glanced at the beads of sweat from his tall glass collecting on the table. "Since when do you drink ale?"

Fynn's lips twitched. "I don't. But it seems to be the drink of choice, so I thought I'd give it a go. The foam is awful."

I traced patterns on the table with the moisture from his glass. At least when I looked at them instead of Fynn, talking was easier. "I'm glad you didn't leave. I'm sorry for everything I said. All of it."

"I'm sorry, too." Fynn's hand covered mine. "Sorry that I had to show you something that scared you. Only when I tried to go, to return to the water like you wanted, I realized I couldn't leave you with the *fossegrim* still hunting here." My heart thudded in my ears as I listened. "Even if I'm a *monster*, too."

Hearing my words repeated back at me stung like a slap. "I didn't mean that."

He squeezed my hand. "I showed you something I doubt most people here could comprehend, let alone accept. But I trusted you when you said you wanted the truth." He laced his fingers through mine. "I *still* trust you."

I drew in a deep breath and met his eyes. "I want to trust you, too. That's why you must tell me everything."

Fynn swept his gaze across the tavern. "Bridey." He spoke my name like a warning, or a plea.

Lowering my voice to a whisper, I leaned forward. "I've seen what you are. Now I need to know *who* you are. And don't spare any detail."

Fynn grimaced. "This isn't the right place for such talk."

As if to prove his point, Ms. Katleen bustled over to our side. "It's so nice to see you, dear." She clamped a heavy hand on my shoulder. "And I've already met your charming friend. Are you hungry?" Her auburn curls bobbed around her chin as she spoke.

Fynn shook his head. I mumbled, "Not really," but a loud growl from my stomach drowned my words.

"What can I get you, then?" Ms. Katleen asked with a knowing look. "Name anything."

"Loaghtan lamb for me, please." I hoped to send her away from the table quickly. "Herrin' for him. And a bonnag to share."

The instant Ms. Katleen whisked her way toward the kitchen, I reached across the table and gently prodded Fynn in the chest. "You lied to me about not knowing the *glashtyn*. You made me fall for you while pretending to be something you aren't— human. So you owe me this. And there will *never* be a perfect time to talk. Now, out with it."

Fynn sighed, but finally agreed. "There isn't much to tell. I was born eighteen years ago at the mouth of a bay near the Welsh coast. My father taught me to hunt."

"Hunt what?"

"Fish, mostly. And seals." He gave an apologetic smile. "He also taught me to speak English, so I could go on land if I chose. But I preferred to hunt in deeper water, where there's bigger game like sharks and whales."

I suppressed a shudder. Dozens of questions raced through my mind, making it difficult to choose just one. "What about your mam?"

"She was human, if my father told me the truth. I never sought her out. When I was ten, Father left me to fend for myself." He paused when I arched my brows. "Don't make that face. It's our custom."

"Well, I think it's terrible." Though I shouldn't have been surprised to hear that the ocean was as brutal a place as I'd imagined.

"Any more questions?"

"We've only just begun." I leaned closer. "What's your real name?"

The question made him laugh, low and melodic, in a way that made my stomach flutter. "Nothing I can pronounce in this tongue. Besides, I like 'Fynn.'"

I hoped the dim lighting would disguise the furious blush in my cheeks. "I'm glad. How long do *glashtyns* live?"

"Longer than you. About a human life and a half." He smiled. "Which just means you'll never have to miss me, assuming you don't wish me to return to the sea."

"What were you doing near Port Coire when the serpent attacked you?"

He regarded me solemnly, shaking his head. "Other questions?"

"Fynn, this is important. There are monsters in the water waiting to kill my family and friends. Were you coming to help the fossegrim? Or the serpent?"

His lip curled. "No. Glashtyns and serpents hate each other. Always have. But if I tell you what I was doing, you have to promise not to think less of me." He took both my hands in his, and a slight tremor passed between us. "I'd gone on land in human form—not this island, but another close by—to hunt a girl."

I reached for Fynn's glass and lifted it to my lips. He raised his brows as I took a gulp of the bitter liquid. It made me cough, but warmth spread through my chest. "Right. Because glashtyns drown women."

Fynn sighed, his breath grazing my cheek. "It's our nature." Seeing my stony stare, he hurriedly whispered, "I would never hurt you. You really did save my life that day on the beach. Glashtyns know of places deep underwater where we can sometimes heal, if we reach them in time, but the sea had spat me out and left me to die . . ."

He fell silent, as though the memory pained him. Then he met my eyes and continued, "When I woke after the fight, there you were. I should have wanted to carry you off into the water, yet all I longed to do was wipe the worry from your eyes. I can't explain why I've lost the urge to hunt. But I have no desire to harm you. Never have, even when I took you swimming."

I took a second sip of the ale, then pushed the glass toward Fynn. I'd had enough. "I can explain the change. Well, a little." Morag's tale of blood magic was still fresh in my mind. Seeing Fynn's wide-eyed look of amazement tugged a reluctant smile from my lips. "I'll tell you later. Right now, I want to know more about—"

"More about what?" a sharp voice asked.

Mrs. Gill stood by our table, her arms folded across her chest. "Bridey Corkill, does your mam know you're here? I daresay she wouldn't approve of the company you're keeping."

I clenched my hands on the edge of my seat, not daring to glance at Fynn. "Mam's the one who suggested Fynn stay with us. We're not the first family that's hosted a tourist here, I might remind you. She trusts me to make my own decisions."

"Well, I'm keeping an eye on you." She spun on her heel and strode away.

I had an urge to chase her, to grab her bony shoulders and shake some sense into her head. But instead of drawing even more unwanted attention our way, I took another sip of ale to wet my bone-dry mouth.

Fynn scrubbed his hands through his hair and sighed. It seemed to have cost him a great effort not to shout at Mrs. Gill. When he finally looked at me again, he said in a soft voice, "Where were we?"

"We were talking about what brought you to the Isle. And the serpent." A cold wave washed over me, sweeping away the warmth of the drink.

"Right." Fynn grabbed the glass, pushing it back and forth between his hands. "I was hunting on land, and when I returned to the water with my catch"—he frowned at the look I gave him, and quickly amended—"with a girl, I encountered the serpent. It wanted my kill, and we fought." Fynn ran a hand gingerly down his injured side. "Needless to say, the serpent won."

Picturing Mam's painting of the two beasts facing off over the drowned girl's body, I frowned. "Had you ever fought a serpent before?"

"No. The ocean is vast, and I've never strayed far from these waters." Fynn paused to take a sip. "I wonder why the serpent is keeping close to this island, anyway. The fossegrim is easier to explain. It likely followed the serpent here, picking off the remains of the larger beast's meals. Or, if it's the same one that murdered your grandfather, it may have remembered this spot as good hunting grounds. But serpents never stay in one place for long."

I told the story of Morag's foot and the half-blind serpent's desire for revenge while Fynn drained his glass.

"Wish I knew why people drink this stuff." He wiped his mouth on his sleeve. "It's disgusting. And I wish I knew how we could get rid of the damned fossegrim before anyone else goes missing."

"And the serpent, someday," I added softly. It had to be stopped eventually, though until it started luring people into the water like the fossegrim, the fiddling monstrosity was our sole concern. "Morag reckons she may have found a way to be rid of the fossegrim. Piercing its heart with steel may kill it. How are you at stabbing?"

"Probably the same as you."

"Hopeless, then."

Fynn shook his head. "Not hopeless. You're strong. Stronger than me, I'd wager, while I'm still healing."

Maybe he was right. I did all that wood chopping for Mam. But I couldn't take the life of a living being, even one as cruel as the monster who took my grandad away. I couldn't even spear a single snig the day Morag sent me scouring the shore. Just thinking about killing gave me a feeling like spiders scuttling across my skin. "We'll find a way." I managed a smile. "At least, I hope so."

"I know so."

I was about to ask Fynn whether he'd ever encountered a *fossegrim* before this one when Ms. Katleen and her mam appeared at our table with our supper and our cake.

"Who ordered the lamb?" Ms. Elena asked.

"I did." As I met her eyes, her waxy hands trembled so hard she nearly dropped the plate in my lap. She banged my dish on the table, and I took advantage of her nearness to whisper in her ear. "There's something dangerous in the water, and you know it. No one wants to listen to me or Morag, but they might be willing to hear you, if you were to try."

She flinched, and hastily straightened as much as her stiff back allowed. "I'm nearly deaf, young lady. I haven't any idea what you said." She gripped the table and frowned. "Now, if you'll excuse me, I have bread in the oven."

As she tottered off, Ms. Katleen bent down and whispered, "I'm sorry about Mrs. Gill. That woman . . ." She pressed her lips together as though biting back the sort of remark that would make Mam use my full name. "Let's just say not everyone here jumps to conclusions just because someone thinks they saw something funny in the water, or because Thomase Boyd is flinging accusations faster than you can say *unfair*. You two are welcome to stay as long as you'd like."

When Ms. Katleen left us to our meal, I lifted my fork and glanced at Fynn's untouched fish. He stared at his plate as though it were laced with poison. "Eat," I urged. "You'll need your strength if we're going to hunt a *fossegrim* and help with a wedding tomorrow."

Fynn picked up his knife and fork, chopping his supper into sloppy portions. "I thought you wanted me to stay away from your family."

I reached for his hand but drew back before our fingers touched. "I'm still angry you lied, but I understand why you did. You knew how I'd react."

He gave a small smile. "Just my luck that I fell for someone who can't stand the sea. You're well within your right to hate me."

"I don't, though. Knowing your secret hasn't changed what I feel for you." Except, when I looked at him now, I saw the beast, too.

Something Mam had said weeks ago echoed in my thoughts, chasing away my vision of his *glashtyn* form. "Besides, the Corkills don't turn their backs on anyone. Your place is with us. That is, if you still want it."

Fynn raised his eyes to mine. "Of course I do. I haven't been sleeping on your sofa all this time out of a love of rocks and trees." With a grin, he stole a piece of my lamb. "This isn't half bad." He hovered over my plate, perfectly poised to steal a kiss. I bent forward, tipping my chin up. Fynn's breath hitched. If I moved another fraction, I could kiss him.

But not today. I drew back. It wasn't Mrs. Gill's threatening words, or the looks of the men at the bar that made me lower my eyes to my supper. Anger was still simmering in my veins. It would take more than the space of a meal to forgive Fynn for keeping so much hidden from me, even if he had his reasons.

As we ate, my mind wandered back through the summer's many strange events before Fynn turned up. The drowned girl. Nessa Daley's disappearance. The false pearl in Da's nets.

"I have one last question."

Fynn paused, a forkful of fish halfway to his mouth.

"The day after the girl washed ashore, I found a giant pearl on the floor of Da's boat, and I saw a fin that looked a lot like yours. Was that—?"

"Me." A smile lit his face. "I saw you protecting Grayse from the birds." Fynn dropped his gaze to the berry bonnag between our plates. "Even before I lost the will to hunt, I thought you were beautiful. Warm and light. The kind of beauty a creature like me, from the cold and the dark, can only hope to grasp for the briefest moment before it slips away like water through human fingers. I just wanted to give you something pretty."

"Then why did the pearl turn into a rock that evening?"

Fynn passed me a slice of bonnag without meeting my eyes. "Nothing from the ocean is meant to survive on land forever."

Suddenly, I wasn't hungry anymore.

CHAPTER SEVENTEEN

The blast of a horn roused me early the next morning. Though its clarion cry was familiar from wedding days past, it sounded shriller than usual. More like a dying seal than a call to celebration. I leaped out of bed, tripped over the edge of our rug, and banged my hip against our bedside table.

"Happy Thursday!" Grayse chirped, throwing back the covers. Liss groaned in her sleep. "Lucky, lucky Thursday!" Grayse's hazel eyes held no trace of tiredness, as though she'd been awake long before the horn blew. "Ready to be a bride-maid, *Bridey*?"

"Maybe tomorrow." I yawned, shuffling over to the window and rubbing my smarting hip. The sky was still a canvas of indigo night and silvery moon, save for a thick line of orange smeared across the horizon. All of Port Coire's fishermen were taking to the water, their boats gliding silently toward the open sea like ghosts retreating into obscurity.

There was no sign of a phantom fiddler hovering over the rocky waters.

As I drank in the star-studded view of the cliffs and our neighbor's chicken coop, memories of yesterday crashed over me like the breaking waves. Fynn the *glashtyn*. Morag's fear of the serpent. Mrs. Gill's hateful words.

Another burst of noise sliced through my pounding head. I flinched and turned to Grayse. "Do you know who Mally charged with sounding the horn?"

Grayse's eyes narrowed to mischievous slits. "The Cretney boys."

I shook my head. "I should have known." I was finally alert thanks to the shrieking horn, and while I didn't feel much like celebrating, it was time to get ready.

Mam had hastily altered one of her old dresses for me. The rosy gown adorned with tiny pearls was like something from a fashion magazine, and Mally pinned a glittering hair-slide behind my ear to secure my fancy knot of braids. Still, gazing at my reflection in all its finery, I couldn't summon a smile.

Perhaps I was simply frustrated that there wouldn't be time to look for the fossegrim, or something metal to kill it with, before the wedding began.

The morning passed in a haze until Grayse, Liss, and I gathered by the door to watch Da and Fynn depart for the church. We each held a thin, reddish osier wand identifying us as Mally's bridesmaids. Judging by the muffled argument that could be heard from the back of the house, we would have to wait a while on the nervous bride.

Tears splashed down Grayse's cheeks as Da and Fynn slipped on their shoes. "I want to go with them!"

"The men always go to the church first, Grayse," Liss said impatiently.

"But I'm bored!" Grayse swung her osier wand, and the supple willow branch swished into Fynn's leg with a thwack.

He shouted something that made Da chuckle and Liss blush. Clutching his leg, Fynn struggled to keep his balance. I tried to disguise my smile with a sudden fit of coughing.

Grayse sniffled and dried her tears. She glanced shyly at Fynn and mouthed, Sorry.

Da thumped Fynn on the back. "We'd best leave before one of us loses a limb, aye?" Grinning, Da opened the door allowing in a gust of warm, sultry air and stepped outside.

"I'll be there shortly," Fynn called. He turned to me. "You look beautiful." He'd never sounded so cautious with me before. His hangdog expression made his angular features appear softer than usual.

After checking that Grayse and Liss were occupied, I put my lips to his ear, inhaling the scent of spring that clung to his skin. He must have borrowed Da's ancient bottle of aftershave. "Cheer up. This is a wedding. You're supposed to be happy."

"I'll be happy if you forgive me."

"I'm trying." The trouble was, when I pictured kissing Fynn again, the image of him in his sea-monster skin flashed to mind. I shivered.

Fynn gave a strained smile, then slipped out the door. For once, I wasn't entirely saddened to see him go.

Minutes later, Mally emerged from the room that would now be mine. My pulse quickened at the sight of her in Mam's wedding gown. Over the years, it had faded from pristine white to buttery ivory, but she looked radiant with waves of her honey hair cascading down her back.

"Isn't it gorgeous?" She twirled around the main room, a butterfly in flight.

"Yes," I managed, despite the leaden feeling in my stomach. "Artur will be speechless."

Seeing her in the gown made Mally's imminent departure a reality. She would go to England tomorrow, taking the boat ride I had dreamed of for ages. *We* had dreamed of. I wasn't ready to watch her leave.

"Ready, bird?" Mam snapped her fingers, calling my attention. "What's that you're wearing?" Frowning, she touched the string of my Bollan Cross, but the high collar of my dress hid the charm.

"It's a necklace." I turned away from her and hurried down the hall. "Give me one more moment!"

The extra crosses from Morag rested in a jumble on our dresser. Perhaps I could convince Mally to wear one on her journey tomorrow. I pulled three crosses from the pile and rushed back to the main room.

"Here." I offered a cross each to Liss, Mally, and Mam, who gave me identical blank looks. "They're necklaces. I thought it would be nice if we wore them to the wedding, to show we're family."

"Everyone knows that already." Mally took a necklace first. "It's a *bone*."

"Aye. But it's pretty, right?" I dangled the second Bollan Cross in front of Liss until she took it from my hand. "Put them on."

"I don't know. They're kind of horrible," Liss grumbled, but she and Mally slipped the crosses over their heads. After a strange, almost startled look at me, Mam did the same.

"Let's go!" Grayse urged.

As we neared the church, time seemed to speed up. We walked three circles around the churchyard with Artur's attendants, a tradition I'd never understood. Then we stood by the altar inside the stuffy sanctuary, listening to Pastor Quillin's voice rise above the sniffles of the small crowd as he blessed the couple.

Only about half the residents of Port Coire lined the pews.

"So many are missing," Liss whispered, leaning in. "Probably all friends and relatives of Mally's former beaus." She frowned. "Never mind them, though. She doesn't need their approval to enjoy her day."

I made a faint noise of agreement, but I knew better. Not even the gossips would miss an opportunity for dancing and feasting. They'd slurp our broth and gorge on our geese while muttering behind their hands.

No, those who had chosen not to attend the ceremony were avoiding me.

Mrs. Kissack was notably absent, though one of her friends nudged another woman's shoulder and glanced my way. The women exchanged a look and shook their heads, but I fixed a smile on my face and focused once again on Mally and Artur.

In a blink, the ceremony was over and the guests rose to their feet. Applause echoed off the church walls as folk tossed hats and handkerchiefs into the air. The Cretney boys threw the wedding horn, and Grayse tossed her wand. It was a miracle no one lost an eye.

Fynn stood in the front row of onlookers keeping a healthy distance from the Gills. I was surprised they'd even bothered to come. I shook my head at them, then pretended to glare at Fynn until he acknowledged me with a grin.

In so many ways, he was still the boy I'd come to know. And yet . . .

Our neighbors sucked in their breaths, heads turning toward the altar. I glanced up just in time to witness Mally and Artur's first kiss as husband and wife. He dipped her to the floor in his enthusiasm and nearly dropped her.

Someone whistled. The tips of Artur's huge ears turned pink.

Scattered applause followed the newlyweds as they retreated down the aisle. Mally caught my eye and waved as Artur ushered her out the church doors. I returned the motion, though I doubted she'd seen, then dodged the copper-haired Cretney boys to reach Fynn's side.

"I'm counting to ten, lads!" a woman's deep voice boomed. "How many times have I told you, there's no playing chase in the Lord's house!"

Seeing me approach, Fynn sat straighter in the deserted front pew.

Aside from my parents, who spoke in low voices with Artur's mam, and my sisters, who were entertaining a few lingering guests, the church had emptied.

"Care to explain why everyone's gathering out front?" Fynn asked, nodding toward the windows, which offered a view of the weed-choked churchyard. Young men were stretching their legs, preparing for a run in their Sunday best.

"They're getting ready for the race." I smiled. "Whichever lad reaches the market first gets to break a bonnag over the bride's head. Then the girls grab cake to put under their pillows so they can dream of their future husbands."

"That seems like a waste of good cake." Fynn shook his head. "And a useless way to find a husband. Why are they going to the market?"

"That's where we hold the feast. Wedding celebrations are always in the market."

Fynn found my hand on the wooden seat and looked at me, a question in his eyes. When I nodded, he twisted his fingers around mine and, to my relief, they felt normal, hot and slightly rough. Certainly nothing like the rubbery skin of a flipper.

He lowered his voice as my parents' conversation faded. "Care to share what's bothering you? Do you have more questions for me?"

"It's not that. I wish we'd had a bigger turnout, is all." My stomach ached as I surveyed the empty church again. "I can't blame the folk too nervous to risk being out at dusk, but . . ." I shrugged. "I wonder how many wished to avoid me. Seeing you win the race, though, that might lift my spirits." I pulled my hand from Fynn's and shoved him off the pew.

He bowed quickly. "If I get there first, the cake is yours." His eyes flashed. "You could even eat it and save Mally from the humiliation of crumbs in her hair."

"And spoil all the fun?" My lips turned up in a grin for the first time in days as I glanced to the windows again.

Out in the churchyard, sandy-haired Thomase elbowed stout Martyn Watterson in the ribs out of pure meanness or to give himself more space to stretch. I couldn't be sure. Lugh was there, too, standing apart from the others and watching the sky.

I walked to the door with Fynn. *"Aigh vie!"* I called as he went to join the lads. "That means *good luck!*" He waved, and then, to my surprise, strode toward Lugh.

My old friend tensed. Fynn stepped closer, his lips moving rapidly. Lugh squared his shoulders, scowling deeper, and replied. They stared at each other for a long moment.

Leaning against the church door, I strained to hear, but their voices blended with the murmur of the other lads.

With a jerk, Lugh's open hand shot toward Fynn. Fynn gripped the hand with both of his, and Lugh's shoulders relaxed. They nodded stiffly and dropped their hands, then went their separate ways.

I sighed. Regardless of what had passed between them, they both seemed at ease now.

"Are we heading to the market soon?" I called to Mam, glancing over my shoulder into the church. I wanted to greet Fynn, Lugh, and the others at the finish line, and they looked ready to take off at any moment.

"Soon," Mam's voice drifted from the altar.

"Or we could go now."

I whirled around. Cat stood beside me in a pale green dress. To my dismay, she wore a string of her mam's best pearls instead of the Bollan Cross I'd asked Lugh to give her. Shadows ringed her eyes, and her smile was faint, but at least it was there. Like old times.

She propped her hand on her hip. "How about it? Be my escort?"

With effort, I returned her smile before looping my arm through hers. "You've got to stop scaring me like that."

"Please," Cat scoffed. "Seems to me you need more excitement in your life." She waved to Lugh and Fynn as we passed. "I got your present. The necklace. I would have worn it today, but my mam insisted I borrow her pearls. I don't like to upset her since Alis . . ." Cat twisted the strand of pearls between her fingers. "Did you make it yourself?"

"Morag did."

Cat raised her dark brows, her eyes widening. "It's not human, is it?" We veered left, following the dirt path through a copse of tired, bent ash trees.

"No." Cat's shadowed eyes demanded the truth. "It's a charm to prevent drowning. When you return home, put it on and don't take it off. Even if you don't believe me."

"I won't." Cat raised her voice as the sound of frantic feet grew louder. "I know Alis didn't wander off with Nessa or Eveleen." Her lips trembled. "Mrs. Kissack told me what you said, about seeing the monster that killed your grandad, and—"

"You think I'm mad, too?"

"No. And neither does Lugh. I'm not sure I believe in sea monsters, but I know you wouldn't lie, either." She squeezed my hand. "There's something strange happening here. And after all that's passed, I'm not sure I'm ready to hear the truth."

I took a deep breath. "I understand. Better than you think. But the necklace will keep you safe."

"Will it? It's just a disgusting old bone, as far as I can tell, and I don't trust witchcraft." Cat met my gaze and held it, heedless of the crooked path ahead. "But I trust you, Bry."

CHAPTER EIGHTEEN

We barely had time to perch ourselves on the edge of the fountain before the lads dashed into view. Harsh breathing and the slap of bare feet on hard-packed earth rang through the air as they drew nearer. Thomase was in the lead, Lugh and Fynn following hard on his heels.

"Come on, Martyn!" Liss clasped her hands against her chest.

Personally, I didn't think Martyn was likely to catch the others. He was near the back of the group, along with one of the scrawniest Cretney boys, looking as though he'd soon keel over into the bushes.

As the lads scrambled toward the tailor's shop—the tiny building declared as the finish line—I was sure for a moment that Thomase *would* win. But then he tried to elbow Lugh in the ribs to ensure his victory.

Lugh shoved him. He'd always loathed cheaters. They landed in the dirt together, a tangle of limbs punching and kicking. All the frustration and sorrow both lads had endured thanks to the sea seemed to be pouring out as they struggled. I winced as Lugh landed a blow that was sure to give Thomase a black eye.

Fynn flew past them, making my heart skip as he breezed into the lead. But Adam Radcliff, another of Mally's former sweethearts, darted ahead at the last second. He slapped his hand against the wall of the tailor's in the space of a blink before Fynn rammed the building with his shoulder.

While the crowd applauded, Ms. Katleen presented Adam with the bonnag. As a girl tossed flower petals, Mally glided over to her side.

"I'm glad that's done," Liss muttered, leaping to her feet and smoothing her dress. "I'm going to check on Martyn."

Fynn dropped into Liss's vacated seat. Dark patches soaked Da's old suit. Mam had made her best effort to hem the garments to Fynn's lean body, but it was a haphazard job.

"That was interesting," he panted, slicking back his disheveled hair. "I'm surprised that idiot didn't try to trip me instead of your friend."

"Oh, I'm not," Cat said, nudging me with her shoulder and pointing to the spot where several lads were attempting to pull Thomase and Lugh apart. "That Boyd lad is nothing but trouble. Handsome trouble, though."

I groaned, but Cat didn't appear to hear. She turned, splashing cool water from the fountain on her face. "I'm going to see if I can grab a piece of the bonnag to put under my pillow. Want to come, Bry?"

I glanced at Fynn and shook my head. "I'll just watch."

"You don't want to dream of your future husband tonight?"

"I don't want to dream of anything. I'd welcome one night of uninterrupted sleep."

"I do!" Grayse jumped up from her seat and reached for Cat's hand. They hurried to join the group of girls gathered around Adam and Mally.

When Cat and Grayse were out of earshot, I whispered to Fynn, "It's a silly superstition." He arched his brows. "Not that all superstitions are silly. Some, as we know, are quite real."

Fynn nodded gravely and leaned against me. I stiffened, my heart quickening, and as though he sensed my discomfort, he pulled away. That only made me feel worse.

As we listened to the shouts of girls vying for a piece of the dreaming cake, I prayed the happy sounds wouldn't turn to screams when dusk fell on the wedding feast.

Though the girls' struggle was usually a spectacle worth enjoying, I kept my gaze trained on the hill to the north, hoping to see a gray-haired figure ambling toward the gathering. But Morag's foot must have been bothering her. Or else she didn't want to brave the harsh tongue-wagging of the townfolk.

When Mally announced supper, everyone claimed their seats. Fynn and I hurried to the table where Mam and Da were seated, the Gills beside them. Da commanded one end of the table, and gestured for Fynn to sit at the other.

"Is that wise, Peddyr? Letting a murderer preside over your family's meal?" Mrs. Gill demanded, her jowls quivering. Her round face had seemed so friendly when I was small, though that was a long time ago.

Fynn drew out his chair and sat without so much as a glance at Mrs. Gill, but Da frowned at her. "That's a mighty strong word to throw around without proof, especially at a wedding."

She sniffed, looking suspiciously at Fynn. "I stand by it. I can't recall a summer tourist ever staying as long as this lad. And until he turned up, our girls didn't fear disappearing from their beds. It doesn't take a law man to piece these things together."

Da sat taller and narrowed his eyes. "If you have a problem with anyone at this table, there are plenty of seats elsewhere."

"Your choice," I added as I dropped into a seat and smiled sweetly at her.

Mrs. Gill rose stiffly from her chair. "Fine. Let's go, Danell." She tugged her husband's arm. "We aren't welcome here. The Corkills can enjoy their meal with the murderer and their witch-loving daughter without us."

As they shuffled away, Da rubbed his hands together. "Now that that's behind us, where's the first course?"

Broth arrived in wooden piggins, and hardly anyone spoke as we scraped the steaming liquid up with large mussel shells. Next came a platter of capons, followed by goose. Grayse's mouth fell open as Da carved slivers of meat from a roasted hog. It was all more than we could afford, especially with fish still scarce, but friends and neighbors had pitched in to make the feast one to remember.

As I ate, my gaze traveled to Morag's hill. Still, no hunched figure limped into view.

Perhaps she hadn't understood that my invitation was sincere. Yet, she'd fixed me countless cups of tea, helped me begin to accept Fynn's *glashtyn* side, and trusted me with the real story about her foot. In the space of a summer, she'd become like a grandmam to me. She had more than earned her place at our table.

Mam pushed back her chair. "I can't eat another bite! Shall we dance as we used to, love?" She ushered Da from his seat as a group of musicians struck up a popular dance hall tune.

Someone tapped my shoulder. "Care to take a walk?" Fynn offered me his hand. "I'd ask you to dance, but I don't know how."

"All right." I glanced around the square. Mally's white dress and Artur's dark suit stood out among the paltry crowd of revelers. Liss led Grayse and a few younger girls in a dizzying circle dance. Lugh spoke with Martyn while Thomase skulked nearby, kicking stones. There was no sign of the Gills.

Fynn shot me a hopeful look as I gripped his hand. "You're not afraid to be alone with me, then?"

I shook my head. "Are your wounds healed enough for an uphill climb?"

"It's not what I had in mind, but I think I can manage." Fynn raised his brows. "Besides, it's past time I met Port Coire's famed witch."

I shielded my eyes against the setting sun. "Aye. Help me find a plate, would you? Morag might like some supper."

Slipping away wasn't difficult, especially when drinks were flowing freely courtesy of Ms. Katleen. Balancing a napkin-covered plate of meat and rolls in one hand and holding Fynn's arm with the other, I slid between the long shadows of the bakery and the tavern.

Strangely, even though his nearness made me picture the *glashtyn* again, I didn't feel the slightest hint of nerves. That is, until I began thinking of what I was to do if he tried to kiss me again.

Fynn sang under his breath, seeming to gain confidence in the tune as the rush of ocean waves drowned the noise of the celebration.

"What's that you're singing?" I asked.

Fynn shrugged. "A chanty I picked up listening to sailors. I regret that the words aren't very—" He frowned at something in the distance. A girl-shaped something, running toward us with alarming speed.

"Roseen!" I gasped.

When she reached us, Cat's cousin doubled over panting. Her eyes were wide, her face red as a beet. "Catreena," she wheezed, pointing back the way she'd come. "Catreena."

My blood turned to ice. "What about her?"

Roseen gestured frantically toward the sea. "We were on the beach. She just—swam—wouldn't answer me." She shuddered. "You have to help her!"

Fynn disentangled his arm from mine and bolted toward the nearest strip of beach, casting off Da's suit jacket as he ran. If anyone could get to Cat in time, it was he.

"Don't just stand there! Go after him!" I shouted at Roseen, heart thudding in my ears. The plump girl looked about to keel over. "Hurry! Fynn might need—oh, just go!"

Roseen nodded, still breathing hard, and dashed off.

Satisfied she would at least try to help, I dropped Morag's plate and sprinted back toward the party. The distance from the beach to the market had never seemed so great. I needed to find Da. He would find something sharp and fight the monster, for surely it was the fossegrim that had called my best friend into the sea.

"It's Bridey!" someone called as I ran through the market. "How are the fish, Bry? Still whispering death threats from the waves?"

Shaking my head, I rushed to the nearest table, scattering napkins and plates in my search for anything metallic and sharp. There was a platter of leftover goose. Clumps of flowers. An empty bread basket. A hog's rump with a carving knife stuck in the side. I pulled the steel blade out and hid it in the folds of my dress.

Peering through the crowd, I found Da in the shadow of the carpenter's shop, sipping a mug of ale. I could run to him now and tell him Cat was in trouble. I could press the knife into his hands and explain what he needed to do. Follow him, wringing my hands, while I helplessly watched the rescue.

Drawing a deep breath, I turned away from the party. Fynn was already on his way, and he was a stronger swimmer than Da. And the *fossegrim* was mine to challenge. The constant dread of losing anyone else I loved would end tonight.

I tore past the bakery and the tavern, patting the lumpy Bollan Cross hidden under my dress. It lent me silent reassurance as I rushed by Fynn's discarded jacket.

When the earth beneath my feet changed from packed soil to sand, an eerie chant echoed in my ears. The sky darkened to lavender, making the filmy figure hovering in the waves easy to spot. But there was no sign of Fynn or Cat in the murky water. Roseen stood alone on the beach, arms wrapped around her waist.

Come to me, a voice crooned. *I've been waiting so long.*

The last time I'd heard this melody, it had made all rational thought impossible. My legs had jerked forward of their own accord. But with the cross around my neck, my mind was clear and my feet only moved as I told them to. If I lived through this, I'd have to tell Morag how well her charm worked.

Let me hold you, my treasure, an hour or two.

Mouth dry, knees banging together, I crossed the sand, heading straight for the crashing surf.

At the water's edge, I froze. Facing down the sea had been so much easier with Fynn at my side. With no one to walk beside me, my courage fled in the thundering waves.

The wind picked up, knocking a swell sideways and revealing a glimpse of dark, curly hair.

Cat.

If I didn't move quickly, my best friend would forever belong to the sea. The salty waves had already taken enough from me.

Stomach lurching, I staggered into the water. I clutched the carving knife with both hands, terrified a wave would knock me over and I'd lose the blade. Roseen called out, but I didn't turn to acknowledge her. If Fynn didn't reach Cat soon, she would drown.

We'll dance in the waves to your heart's delight.

Chill water crept up my legs, soaking my dress. I shivered, kicking to untangle myself from something slimy, then continued slogging against the current. The fossegrim floated just beyond the peaks of the waves, pulling a bow tenderly across a small fiddle. He was still too far away. I still couldn't swim, and the water would close over my head before I reached him.

My love, my life, you'll make a beautiful wife.

I fumbled with the knife as a wave smacked me square in the chest. The ocean numbed my fingers. I wondered how I could ever get close enough to the monster. But I'd die before I let this creature have Cat.

"I'll do it! I'll marry you!" I shouted over the anguished cries of seabirds. Concealing the blade behind my back, I planted my feet in the mucky sand and willed myself not to think about what might scuttle over them.

The fiddle's sweet notes faltered. The fossegrim raised his colorless eyes to meet mine and a smile stretched across his pallid face. He glided over the water, his wavy hair and ruffled shirt blowing in the breeze.

That was a good sign. He looked transparent as a ghost, but if the wind could touch him, so could I.

"Bridey!" Fynn's call was clear above the roar of the water.

I tried to answer, but the words died in my throat as the fossegrim surged forward. Up close, he wasn't so handsome. His face and neck were mottled green and gray, his eyes milky like something left to decay at the bottom of the ocean. The clothes he wore hung in tatters off his gaunt frame, and clawlike hands curled around his fiddle. The instrument's body appeared to be carved from driftwood, and its strings resembled fine braids of blond human hair. If this was what Lugh's mam and the girls had seen when they leaped from the cliffs, it was no wonder they'd panicked and drowned.

The creature spread its bony arms and hissed a single word: *come.*

Now was my chance. I held the carving knife at my side beneath the water, careful to keep it out of sight of the *fossegrim.* I crept forward until he and I were more than close enough to touch.

The *fossegrim* lifted a hand, palm open. I flinched, anticipating a blow, but he merely ran a long, thorny finger down my cheek. My skin burned, and the odor of smoke invaded my nose and throat—the stench of rotten meat sizzling over flames, of gutted fish, and spoiled milk.

Resisting the urge to rub my cheek, I locked eyes with him. "What are you waiting for?" I managed, despite my constant shuddering. "I'm right here."

This time, he reached with both hands, mouth gaping in a horrible imitation of a grin. Fragments of bone littered his mouth, though they were too irregular and misshapen to be called teeth. Ripples of cold rolled off his body and crashed into me, making it even harder to stay on my feet. The faces of Cat, Grandad, and the missing girls flashed before me, steadying my shaking legs as the monster wrapped a hand around my waist.

Unable to utter a cry or even draw a breath, I jerked back and raised the knife, aiming for the creature's heart. A claw-curled hand swiped at my arm, but trying to stab a monster wasn't so different from chopping wood. I had to follow through with my swing or risk losing my balance. The sharp points of his nails raked my forearm, yet I pushed through the searing pain.

The carving knife rammed into the fossegrim's chest.

He howled, grabbing me by the throat, but as his life bled away, so too did his strength. Using both hands, I drove the knife in deeper, recalling the faint music playing on the wind as Grandad jumped. No one else would have to die for the fossegrim's pleasure.

The creature shuddered, his milky eyes bulging. For a moment, I thought he would simply sink beneath the waves. Then a loud pop rang out as his body burst into wet chunks of sticky, greenish foam. The sight reminded me of the dyed seeds girls would throw at the end of Mally's celebration. Bits of fossegrim stuck to my face and hair, cold and reeking of ash, while other pieces fizzled in the waves. Wiping muck from my brow, I lunged for the knife that had served me so well, but it had been lost to the sea along with the fossegrim's gruesome instrument.

Someone crashed through the water yelling my name. Fynn struggled against the waves. His trousers clung to his legs like a second skin, but his chest was bare. Rivulets of water ran down his face.

Finally remembering how to use my legs, I sloshed forward into his waiting arms. Even in his other form, Fynn was nothing like the horror I'd just faced. I held tight to his waist, finding his warmth a relief after the fossegrim's intensely cold touch. My right arm throbbed, but I was past caring about the pain.

"Don't take offense," he muttered shakily, holding me close, "but you stink."

A laugh escaped my dry throat as I glanced around. "Where's Cat?"

"Safe on the beach." Fynn cupped seawater in his hands and used it to clean more thick slime off my cheek. "I had to wrestle her out of the water. Roseen helped me hold her down." He picked a clump of fossegrim out of my hair and lobbed it out to the horizon. "I don't think either of us alone could have kept Cat from heeding the monster's call, she was struggling so, but I wish I could have come for you sooner. I *should* have come for you sooner."

"You did what you had to. Thank you for looking after my friend." I rested my head against his shoulder. A pale moon appeared through the broken wall of clouds. "If we're waging war against the sea, I'd say we just won a battle."

Fynn's face lit with a fierce pride, and I managed a strained smile.

"But, did Cat and Roseen . . . ?" I wasn't sure how to ask whether they'd seen him in his *glashtyn* form. I dreaded his answer.

"They didn't see anything I care about," Fynn answered. "Even in this skin, I'm a strong enough swimmer to handle a spell-touched girl." He glimpsed my bloody arm and held it above the water. The stinging dulled slightly, but the four slashes there looked deep enough to leave scars.

I swayed against Fynn, lightheaded. "I need to get to shore." He obliged by picking me up and splashing through to the shallows. "I like you, Fynn. Rather a lot. No matter what you are," I murmured, gazing up at him. "Have I told you that?"

A smile lit his face. "Even if you didn't, I think I already knew." He smoothed my hair away from my forehead. "Does this mean you've forgiven me?"

"I can't seem to stay away from you, any more than you can return to the sea. So, yes." I closed my eyes, content for once to listen to the ocean's whispered secrets.

On shore, Cat inspected my arm with a frown. "We'll have to put something on your cuts. They look terrible." Her dark curls were plastered to her head, and like Fynn and me, she was soaked from head to toe. "Roseen went to get blankets. And to tell our parents how you and Fynn rescued me when I tried to swim and got in too deep."

I blinked. "Isn't she going to tell them about the—"

"Monster? Fairy? Ghost?" Cat shivered in the brisk evening air. "No." She met my eyes. "No one believed you when you tried to explain what happened to your granddad. And no one would believe us now, no matter how well we explained it." She laid a trembling hand on my shoulder. "I'm so sorry I never believed you."

Pulling Cat into a tight hug, I murmured, "It's all right. There are a lot of things I wouldn't have believed until recently."

Grandad told me many stories when I was small, but my favorites were the ones in which clever girls outsmarted dangerous beasts. If he were here, he'd be proud of what I had just done, and that thought made me stand a little taller.

"I know the feeling," Cat said at last, shivering hard. "Roseen and I were walking on the beach, collecting seashells for Alis's memorial. Out of nowhere, I heard beautiful music, and the next thing I knew I was in the water. I didn't even care that I was going to drown. Only the music mattered." Cat heaved a shuddering sigh. "Then Fynn was holding me while Roseen covered my ears, and you were facing a—what was that thing, Bry?"

Fynn gave me an encouraging nod. Cat needed the truth now.

I gripped her shoulders. "It was a monster. And there are more like it. That's why I gave you the hideous fishbone necklace."

She nodded, her eyes round like twin moons. "I still don't understand how you killed a monster. You were so brave!"

My cheeks warmed. "I didn't feel brave. And besides, I don't think killing means you're brave. I just did what I had to, to keep you safe." Cat made a soft noise, a sob or a muttered word. "It was Morag that gave me the idea about piercing the monster's heart with steel. In a way, she's the reason it's dead and we're still here."

We moved farther up the beach, trailed by Fynn. "I always thought Morag was a horrible old woman," Cat said softly. "Yet it seems she's smarter than anyone else in these parts." Cat gave a weak chuckle. "Now I wish I wasn't so fond of sweets. Maybe then my mam would have apprenticed me to a witch instead of a cake maker."

I squeezed her hand and smiled.

It was over. The disappearances would finally end. It was over. Against the vast, uncaring sea, we had won.

Chapter Nineteen

A fist pounded on our front door, jarring me from the memory of watching Mally and Artur's ship departing the harbor at dawn. I turned away from the hearth where I'd been feeding the flames a bundle of herbs, and Da peeled himself out of his chair. Mam hurried after him, her hands still wet from washing dishes, followed by Grayse.

Mr. Gill stood on our step, his face brighter than a spring radish. "Found—bodies—harbor," he wheezed, chest heaving.

A thorn of cold jabbed my gut as names and faces flashed to mind: Cat, Lugh, Martyn, even Thomase. But I'd killed the *fossegrim*. This couldn't be happening. Unless the serpent somehow . . .

"Who?" I choked out.

But Da was already speaking. "What are you going on about, Danell? There were *murders* at the harbor, is that what you mean?"

Mr. Gill brushed aside the gray curls plastered to his brow. "I've called a meeting," he panted. "My house. In an hour. I'll explain there." He turned without another word and jogged toward the next house down the row.

"Wait! Whose bodies did you find?" Da shouted after him, but Mr. Gill didn't glance back. "We have to go to that meeting," Da said, resting his eyes on each of us in turn.

I nodded, lost for words as I tried to imagine any explanation other than another monster.

Mam's face turned ashen. "But Peddyr, I don't know that I want Grayse hearing—"

"I want to go." Grayse stomped her foot, nearly knocking over the paraffin lamp that sat near the door.

Sighing, Mam leaned against the wall. If the shadows beneath her eyes were any indication, she hadn't slept well despite draining a mug of Morag's healing draught. In fact, she hadn't looked at ease since she examined my arm last night.

Fynn cleared his throat and turned to Mam. "I'll stay with Grayse so you can attend the meeting, ma'am."

"You will?" Mam's eyes brightened. Since learning that Fynn had been the one to bring Cat back to shore, Mam and Da had been treating him like a hero, forcing extra helpings on him at breakfast and shooting him looks of admiration.

"Of course." Fynn grinned at Grayse. "You can teach me a new game, if you'd like." Grayse reached for his hand, her pout vanishing. Fynn's eyes met mine for the briefest moment before he disappeared into the main room, and I mouthed my thanks.

"And you girls?" Mam asked, looking between Liss and me.

Liss started toward our bedroom at once. "I'm going to change. I'll be ready soon."

Mam's gaze shifted to me. "How's your arm, bird?" She lightly touched just above the salve-stained bandages covering me from elbow to wrist.

"Mally's salve burns worse than the cuts themselves," I muttered, "so I think everything's healing as it should." I didn't quite trust that Mam believed the story we'd given her about Cat scratching me in her confusion during the rescue. Still, there were more pressing concerns at hand.

Mam smoothed my hair, frowning. "Do you want to come with us? You can stay here if your arm's hurting more than you're letting on."

"No. I'll come." As Mam narrowed her eyes, I hurried to add, "It hurts a bit. But I want to go." I had to find out who had been lost this time. And I didn't mind the pain, as I'd told Fynn the night before as he carefully bandaged my arm. Each time it throbbed, the wounds reminded me of what I'd won.

That the creatures from my nightmares could be slain. Of course, I didn't want to face another so soon, but I had sisters to protect. And now, Fynn.

"Don't leave without me."

I breezed into the bedroom and found the four remaining Bollan Crosses on the dresser where I'd left them. I shoved them into my pockets. The meeting would be a good time to offer the crosses to anyone willing to listen to a witch's apprentice.

Near the bed, Liss stared at two skirts with shimmering eyes, as though the mention of more bodies had bothered her more than she cared to show in front of Mam.

I paused, wanting to offer words of comfort, but found I had none.

The Gills' house was stuffier than usual, packed with more than half the town. In the crowd, I spotted faces I hadn't seen since the start of summer, and many who hadn't deigned to attend Mally's wedding. People crammed themselves into every available corner, glancing around and conversing in terse mutters. I followed Mam and Da to the back of the room. The Gills themselves were nowhere to be seen.

Mam, Da, Liss, and I squeezed in beside Lugh and his da by the hearth. I caught Lugh's eye, and he gave a strained smile. His da nodded curtly.

Perhaps he thought I was mad, too, but the stares and whispers bothered me less now. Maybe, in time, my skin would grow tough and leathery like Morag's, an impenetrable armor against the nonbelievers.

Sweat beaded on my neck and trickled into the collar of my dress as the minutes wore on. Mr. Gill couldn't expect us to sit here patiently for hours, waiting for a better explanation than the one he'd barked at our doorsteps.

Someone shook my shoulder, startling me from my thoughts.

"Do you think old man Gill will be here soon?" Lugh leaned around his da, studying me, his brow furrowed.

"You have a really strong grip." I rubbed my shoulder. "And I certainly hope so." I scooted across a few feet of rug, claiming the small space between Lugh and the Gills' firewood basket.

Lugh touched my shoulder again, lighter this time. "How's your arm?" Before I could respond, he added, "I heard the whole story from Cat's mam this morning in the market." He dropped his voice to a whisper. "My da's been sending me for Samson almost every day lately. Says it calms his nerves."

I glanced at my bandaged arm. "It feels like Mr. Watterson's dog gnawed on my arm. But I'll mend. Cat's safe, and that's what matters."

"Still." He touched his forehead to mine. "I hate seeing you in pain." My breath hitched. Deep in my chest, something twinged, a duller ache than the one in my arm. Then I thought of Fynn, at home trying to make Grayse forget her worries for a little while, and the ache faded.

"Where is Cat, anyway?" I peered at the newest arrivals tramping through the door.

Lugh frowned. "I haven't seen her or her mam yet. They probably stayed home. They're sick of hearing about death and disappearances."

"Who isn't? But it's better to know what's happening than to sit home and wonder. The things I imagine are usually worse than the truth." I sighed. "Even if the truth is horrible."

The Stowells weren't the only people missing the gathering. Thomase and his mam were absent, as were Ina Cretney and her brood. Lugh, Liss, and I were the youngest people in attendance. Parents must have been trying to conceal the grisly details of this latest tragedy from their children.

The buzz filling the house suddenly faded to whispers, as if I'd plunged my head underwater. Everyone looked toward the foyer where Mr. Gill and his wife appeared.

Mr. Gill squared his shoulders and began in a weary voice, "Thank you all for your patience. I've been struggling to find the right words, but we have little time to waste. The bodies of Nessa Daley, Eveleen Kinry, Alis Stowell, Nanse Doughtery, Austeyn Boyd, and Brice Nelson were found in the harbor late this morning."

Lugh tensed beside me, sucking in a sharp breath. I put my hand over his and tried to disguise my exhale of relief as a cough. There was no new murderous sea beast. Just the *fossegrim*'s victims washing ashore at last.

Mr. Gill raised his voice as cries of shock and horror burst from many mouths. "Adam Radcliff and his brothers made the discovery when they went to check their traps just before noon. There's no doubt they were murdered."

The murmurs grew louder, making it nearly impossible to hear Mr. Gill above the din. "Not Brice," a man groaned. "Not my oldest friend."

"*Murders in the harbor?*" a woman shrilled. "I think it's time we gather our things and leave this town before we're murdered, too." She paused for a moment, then snapped, "I don't care if we go to the poorhouse! Poor is still better than dead, last I checked."

"What if it's me, next? I have to protect my baby." An older girl with dark hair clutched her belly, her face pale as a gull's wing. Lugh looked like he might be sick. Not only had he lost his mam, but Mr. Nelson had been a great friend to his family.

"Do you need some air?" I asked Lugh. He didn't seem to hear me.

The conversations had become a shouting match.

"Would everyone just be quiet!" Da was on his feet, shoulders shaking. Silence descended on the house. "Better," he grunted. "Now, let Danell finish." Da sat again, folding his hands in his lap, and nodded at Mr. Gill.

"Yes. Well." Mr. Gill coughed. "Thank you, Peddyr." His expression darkened as he surveyed the crowd. "As I was saying, seven deaths on our shores in one summer is the greatest tragedy in the history of Port Coire." He eyed each of us as sternly as though we'd confessed to the murders. "Someone in our fair town has developed a thirst for blood, and we need to decide how we're going to stop the offender before he strikes again."

I shook my head, filled with unease at the thought of a hunt for the murderer. Now that I'd slain the *fossegrim*, there was no culprit for Mr. Gill to condemn.

"How were they killed?" Da demanded.

Mr. Gill mopped his brow with a handkerchief and sighed. "We aren't certain. Their bodies were in a terrible condition, made worse by time and the water. We'll share full details with the authorities so they can determine the cause of death, but the reason I've called you all here is to discuss how we can keep our community safe in the meantime."

Adam Radcliff stood, arms folded across his barrel chest. "It looked like something—or someone—ate them." He swallowed. "Well, ate parts of them, anyway."

"That's enough!" Mr. Gill snapped. "You'll frighten the women and—"

"Whoever it was left their heads, and a few fingers behind. And several of these." Adam locked eyes with Mr. Gill as he held up what looked like a long, red-stained piece of bone. "I apologize if I've upset anyone. But sharing these details may help us find the killer."

Gooseflesh covered my sweaty skin. That was no ordinary bone shard.

It was a serpent tooth, just like the one that stabbed Lugh's foot on the beach. The serpent had eaten the *fossegrim's* victims. I thought of Fynn's tale about fighting the serpent for a drowned girl to eat, and wondered if the serpent attacked those poor people once the *fossegrim* lured them into the water. Not that it mattered.

I thought I'd saved our town, but I was wrong.

What mattered now was stopping the serpent before it made a meal of anyone else, on land or at sea.

"We must seek out the murderer today!" someone cried, to scattered applause. "We can't continue to live in fear!"

"This is the work of the Little Fellas!" a woman argued. "They've put a curse on Port Coire, and we'll all have to make a sacrifice if we're to break it!"

"What kind of sacrifice?"

"Enough babble!" With a rustling of skirts Ms. Elena shuffled to Mr. Gill's side. She peered into the crowd of faces until her eyes found mine. "I've been silent far too long. No man would do anything this hideous. Nor would the Little Fellas."

She raised her paper-dry voice over the murmuring of the crowd. "The Little Fellas live for their tricks and revels. They might curse the life of a lone mortal who crosses them, but they aren't *killers*."

Mr. Gill made a noise like a dying goose. "Now see here, this isn't a children's tale! There's a dangerous—"

"No, you see here, Danell. I remember when you were this high," Ms. Elena motioned to her knee, "and I gave you a thrashing for making birdcalls during the Sunday sermon. You're still a little boy who needs to shut his mouth and listen." She paused, breathing deeply. Mr. Gill's face turned white and red and purple all at once. "We must look to the sea. There's a monster, called forth from the deep—"

"Sea monsters again? Ha! The old woman's as mad as Bridey Corkill." Mrs. Kissack rose to her feet and pointed an accusing finger at me, as though I'd somehow caused Ms. Elena to stand up and support my claim.

Every head in the room turned toward me, and I dropped my gaze to the floor.

"Danell Gill is right," a deep voice said. "There's a murderer in our midst, lads, and we need to do something. I have to protect my family! Who's with me?"

Cheers rang through the house. There was an inhuman quality to the voices of my friends and neighbors that made me shiver.

"The first order of business," Mr. Gill called over the babble of voices, "will be to impose a curfew. Anyone roaming town after dark will be considered suspect and held for questioning." Several people nodded. "Are there any volunteers to patrol the roads and cliffs tonight? We need enough men for two shifts: six to midnight, and midnight to dawn."

Da's hand shot up, as did Lugh's. Then Lugh's da put his hand up, and father and son exchanged a rare smile. Mr. Watterson and a smattering of younger men came forward, all willing to sacrifice their sleep for the good of the town.

I shook my head. The most disagreeable thing they were likely to find was a stray Manx cat in heat. Unless their eyes were trained on the sea, and the moon swelled to its fullest, they wouldn't find the culprit slinking among the waves.

Every moment they spent arguing over details of a pointless patrol was another moment that the serpent was free to claim another victim.

And if the serpent was as terrible as Morag described, fighting it would be a far greater challenge than the fossegrim. I knew the truth; I couldn't waste any more time.

Climbing to my feet, I pulled the four remaining Bollan Crosses from my pockets and strode to the front of the room. Before I had a chance to think of the eyes upon me or the laughter that would drown out my words, I addressed the group. "These are Bollan Crosses," I mumbled, staring at my feet. "They're a charm to ward against drowning, and I thought—"

"Speak up!" a dry voice commanded. I raised my head, clutching the crosses to my chest. Ms. Elena gave me a faint nod of encouragement.

After a slow breath, I tried again. "These are Bollan Crosses. They're just wrasse bones on string, but they'll keep those that wear them from drowning."

The house was silent.

Meeting Lugh's bright eyes helped me continue. "I rescued my best friend from the ocean last night, and my charm worked quite well. Morag Maddrell made them." I knew how most people felt about Morag, but she deserved credit for her work. Anyone too proud to touch a gift from a witch would have to accept whatever hand fate dealt them.

"How do we know old Morag isn't the one who put a curse on us?" Mrs. Kissack cried.

"Can witches charm someone's head off their body?" a voice countered.

"How do we know the hag's even still alive? When was the last time anyone saw her?"

I set the crosses on a small table with shaking hands. "You're all welcome to them. There are only a few, but I'm sure Morag can make more."

"I have one," Lugh called loudly, over the throng of people who were now discussing the possibility of Morag's involvement in the gruesome deaths. "You can scoff at sea monsters, if you must, but surely some of you are wondering how one man—or a few—could cause such a rash of murders so quietly in your own backyards." Lugh locked gazes with me from across the room, and I mouthed a silent *thank you*. "Are you willing to risk your lives? If there's even the smallest chance these charms work—what's the harm?"

No one stepped forward, but at least I'd tried, and so had Lugh. I wove between close-pressed bodies to reach Mam's side, aware of the disapproving glances following me.

"You were splendid up there," Mam whispered fiercely. "Morag would be as proud as I am if she knew." Her gaze slid out of focus, and she rubbed her temples. "She taught me about those crosses when I was younger. I remembered after you gave me one to wear for the wedding, but I hadn't had time to tell you . . ."

I threw my arms around Mam's waist and squeezed. "I'm going. I'll see you at home."

A current of gossip swirled in my wake as I crossed the foyer. As I stood outside, letting the breeze dry the sweat on my brow, movement from the front window caught my eye. Fenella Kewish, the town gossip, picked up a cross and slipped it on. Snowy-haired Ms. Elena took one next, followed by Martyn Watterson.

I touched my fingers to my forehead in a quick salute, and turned away.

While the town argued over murderers and how mad I was, I had work to do.

Chapter Twenty

The sun hovered above the treetops as I ran home. There were still a few sunlit hours in which I could scour the land for the few poisonous plants I knew. If I was quick about it, there might even be time to deliver my finds to Morag before curfew.

Fynn glanced up from the hearth as I rushed inside. "What's wrong?" He dropped the wood he was about to feed to the flames.

"Too many things," I panted, running a hand through my damp, sticky hair. With hardly a moment to catch my breath, I recounted every detail of the meeting. When I finished, silence fell over the house.

We needed to act quickly, for the sake of anyone near the water.

"Fynn?" I laid a hand on his arm. The touch seemed to recall him from whatever vision had claimed him.

"The serpent sounds angry," he muttered. "Hope I at least gave it a good scar, or—"

"Where's Grayse?" I interrupted. I'd forgotten she was supposed to be with Fynn. The remnants of a card game lay on the floor, but there didn't appear to be a mischievous blonde head behind any of the furniture.

Fynn nodded toward my bedroom. "She's taking a nap. Cheating at cards exhausted her."

I hurried toward the door. "I'm going to wake her. We'll drop her off at the Stowells'—they weren't at the meeting, so they must be home—just in case Mam and Da are out discussing the new curfew a while longer."

"You could tell *me* where we're headed, while you're at it," Fynn said.

I paused to offer him the ghost of a grin. "We're collecting herbs for Morag. I'll explain on the way. If you want to come, that is." I opened the door, calling over my shoulder, "Whatever you decide, I need to go *now*. . . ."

Fynn hurriedly pulled on his boots. "Then I'm with you."

We maintained a brisk pace after dropping Grayse at the Stowells' cottage, slipping behind a row of tall houses as a shortcut to the overgrown field that bordered the forest. The usual scuffing of feet and shouts of *hello!* were absent, leaving only the sighing of the wind. Unease clung to me like cobwebs as I explained to Fynn how Morag would make serpent poison with whatever we found today.

"I'm certain I remember seeing a clump of pennyroyal over here," I muttered, mostly to distract myself.

Fynn shot me a look. "Pennyroyal?"

I pressed my hands to my hair as a gust of wind blew strands into my face. "The flowers are bright purple and puffy like dandelions. You can't miss them."

He darted ahead, kicking rotten strawberries from his path. I bounded after him through the waist-high grass, glad to leave the quiet of town.

"Is this it?" He waved a fistful of spiky purple stalks. I nodded and hurried to join him. "You're sure this is poison? It looks more like one of Mally's wedding decorations."

I crammed the flowers into my pocket. Smashed or not, they'd be effective. "I'm sure. Animals die if they eat it. People, too." I paused to rub a stitch in my side while Fynn prowled the field.

"What else am I looking for?" he asked.

"Caper spurge. If the serpent gets a taste, he won't be able to stop vomiting. It's a tall plant with heart-shaped leaves. It should be bearing small green fruit this time of year."

Fynn parted the grass, pulling up a reddish stalk of rhubarb. The plant's leaves contained a mild poison that would do little more than give the serpent a stomachache.

"That's no good. We're trying to kill the monster, not give him indigestion!"

Breathing easier now, I combed through a part of the field Fynn hadn't visited yet. Yellow heads of cushag bobbed in the wind, and strands of delicate bluebells brushed my knees, but a rotten odor lingered beneath their fragrance. My gaze fell on a dead mouse baking in the sun, and my throat tightened. I hurried in another direction.

"How about this?" Fynn held up more flowers for my inspection.

Shielding my eyes against the glare of the sun, I studied the blue petals in his hand. "No, no, that's gentian. It's used for healing."

Fynn shrugged, tossing the flowers to the ground. "I thought all the pretty ones were poisonous." He cut a path toward me, reaching my side in a few long strides.

A smile warmed my voice. "Only some." I took his hand. "This way. I know another place we can try, but then we'll have to bring whatever we've found to Morag. If Mally and Artur's boat had any trouble, they could still be at sea right now . . ."

We exchanged a look, and Fynn nodded gravely. Without another word, I guided him toward the woods at the base of my favorite hill, but instead of beginning the climb, we continued straight through a thicket of young oak trees. "There's a valley just up here," I explained, ducking under a branch. "I haven't been this way in ages, but I think we'll find more herbs than we need there."

"Bridey," Fynn murmured as we picked our way through the tangled branches. "There's something I've been meaning to tell you since last night. You won't like it, especially not after what the serpent did to those people, but I don't think I have a choice." He halted, turning to face me. "Your father asked me to go fishing with him tomorrow morning. An overnight trip."

"What? When did he ask?" I demanded, taking a step closer. A gnarled root caught my foot and I stumbled, reaching for a branch to steady myself.

"Careful." Fynn snagged me around the waist. "He asked at the wedding feast."

I gripped his shoulders. "Well, you can't go. Not when the serpent is so close. We have to keep Da ashore until Morag makes her poison and we've slain the beast."

Fynn shook his head. "We both know there's nothing we can say to keep your father on land. Fish are still scarce, and he doesn't—"

"—believe in sea monsters," I finished, bowing my head. Fynn was right. There was no stopping Da from sailing, no more than I could stop the sun from setting.

"The best I can do is go and try to keep him safe."

"And who will keep *you* safe?" A startled thrush took flight as my voice rang through the trees. "The serpent nearly killed you once already!"

Fynn put a finger to my lips. "Maybe your father won't want to go after what's happened. But I thought I should warn you." He touched his forehead to mine. "I'd die before I let anything hurt your father."

"That's what I'm afraid of," I muttered against Fynn's finger. "Promise you're coming back to me."

"I will. If you promise me something in return." He smiled and looked away, suddenly shy.

"Name it."

"Teach me how to read." He met my gaze again. "Once the serpent is dead."

I peered deep into Fynn's eyes, searching for a glimmer of teasing, but found none. "All right. I promise to teach you to read, if that's what you wish."

"It is. Though while we're on the subject, there are a lot of things I wish I had . . ." Fynn bent his head and kissed me, running his tongue along my bottom lip. "Like your heart."

I longed to say something clever, but with Fynn so close, I could barely stammer, "Well, then, take it."

It had been only days since our last kiss, and yet, he clutched my arms as though we'd been apart for months. My heart pounded in my ears, a dizzying refrain, as his lips collided with mine again. He tasted of salt and sunlight and the hottest days of summer.

And when I returned the kiss, I tasted something far stronger: the swooping, soaring, intoxicatingly sweet rush of fearlessness. I wanted to stay just like this, our lips touching even as we gasped for breath, until I'd memorized his taste. Maybe then, I could carry that soaring feeling, and him, with me forever.

But the serpent couldn't wait. We'd already wasted so much time standing there. "We need to take the herbs to Morag's before the new curfew," I murmured.

Yet as I untangled my hands from behind Fynn's neck, something he'd said not long before drifted back to me: *Nothing from the ocean is meant to survive on land forever.*

"Remember," I whispered as Fynn and I stood in the gloomy hallway early the next morning, listening to Da prepare to go to sea. "Be sure you aren't the third boat out of the harbor. It's bad luck, and that's the last thing any of us needs."

I laced my slender fingers between his larger ones. My eyes remained dry, but my pulse quickened every time I glanced at the two pairs of boots and weatherproofed cloaks Mam had set by the door. Until Morag's poison was finished at sundown—she swore it took a full day to brew—there was nothing I could do to protect Fynn or Da, or anyone else.

I hated this restless feeling, waiting on others before I could act, worse than the idea of fighting another *fossegrim*.

Fynn lifted our joined hands and kissed the backs of mine, jolting me back to the present. "It's only for a day and a night. I'll be fine. It's not as if the serpent attacks *every* boat. Your town would be missing a lot more fishermen."

I shuddered. It was far from a comforting thought. Clutching the front of Fynn's shirt, I whispered, "But if you do see the monster, go for its good eye."

"And you," he whispered back, his eyes as solemn as a funeral-goer's, "promise me you won't try to poison the serpent without my help."

I opened my mouth to say yes, but the word stuck in my throat.

"Are you ready, lad?" Da's gruff whisper cut through the dark house, sparing me from making a promise I couldn't keep.

"Time to go," Fynn replied. His lips brushed my cheek, sending a pleasant shiver through me. "I need a proper send-off."

I turned my head, lips lightly touching his. "That can be arranged."

A door creaked open behind us, and we jumped apart. Liss bustled down the hallway, jostling me as she passed.

"Sorry," she mumbled sleepily, rubbing her arm like she was the one who'd been bumped. Already dressed for the day, she had a light shawl wrapped around her shoulders.

"Where are you off to? It's early!" I whispered, mindful that Grayse was still asleep.

"Liss is going to sea with us, of course," Fynn said. "She's volunteered to bait our hooks."

"Oh, very funny." Liss scowled. "I'm tutoring Martyn before his da opens shop. Today is his first day as official bookkeeper." She ran her hands down her braids, checking for loose strands. "Mam knows." I looked skeptically at her, and she frowned. "I did tell Mam. I'll be back around noon."

Liss started for the door, but paused and glanced over her shoulder. "Be safe out there today, Fynn," she said before continuing on her way.

"Now," Fynn said, "where were we?" He leaned in for another kiss, but I drew back to pull a knotted handkerchief from my pocket.

"You can't forget this."

"Thank you, but—what is it?" Fynn turned the handkerchief in his hands.

"Knots for wind." I smiled as he continued to look at the bundle, puzzled. "Keep it with you whenever you're on the boat, and the wind will always be at your back." I toyed with one of the knots I'd tied the night before.

"Did Morag teach you that?" He gave a faint smile before tucking the handkerchief away.

"No, every girl on the Isle knows the magic knots. I made one for Da when I was small. He still carries it."

Fynn leaned in for one last kiss, and seconds later, he and Da trudged out the door armed with fishing rods, tackle boxes, and a hamper packed by Mam—all the things Da didn't keep stored in the boat with his nets and traps.

I joined her in the doorway, watching as Da and Fynn disappeared into the heavy mist.

"*Cair vie!*" I called as soon as I could talk around the lump in my throat. Da acknowledged the words with a wave, but Fynn paused.

Mam rested a hand on my back. "Use your English, bird."

"Fair winds!" I shouted. But they had become nothing more than two blurry shadows fading into nothingness.

There was nothing to do now but wait for sundown.

CHAPTER Twenty-One

Liss didn't return home by noon. Or even more than an hour later. I huddled on the sofa with Grayse, watching Mam tread a path from the kitchen to the main room and back. Her pacing made my head spin.

"I could go to the Wattersons' and see if she's there," I offered for what felt like the hundredth time. If Mam didn't agree soon, I resolved to go anyway. There was nothing else for me to do until sundown, in any case.

Mam paused by an armchair, blinking at the dish rag she'd been clutching for an hour without using it. "No. Thank you. I'd best fetch her myself." She started toward the peg that held her cloak.

"Don't be cross, Mam." Grayse nibbled the ends of her fingernails between words. "Liss probably forgot the time. Maybe she's running home now."

Mam turned, halfway through shrugging on her cloak. "Of course, little fish."

Grayse might not have glimpsed the lie in Mam's eyes, but I did.

Perhaps Liss *was* in danger. The thought made my skin crawl. But she had no reason to go near the sea today, not when she was so excited to meet her secret beau at his da's shop. Liss was on an adventure with Martyn somewhere, no doubt, and things would go much better for her if I found her first.

"Watch your sister, Bridey," Mam said, ushering me back to my senses.

I leaped up. "Why not take Grayse with you? You can search faster with my help. I'll start at the Wattersons' while you try elsewhere, and we'll meet in the market."

Mam's shoulders slumped. "Very well. Grayse and I will go ask at the neighbors', and we'll meet you at the fountain in an hour. And Bridey—" She waited until I raised my eyes to hers. "No delays."

I hurried north, my skirt swishing around my knees. An hour wasn't long to check all the trysting spots Mally used to frequent, so starting at the Wattersons' house seemed a sensible plan. Liss and Martyn might have mentioned something to his family about where they were off to.

Town was quiet in the afternoon gloom, but fires cast their ruddy light in the windows of most homes.

I rapped on the Wattersons' door and fixed a pleasant expression on my face, turning my back to the sea. I could hear muffled voices inside, before heavy steps trudged toward the door. Seconds later, Martyn's face appeared.

When he saw me, he smiled warmly. "Afternoon." He clapped me on the shoulder, shooting pain through my bandaged arm. "How's your wound?"

"Grand," I gritted out, "when no one's touching me." Martyn's smile turned sheepish. "Where's Liss? She needs to come home now. She's over an hour late!"

But Martyn's brow furrowed. "She isn't here."

I stared. Was he always this thick? "Of course she is." I peered into the house. "Li-iss!" I called in a singsong, my pulse quickening. "Do you have any idea what time it is? Mam's beside herself!"

Martyn's face slowly turned the color of clotted cream. "I haven't seen her today," he insisted. "I waited at the shop for hours, but she never came. I thought—I thought she was busy and couldn't come. She'd warned me your mam might not let her out, given the news of those poor folk at the harbor."

My fingers worried at my Bollan Cross. "When has Liss ever been too busy to keep her word? You didn't think to look for her?"

"I didn't think—"

"Didn't think at all, did you?" The harshness of my words startled even me. I offered Martyn an apologetic look. "I'm sorry. Liss left at dawn and . . . if she's not here . . ."

Martyn rubbed the back of his neck. "What can we do?"

I jumped off the front step and started running. "Go. Tell everyone Liss is in danger," I called over my shoulder. "They won't believe me, but they might listen to you!"

"Wait!" Martyn shouted. "Where are you going?"

"To help my sister, same as you!" When he still didn't move, I urged, "Raise the alarm! Hurry!"

I veered left, heading for the spot where the fossegrim had attacked Cat. I hoped Liss was wearing her Bollan Cross. Nothing else could keep her from drowning if the serpent had dragged her underwater.

My pace slowed as the ground shifted from dirt to sand. I loped down the beach, stopping just shy of the waves. Eyes narrowed, I scanned the gray-blue horizon for a flash of blonde hair or the gleam of inky rubber skin. But aside from the whitecaps, the only things stirring were massive rainclouds hovering over the sea, not quite ready to unleash their fury.

I prowled the sand, watching the water. My toes dug into something soft that wasn't sand. Heart sinking, I glanced at a familiar scrap of dyed wool lying among broken oyster shells. It was the shawl Liss had worn when she left the house this morning.

Clutching the familiar blue garment to my chest, I glowered at the water. "Take me next! If you want a fight, I'll give you one!" My breath came in quick sobs. "I'm through being afraid. Come and claim me! Just leave my sister be."

A gust of wind blasted loose sand around my ankles, but no half-blind serpent emerged to heed my challenge.

Whirling away from the ocean, I wrapped Liss's shawl around my shoulders and dashed toward the market to meet Mam. I'd convince her we needed someone with a boat to call Fynn and Da in to shore. Fynn was the only person capable of helping Liss now.

He could go where Mr. Gill and his patrolmen could not, and find my sister.

"Hold on, Liss," I whispered, hurrying over to Mam and Grayse. They stood near the fountain, talking to Mr. Gill, the water's merry babble failing to disguise their low, urgent tones. "Please, hold on."

I spent the rest of the long afternoon at home minding Grayse, playing games I wasn't thinking about, and preparing food I didn't touch, while Mam found someone to bring Da and Fynn back from sea. She didn't understand why I was so frantic, but she agreed to have them fetched anyway. She seemed to have little faith in the search party Mr. Gill was gathering.

Grayse hardly said a word as we passed the dragging minutes, and every time something reminded her of Liss, her eyes brimmed with tears. Mam would have been better comfort, but she'd begged me to take care of Grayse while she waited at the harbor.

"For my sake, please stay here. Stay safe. I can't stand the thought of losing another daughter," she'd pleaded.

I'd tied Liss's shawl around Mam's shoulders, pressing a stack of slightly stale biscuits into her hands before she departed.

By the time the front door creaked open, it was an hour or so before sundown. Morag would be waiting at the cottage with the poison. Grayse was sprawled on our bed, asleep early with her thumb in her mouth.

I scrambled off the sofa, peering past Mam as I hoped for a glimpse of Da and Fynn. "Where are they?"

"Almost here. I left to check on you girls the moment I saw their boat on the horizon." Mam collapsed on the warm spot on the sofa I'd just vacated, and her hollow gaze said enough. Her hair and Liss's shawl were damp, crusted with sand.

"Go rest with Grayse," she whispered.

"But I'm not the least bit—"

"Go." Her shoulders quaked, but her reddened eyes had no tears left to shed. Softer, she added, "All these years . . . Morag has been right to fear the sea. I'd never given it more than a passing thought, when all this time, I should have been guarding you girls against it."

I put a hand on her arm, but before I could tell her how right she was, she seemed to snap out of a daze. She shook her head and loosed a breath of nervous laughter. "Oh, what am I saying? I'm out of my mind with exhaustion. Forgive me, Bridey . . . Sea monsters belong in bedtime stories, along with fairies who like to clean people's houses."

"But, Mam." Perhaps I ought to tell her about her dreams. Maybe Morag was mistaken. Maybe Mam was ready to accept the truth.

"Go sit with Grayse!" Her tone told me she was far from ready after all. "I need you to keep her out of your Da's way when he gets home. Now!"

Tiptoeing into the bedroom, I snuggled up next to a sleeping Grayse and stared out the window at the gray clouds swollen with rain. I had half a mind to climb through the window and run to Morag's for the poison now, but I needed Fynn as much as I needed the deadly witch's brew.

It was only a matter of agonizing moments.

Raised voices sounded from the front of the house, startling me into alertness.

The window was now streaked with raindrops, and the sky beyond it still steely gray, though my empty stomach told me it was nearing suppertime. I hurried into the hall, shutting the door with care to avoid waking Grayse.

Fynn and Da weren't in the house.

Mam, tousle-haired and clad in a robe, stood in the doorway. She didn't acknowledge me when I peered over her shoulder and asked what the fuss was. But I answered my own question as I took in the bizarre gathering on our lawn.

Standing on one side of the road, soaking up the rain, were Da and Fynn. Their fishing gear lay in a heap at their feet. They glared at five figures opposite them: Mr. Gill and four surly men who often smoked pipes at the tavern. Mr. Gill held something long and thin in his hands, and Fynn's gaze was trained upon it.

"He has to come with us, Peddyr," Mr. Gill insisted, gesturing at Fynn.

Da shook his head. "He doesn't have to do anything. He's a guest here. My guest."

Mr. Gill shifted his weight. "I know you're not happy about it, but Mrs. Kissack swears she saw the lad outside her window not an hour ago, leering and beckoning her to come outside. And when she did, she saw footprints leading over the cliffs!"

I clenched my hands at my sides. Mrs. Kissack had surely been dreaming.

Da scoffed, too. "Fynn was at sea with me! Whoever she saw, it couldn't have been him. Danell, think, man! You stopped us on the way back from the harbor with our fishing gear!"

Mr. Gill cleared his throat. "Yes. Well. Even if she is mistaken, there are plenty of folk here who'd as soon take her word for it. And don't tell me you can't imagine why. He shows up just days after that unfortunate girl drowned, claiming he remembers nothing, hardly says a word to anyone—"

"And why should I?" Fynn's eyes flashed. "I can recognize an idiot without having to engage one in conversation." He crossed his arms, and one of the men imitated him.

Da clapped a hand on Fynn's shoulder. "He's been with me since before Liss went missing. He even reeks of fish!"

Mr. Gill tugged at his collar, his eyes bulging slightly. I hoped his shirt would choke him. "Still, he's one of the only suspects we've got. He has to be taken in for questioning. And should he fail to provide answers to our satisfaction, a constable from Peel will take him someplace more . . . permanent."

Take Fynn *where*, exactly? And what did he mean by *permanent*?

"Come with me, son," Mr. Gill commanded, extending a hand to Fynn. Then I understood. He meant a cell, confinement, sentencing for crimes Fynn hadn't committed. All to lure the town into a false sense of safety that would crumble the moment someone else's head turned up in the harbor. Like Liss's.

Mam shook her head and pressed her fingers to her lips. "Danell! How do we know *you're* not the one behind these murders? Has anyone questioned you? What if I saw you outside my window, hmm?"

Mr. Gill's lips twitched, but he didn't spare a glance for Mam. He and his men advanced, forcing Fynn back. Da reached for something on his belt—a knife—but Mr. Gill was quicker. He aimed the long, thin object toward the sky, his face expressionless.

A bang reverberated through the still morning air as the end of the old hunting rifle exploded.

"Peddyr!" Mam's cry drew neighbors from their houses with a chorus of front doors creaking open.

"Stop it!" A scream ripped from my throat as I pushed past Mam, running toward the men. "You have no idea what you're doing. You're only making things worse! Fynn is the only person who can help Liss. If you take him, she's doomed!"

"Stay back, Bridey!" Da growled as I neared him, his eyes narrowed at the rifle.

"Wait!" Fynn held up his hands. "I'll go." He walked stiffly to Mr. Gill's side, avoiding my gaze. "Lower your weapon. I'll go." The two broad-chested men seized him, securing his arms behind his back.

Mr. Gill lowered the rifle. "That's as it should be."

I ran toward Fynn but the men blocked my way. "I hate you!" I didn't care who heard me. Weak Mr. Gill, his supporters, the neighbors who stared from their front steps like I was the evening's entertainment. "I hate all of you!"

Mr. Gill turned, a sad smile on his graying face. "Go chase your sea monsters, lass, and forget this troublemaker."

As he marched Fynn onto the road, I started after him, but Da swiftly grabbed me.

"Bridey! Get control of yourself!" He pinned my arms at my sides, and I struggled against him. "Ouch!" He winced as my foot connected with his shin. "We have to let Fynn go for now. But we'll fight this. Don't you doubt it for a second."

I peered up the road, trying to spot Fynn in the group, but the figures all blurred together.

As Da lifted me into his arms, Mr. Gill's voice carried on the wind. "Soon as we lock this one up, we'll pay a visit to the witch."

Morag. I had to warn her and get the poison so I could use it, with or without Fynn.

I twisted in Da's arms, but his grip was firm. "Easy, bird." He brought his face closer to mine. It was as blurry as the figures striding up the road.

Inside, Mam poured tea and made toast, but I said I'd rather go to bed without supper. I'd have to sneak out my window— there was no way Mam and Da would let me out of the house tonight. As I reached the bedroom door, I turned back, watching my parents sip their tea with shaking hands.

For a moment, I considered telling them the whole story. About the fearsome creatures hidden in the deep, and Fynn's secret. But I knew as I studied their faces, even as they discussed curses and the Little Fellas in hushed tones, that there were certain things people just couldn't believe until they saw for themselves.

That, and there wasn't time to talk.

As I slipped into my room and shut the door behind me, Da murmured, "Mureal, where did you put my boots? I'm heading back out to look for Liss myself. Danell Gill and his search party are as useless as a fish trying to walk on land."

A chill stole over me as I thought of Da rowing his boat into the serpent-infested water. It was all the more reason to hurry.

Hoping Morag's poison would be ready, I crossed to the window, popped the latch and slid open the glass panel. It would be just a short drop to the muddy ground.

"Where are you going?"

I turned, pulling back my hands from the window ledge. Grayse blinked up at me, half-awake and stretching.

I tried to smile. "To save Liss. And Fynn and Morag, too, if I can manage it."

Grayse threw back the blankets. "When will you come home?"

"Soon, I hope. Tonight." I forced a smile. "But I need you to do me a favor." Grayse bobbed her head. "Good. You can't tell Mam I'm gone. Don't even let her in our room. Understand?"

Grayse nodded again, looking more alert as she warmed to the idea.

"If she wants to give me anything—food, tea—insist on bringing it yourself. Tell her I'm exhausted, and I don't wish to speak with her right now."

"Can I eat the food?" Grayse widened her eyes hopefully.

"You can eat it all, if you like. Just make sure you get sick out the window, not in here where Mam will have to clean."

I hitched up my skirt and threw one leg over the window ledge. There was no screen to push away. It had fallen out years before.

"Come back soon," Grayse whispered.

"I'll try, little fish. I love you. Tell Mam I love her, too."

I landed in a cold puddle, spattering mud up my once-white stockings. After a gulp of fresh air, I took off running through the rain, hoping the light would last long enough for me to find Liss.

CHAPTER TWENTY-TWO

Folk watched my dash up the road. No doubt they'd all heard the gunshot earlier—not to mention the screams—and longed to ask if the gossip was true, or to confirm I'd completely lost my mind. Perhaps I needed to build my own cottage on my favorite hill, just across the way from Morag's. We could wave to each other from our private mountains, and never have to endure the ogling of those too blind to see danger staring them in the face. They spread fear and speculation faster than flames on dry kindling, and in doing so, they made evil witches where there should have been only magic and wonder and a lonely old woman.

I charged up the hill, the cool rain pleasant on my face until I reached the trees.

Minutes later, I was pounding on the rotting door. "Morag! Open up!" Something rustled inside. "Liss is missing! I found her shawl on the beach. The serpent must have taken her, and now Da's gone to sea to look—"

"In this weather? At this hour?" The door flung open, hinges screeching in protest. "Has he lost his mind?" Morag's eyes watered, and an unpleasant odor tickled my nose. It seemed to be oozing from the black paste on her hands.

Before I even opened my mouth to ask, she demanded, "Where's your *glashtyn* friend? He wouldn't have trouble finding your sister, storm or no."

I ducked under the cover of the dripping cottage eaves. "Fynn was arrested! The missing people all turned up in the harbor. At least, parts of them did. And Mr. Gill thinks Fynn is likely responsible." I brushed rain and tears off my cheeks. "I'm afraid Mr. Gill and his men are coming for you next. I came to warn—"

"Gill's an old fool!" Morag drew herself up. "I knew his da once. Not well, mind you, but it's no surprise his son shares his mulish ways."

"Then you understand why you have to hide!" I glanced over my shoulder, reassured by the sight of the empty path. "But I need your help first. They're searching for Liss by land, but we both know I can't hope to save her without the poison."

"And it's ready." Morag smiled, holding out her messy hands. "Now come inside before you melt!"

"This isn't a social call!" I stomped my foot, splashing mud in all directions. "There's no time for tea or cake. I need the poison, and you need to find a hiding place if you don't fancy spending the rest of your days in prison, or worse!"

"I know," she answered calmly. "But there's no sense in getting soaked while I put the poison in a jar." She made a sweeping motion toward the cottage interior. "Warm yourself by the fire a moment."

A black pot sat on Morag's hearth, full of stinking goo identical to the paste on her hands. I peered into its depths, half-expecting something to bubble up and snarl in my face.

Morag kneeled at the hearth, clutching a glass jar. "In order for the poison to take full effect, the serpent has to ingest it." Seeing the puzzled look on my face, she added flatly, "He has to swallow it. Though I won't complain if you use some of this to blind his good eye."

"I know what *ingest* means. I'm just wondering, if the goo is so deadly, why is it all over your hands?"

Morag held her jar above the pot and smiled, showing off her remaining teeth. "This poison is only mildly irritating to the skin. I'll have blisters by tonight, but . . ." Her smile widened. "Someone had to test it. I fed some to a rat that's been stealing my bread."

My lip curled in disgust. "Poor longtail! Couldn't you have used a spoon?"

She scooped the green-black sludge into the jar and murmured, "That'd be taking the easy way, wouldn't it?"

Running a hand through my damp hair, I studied the jar. "I just pour this in the serpent's mouth?" My hands tingled as I considered how close I would have to get to the giant needle-teeth. "I couldn't, say, dump it in the water and hope it swallows some?"

Morag arched a brow. Her silence was answer enough.

"Well, I killed the fossegrim during Mally's wedding feast with a carving knife. I'm ready to slay bigger monsters, like King Arthur's knights did in the old stories. You can call me Sir Gawain."

"Not Lady Guinevere?"

I wrinkled my nose and frowned. "She never got to do anything important."

I studied the old woman's mangled foot, the careful way she kept her balance, the power with which she flexed her gnarled fingers. "But you can. Come with me. Help me stop the serpent, so you won't have to live in fear anymore."

Morag shook her head. "Killing a fossegrim took tremendous strength, Apprentice Bridey. You have more courage than any knight. More than me." She struggled to her feet and started rummaging through a cupboard. "But taking on the serpent is another matter, given its sheer size—"

"I know." I plucked the poison jar from the hearth and cradled it. If I lost the precious liquid within, Liss would be gone forever. She probably already was. All I had was hope. Foolish hope. "And just so you know, I missed you at the feast."

The sound of Morag pushing aside mugs and glasses stopped. She paused, a whiskey jar in her right hand.

"But I understand why you didn't come. Most folk here are keen to believe the worst. Why, you're a better friend to me than nearly anyone has ever been."

It was strange to think that when I had arrived at the cottage that first day, I'd worried Morag might chop me up for her evening stew. She was blunt, even cold at times, yet she had never questioned the things I told her. Never made me feel like I'd taken leave of my senses and conjured a world of sea monsters for my own amusement. Now, being in her presence filled me with a sense of calm and purpose.

I glanced up from the floor. It was difficult to see in the dim light, but Morag's body shuddered with sobs. Abandoning the mess, I hurried to her side.

"You shouldn't call me a friend." She pushed the whiskey jar back into the cupboard's depths, her sea-foam eyes streaming. "I'm a coward and a fool," she declared shakily. "But I refuse to face the serpent again."

"I understand," I murmured, though I didn't really. I longed to hide from the sea the way Morag hid from the beast that had left her crippled, but I couldn't any longer. "I have to go now. Liss needs me." I strode toward the door, Morag hobbling at my heels. "You might be able to survive up here all alone, but I can't live without my sister."

I darted into the gloomy afternoon. Gaps in the treetops revealed steely clouds, and cold rain dripped from the leafy canopy. Droplets smacked the top of my head as a distant rumble of thunder rocked the sky.

"Bridey! Wait!" Morag stood in the doorway, holding a crumpled, yellowing piece of paper. "I almost forgot, I found this for you!" Even from a distance, I knew what it was—the missing page of Morag's monster book.

I hurried back, prepared to snatch the paper and run for the harbor, but Morag's fingers closed around my wrist. The more I struggled, the tighter she held on.

"At least let me tell you what it says before you go running off. You need to know what you're up against!"

"Fine. I'm listening."

Her grip on my arm relaxed. "Serpents answer to no one. They have no laws, no ruler, because they consider nothing to be above themselves. *Glashtyns* are one of their few adversaries."

"How will this help me fight one?"

"I'm getting there! Serpents are ancient beasts. The book claims they're as old as Earth itself. And they're powerful illusionists, capable of making men experience the most realistic visions."

I gave a small shudder. That explained why Thomase swore he saw Fynn at a time when he was really with me, running from the *fossegrim*. And why Mrs. Kissack swore she saw Fynn beside the footprints on the cliffs.

Morag hurriedly skimmed the wrinkled paper. "According to this, serpents come from trenches. Yawning caverns on the ocean floor seemingly without end."

This sounded rather far-fetched, even after everything I'd learned over the summer. "Everything has an end—"

"Not necessarily." Morag frowned. "Men build boats, they drop anchors and cast fishing lines, but all they do is skim the surface. Maybe some wonder what's in the deep, far beyond their reach, but none of them *know*, and they never will." Her frown deepened. "For most of them, the truth would shatter their narrow minds."

I hugged the poison jar to my chest and glanced at the path. "I'll remember that. Now I *must* go, and so should you, before Mr. Gill turns up with his rifle."

Morag nodded. She grabbed a ratty cloak and a lantern. "I'm coming with you. I may not be able to go near the water, but there must be something I can do." There was an urgent note in her voice I'd never heard before. "I owe it to you, and to your grandfather."

"My grandfather? You mean Grandad?"

"Not him." Morag tucked her braids into her hood. "I mean your mam's father." She paused, her eyes glistening. "He stole my heart when I was just a girl of thirteen."

I dug my toes into the mud, trying to digest this startling detail. "Look, Da and Liss need me." I offered Morag my arm. "Walk with me toward the harbor, but keep your voice down." Morag slipped her frail arm through mine.

She kept a steady pace, bumping my side when the road dipped unexpectedly. "I admired Turner—your grandfather— from a distance for years. And after a sickness claimed every- one in my family but me, Turner's parents took me in. That's just the kind of people they were, the sort who never knew a stranger."

She smiled at something I couldn't see. "We were always friends, never sweethearts, no matter how I tried to get his attention. He fell for another girl in town. She had eyes like yours, and a voice sweeter than dolphin-song. For years, I believed I could change his mind."

"And did you?" I guided us off the road, casting anxious glances at the lit windows of nearby houses.

"No. But by the time I realized I couldn't capture his heart, I'd grown accustomed to living alone." The farther we went, the more Morag relied on me to steady her. My arm went numb from the pressure.

"Your grandfather provided for me after the serpent nearly took my foot, and when he died, I wanted to be left alone more than ever. But children harassed me. They threw rocks at the windows in the middle of the night. Left rubbish on my lawn. Shouted nasty things at me when I went into town." Her chin trembled, and we walked in silence for a while. "That's why I started the rumors that I was a witch. To frighten them away."

"I understand wanting to be left alone when it comes to people like Mr. Gill," I whispered, steering us into the cover of trees. "But we aren't all horrible. And I know you love Mam, even if you didn't like my gran."

Morag released my arm and paused beside a tree, breathing hard. "I know they aren't all bad. Why do you think I've been making the Bollan Crosses?" She tugged on her cloak hood, using it to shield her eyes from the driving rain. "I've loved your mam from the moment she was born, just as I loved your grandfather. Just as I care about you—you have the same color hair as him, did you know?" A ghost of a smile crossed her face, quickly vanishing. "I want to help save your sister, however I can."

I considered Morag for a moment, trying to imagine how she would fare in the water with her ruined foot if whatever boat we borrowed suddenly capsized. There was no way she could swim.

"Can you rescue Fynn for me?" I had no hope of freeing him myself, not when I needed to get to Liss as quickly as possible. If there was ever a time I needed a little magic, it was now, though Morag had made it clear she didn't do spells. "He's probably locked in a room at the Gills' house for now."

A gust of wind blew Morag's hood off, but her face broke into a smile as she handed me the lantern. "I may have lost my nerve long ago, but I've never met a lock I couldn't undo." She tugged on something in her cloak pocket, and produced a jumble of rusty keys.

I hesitated. "If those don't work . . ." I was asking her to do something immensely difficult and dangerous, yet Morag merely smiled.

"They'll work."

"How can you be so certain?"

"Magic." Her smile widened, even as I blinked a question at her. "There's a kernel of truth in some rumors. Remember that. I'll find the boy and free him."

There was no time to ask the many questions suddenly on the tip of my tongue. And even if there were, I doubted Morag would answer a single one.

"Thank you," I managed, pushing the questions to the back of my mind for Liss's sake. "Tell Fynn where I've gone." I adjusted my grip on the rain-slicked poison jar. "And Morag?"

She met my gaze, her eyes blazing with unearthly light. "Take care, won't you?"

"I will if you will, Apprentice Bridey. Remember, the serpent can make you imagine terrible things. Don't trust everything you see. And check the caves along the cliffs first. As that page in your hand says, serpents like to make their nests in sea caves. Besides, if it ate recently, it may be saving your sister for later."

I ran faster than I ever had down the familiar path to the harbor.

Nightfall was almost upon us, and there was no telling how long we had until the wicked creature was hungry again.

CHAPTER Twenty-Three

Every boat harbored in Port Coire shuddered, rocking in the high wind. All but one. The creak of ropes straining and the slap of water against wood mixed with the hammering of rain. Everything reeked of fish. As I approached the small craft tied near Da's vacant spot, the source of the stench became apparent. Someone had left a bucket of crabs in their boat. A few shifted restlessly on top of the pile, snapping at one another.

Two battered paddles lay on the dock near the crabber's boat. I grabbed them and leaped from the dock to the vessel, careful to keep low as the little craft rolled with the waves. I couldn't imagine who would miss such a battered thing, should the serpent destroy it. Perhaps the owner would thank me for the excuse to purchase a better one.

I set the poison jar and the lantern by my feet in at least an inch of collected rainwater.

Panic tightened my throat. If the storm worsened and the boat sank, I was doomed. I still couldn't swim. But I had to search for Liss and bring Da home. The rain was simply one more reason to hurry.

Not stopping even to empty the bucket of crabs, which would cost precious seconds, I sat on the wooden plank stretched across the center and dipped the paddles in the choppy water. I'd seen Da steer his boat often enough to have a basic idea of the motions. Within minutes my arms burned, but I was making slow progress out of the harbor.

I guided the boat north toward the sea caves, hugging the shore as much as possible. The shelter of the cliffs provided some relief from the raging wind, and though waves still broke against the prow of my tiny vessel, they were smaller than the ones on the open sea.

The rain had soaked through my innermost layer of clothes some time ago, but that didn't make sitting in a squelchy puddle any more comfortable. I shivered, blinking raindrops from my lashes and wishing for a lull in the roar of thunder and wind. If the serpent sneaked up behind the boat, I would only know by its breath on my neck.

I refocused on paddling. Massive, dark towers of rock jutted up before my boat, shrouded in mist and stretching toward the cold sky. They signaled the start of the network of caves where Grandad used to look for periwinkles, the sea snails he liked to boil for soup.

"Liss!" I shouted. My only answer was the keening wind blowing through holes in the rocks.

Tendrils of mist coiled around my arms and legs, making it difficult to steer. Manannán's Cloak had been Grandad's name for this unnaturally dense fog. I fought the urge to turn the boat around. If Manannán Mac Lir, Son of the Sea, was raising his cloak of mist around the Isle he had once ruled, then I was in more danger than I could imagine.

A horrible screeching assaulted my ears as the boat came too close to a narrow column of rock. I paddled furiously, but something prevented me from moving. The serpent?

A dark shape hovered just beneath the boat. I used one of my paddles to jab at it, but was met with strong resistance. Whatever I'd stabbed seemed much harder than a serpent's body.

With a trembling hand, I reached down to touch the dark shape. Coarse rock scratched my shaking hand. I withdrew it, angry with myself for losing my nerve so quickly. There was no room for fear while Liss's life depended on me.

The thin column of rock was much wider at its base. I tried paddling, but the boat made another screeching sound as it rubbed against the rock.

I rose carefully to my feet and stashed the paddles by the poison jar. Thrusting my hands into the water, I attempted to push the boat free. "Come on!" I shoved the wide rock a second time, then a third, sharp bits of sediment opening tiny cuts on my palms. Finally, the boat shifted, and I freed it with a final push.

My hands stung as I wrapped them around the paddles and moved forward once more.

"Liss! Can you hear me?"

Through breaks in the mist, I stole glimpses into the pitch-black mouths of flooded caves, their beds of gravel and shell submerged by the swollen sea.

"Help!" A girl's petrified scream shredded the air.

I glanced wildly around, holding the lantern aloft with one hand, but there was no one in sight. "Where are you?"

There was no answer.

Letting the boat drift, I scanned the cliffs. At first, there seemed to be no sign of a nearby cave, but then my gaze settled on a low rock overhang. I paddled toward it, fighting the fatigue in my arms with every stroke. The bandage on my injured forearm had begun to unravel, but there was nothing to be done for it now.

"Please don't let me die," someone sobbed as I drew closer.

"Liss?" I yelled, hardly daring to believe that the voice belonged to my sister.

"Bridey!" she shouted. "I'm in here! Oh, God, is it really you?"

I moored the boat on the heap of crushed shells that formed the sea cave's floor. Even knowing Liss was nearby, I took great care to make sure the boat wouldn't be swept away. Cold water sloshed around my ankles as I crouched and crawled through the entrance, guided by my lantern's feeble light.

Running a hand along slick walls, I called out, "Where are you?" My voice echoed faintly. My lantern wasn't strong enough to reach into the depths of the cave.

"I don't know!" Liss sobbed. "It's so dark! Hurry!"

"I'm coming!" The ceiling of the cave rose after a few steps, allowing me room to stand. The stench of decay was as disorienting as the lack of light outside the narrow halo of my lantern. My foot grazed a cluster of barnacles, and my stomach squirmed.

"Just my foul luck." As I stumbled down the narrow passage, frantic breathing filled my ears. "Liss?"

"Bridey! Right here!" A hand swiped at my leg from the shadows, causing me to miss a step. I flapped my arms, the lantern bobbing wildly, but my feet found purchase in a pile of something soft, like rotten logs.

"W-watch your step," Liss stammered. "There are bones in the corners."

"Bones?" I leaped back, splashing myself with chill water.

"Get me out of here!" Liss wailed, her cry echoing off the cavern walls.

"Take my hand." I reached out, trying to take in the state of her. Liss sobbed harder as my fingers closed over her wrist. "Can you walk? I've got a boat at the entrance, but we need to hurry. The storm is getting worse."

Liss sniffled. "I think my leg is broken. The beast—" She shuddered. "When I first heard your voice, I thought it was back. Making me imagine things again."

I remembered what Morag had told me. "Serpents are powerful illusionists." But my sister's hand clutching mine was too warm and familiar to be a trick. I pressed my fingers into her wrist to find her pulse, reassured by its faint rhythm.

Manannán had conjuring powers just like the serpent. It was rumored he could make one man appear as one hundred to any enemies who dared approach the Isle. Perhaps, if I asked nicely, he would aid me in confusing the serpent long enough for me to toss the poison into its mouth. Or perhaps he'd send me the magical red javelin he kept at the prow of his boat to spear his attackers.

Another cry from Liss drew me back to the present moment. "Listen, you'll have to try walking if you want to get out of here. I don't think I can carry you. Use your good leg and lean on me as much as you need to, all right?"

We crept along the short passage, occasionally banging into the walls or stepping on shells despite the lantern's aid. When a fainter shade of darkness appeared ahead of us, I shouldered most of Liss's weight and hurried to the mouth of the cave. The boat was right where I'd left it, paddles and all.

With a groan, I heaved Liss over the side and scrambled in behind her.

The rain, which had been a nuisance before, now felt wonderfully refreshing. I collapsed on the boat floor beside the bucket of crabs, giggling, while my ashen-faced sister stared.

The greenish rainwater now reached halfway up the outside of the poison jar, signaling the loss of more precious time. But I had rescued Liss, and we were free of the dark, decaying-bone cave. That was plenty of cause for giddiness.

"Let's go," I said, reining in my giggles at last. I reached for the paddles, my gaze falling on Liss's outstretched legs. Her skirt hung in tatters, and one of her legs bent at an unnatural angle. Needlelike punctures surrounded the break in her left leg, and the rain had washed away traces of old blood. She must have used scraps of her skirt to staunch the bleeding.

I swallowed hard, fighting a wave of nausea. No doubt Liss could feel how serious the wound was, and there was no point in alarming her more by mentioning it.

"Hang on, Liss." I gave her what I hoped was a reassuring smile. "We'll send for a doctor as soon as we're back on land."

Liss nodded, her face pale and pinched as she toyed with a string around her neck. Her Bollan Cross.

"I was on the way to Martyn's, and I saw him in the waves. He was shouting for help," Liss said, apparently taking no notice of my struggle to push the boat back into the water.

"I swam out to rescue him because it looked like something was trying to pull him under. And when I got to the spot where the water turns from green to blue, he vanished." Her eyes were unfocused, her breathing labored. "The serpent grabbed me, and that's when it—"

I thought she might faint, but she pressed her lips together and drew a breath through her nose. When she continued her story, her voice was steady. "It broke my leg. Then it dragged me to that awful cave. And even though it took me underwater, I could still *breathe*." She closed her fist around the small bone on the end of her necklace. "This thing is really magic, isn't it?"

I forced a smile, hoping to comfort her. "It must be. Pray you never need it again." As I eased the boat back into the misty sea, water continued to rise in the hull. It crept partway up my calves, demanding not to be ignored.

"See that bucket?" I jerked my head toward it, unable to take my hands from the paddles as the waves surged higher. "I need you to dump those crabs in the ocean and start scooping the water out of the boat."

"I can't reach it." Liss's eyes shone with tears.

Of course she couldn't, not with her broken leg. I hooked my right leg around the bucket, drawing it closer, then kicked it toward Liss. "How about now?"

The sound of angry pincers, followed by a gigantic splash, was a welcome reply, signaling that Liss had grabbed the bucket at last.

The farther from the shallows I paddled, the faster the wind rushed around us. Water crashed against the prow, sending a furious spray into our faces. It was all I could do to keep from losing one of the paddles, but at least I put a safe distance between us and the rocky shore.

"What are you doing?" Liss shouted over the clamor. Even with the storm hushing her words, the panic in her voice was clear. "I want to go *home!*"

"We have to find Da first! He's out here searching for you!"

Our boat listed hard to the left, wooden sides creaking in protest. If we came any closer to tipping, I would have to release the paddles to help Liss. In the water, we would be easy prey for the serpent. He wouldn't have gone far.

As we tilted farther, something bounced out of the boat and dropped into the water with a loud splash. The sound chilled my blood.

"Liss!" I gasped. She clutched the boat sides and gazed at me with wide eyes.

The waves shifted, and the boat righted itself as abruptly as it had tilted. Liss whimpered, and I thanked the stars neither of us had fallen in. Drawing a shaky breath, I guided us between two massive swells.

"Give a shout if you see Da."

"I'll try." After a moment's pause, she added, "I'm so scared, Bry."

Manannán's mist rolled with our boat, following us out to sea. It gave me an idea. "How about a song?"

Liss nodded, pressing her lips together as though holding in a cry.

"It was not with his sword he kept the Isle, neither with arrows or bow. But when he would see ships sailing, he would cover it round with a fog. He would set a man, standing on a hill, appear as if he were a hundred. And thus did wild Manannán protect—"

"Bridey, do you see that?" Liss pointed at something over my shoulder.

Without raising the lantern, which I'd left by Liss, I couldn't see much of anything. "No. But do you have any idea what fell when we tipped?"

Liss didn't reply. With a break in the waves, I turned to see her wiping strands of golden hair from her forehead and frowning. She held the lantern aloft, and I followed her gaze to the distant figure of a burly man in a large boat, riding the crest of a tall wave.

"Da?" Liss muttered.

I paddled toward him as quickly as my exhausted arms would allow.

"Da!" Liss cried again, her voice rising.

"Over here!" I shouted. If I didn't stop paddling, we would reach his boat in a few minutes' time.

When we were no more than a stone's throw away, Da's features came into focus. His worn cap, his favorite patched shirt, his broad smile. He beckoned us closer.

"We're coming!" I called. "Liss is hurt!"

Da's smile widened as we approached. He seemed perfectly calm. And his clothes and hair were completely dry.

I stilled the paddles.

"What's wrong?" Liss demanded. "Why did you stop?"

Da continued to beam at us.

"That's not him," I murmured. "The serpent is making us see things."

I turned the boat for shore, but a dark, scaly wall blocked the way.

"He's gone. Da just vanished, like Martyn. He's gone!" A scream ripped from Liss's throat. She must have spotted the massive obstacle in our path.

The serpent's middle was as wide as the spread arms of a grown man. Its body was covered in thick scales like plate armor. Ebony spikes ran the length of the monster's spine. Its body writhed with the waves, but its head remained hidden.

Summoning every last ounce of strength, I paddled harder, seeking a break in the rippling chain of flesh. But the serpent had encircled the boat in seconds. My heart banged against my ribs.

"Hand me the jar!"

"What jar?" Liss cried, swinging the lantern around. "I don't see it!"

The serpent slowly tightened its circle. Huge waves crashed into the monster's side, glancing off its scales like water against rock. A shrill hissing reached my ears, sending a burst of cold down my spine.

"It's the only jar on the boat!" I dropped the paddles. There was no use in steering the vessel while only a few feet of water remained between us and the serpent. The jar had vanished—it must have made the splash I heard when the boat nearly overturned.

Panic clouded my vision, but Liss's quiet sobs kept me from falling to pieces. My sister needed me. If I kept the serpent occupied long enough, perhaps Liss could cling to the boat and drift to safety.

Through a haze, I wrapped my sore hands around the paddle. I wasn't sure I could kill the monster, or even pierce its scaly hide, but if it showed its ugly head, I would make it hurt.

The hissing grew louder as the serpent's giant head finally surfaced. The creature shot upward with a rumble as deep as thunder, sending a wave of chill seawater into our faces. It swayed overhead, taller than any tree. There were no cracks in its black, scaly armor, no weak point in which I could thrust the end of my paddle.

Craning my neck, I took a proper look at its head. One murky yellow eye, the size of a dinner plate, watched our boat. The lump where the other eye should have been was a swollen mass of black and purple. Morag's handiwork.

The serpent opened its mouth, revealing row upon row of needlelike teeth. Most were stained a dull red, as they had been in Mam's painting. The monster released a deafening screech, but still I clutched the paddle.

A thud sounded behind me. Liss slumped beside the overturned bail bucket, her eyes closed.

With another shriek, the serpent swooped toward us, jaws stretching wider as if it intended to devour the boat in a single mouthful. A blast of the monster's cold breath pushed my sodden hair off my face.

It was underestimating me. It thought it could make me cower. Good.

I raised the paddle like Sir Gawain's huge axe, like Manannán's red javelin, prepared to cram the handle down the serpent's throat.

The monster lunged. I struck out with my paddle, putting the strength of all my years of chopping wood for Mam behind the swing. The serpent screeched and writhed as the blow landed between its eyes.

I may not have pierced its throat, but any wound was a victory. I raised the paddle again, taking advantage of the monster's momentary confusion to stab the exposed white flesh on the underside of its neck. I was a knight, and I wouldn't flee from this dragon. The wooden handle met scales and splintered with the force of my attack.

"That's for Morag!" I screamed, though I couldn't hear my words over the ringing in my ears from the serpent's cries.

My second blow had angered the serpent more than hurt it. The beast glowered at me with its good eye, rearing up to strike. I clutched my paddle-spear, but now I realized it was more than splintered at the end—it was useless, cracked all the way down past the spot where I gripped it.

I barely had time to think of my family, of Fynn, and everyone else I'd miss as the serpent bore down upon us. Its mouth slowly closed over the front of the boat, like someone wanting to savor a delicious supper. I scrambled toward Liss, who clutched the lantern to her chest as though it could somehow shield her, hoping to prolong my final moment.

Crack.

Something large collided with the serpent's head and knocked it away from the boat before its teeth could sink into the wood. The waves rocked our vessel, nearly capsizing us. I clung to the wooden seat with one hand and Liss with the other, trying to prevent us from spilling into the water.

"Bridey!" a familiar voice shouted. "Hang on, I'm coming!" Da waved from a boat several yards away. The real Da. Water poured off his hair and beard.

"No!" I yelled, my eyes on the serpent's head and the dark shape repeatedly crashing into it. The impact sent up so much white spray that only the outlines of the two struggling creatures were visible, one much smaller than the other. The great serpent submerged most of its bulk as it fought, leaving plenty of room for me to maneuver the boat.

"It's too dangerous! We'll come to you!" I called to Da. Pushing myself upright, I grabbed the lantern and the remaining paddle.

"What happened?" Liss asked groggily.

"You fainted." Coercing my numb arms into paddling was more difficult than I would have imagined. "But Da found us. I'm taking you to him now."

As we helped Liss into Da's boat, he blanched at the sight of her shattered leg.

The water in the hull was now past my ankles. I released a shaky breath as Da's strong hands slipped under my arms and pulled me into his boat.

"Are you mad, child? What are you doing out here?" Da gave me a little shake. The jarring was nothing compared to the waves created by the serpent and its attacker.

"Finding Liss for you." I tilted my chin up, and he simply gaped. "Some things are worth braving the water for."

Da wrapped me in a tight embrace, then picked up his paddles. "I never knew we had another sailor in the family. Now let's get away from that damned thing." He jerked his head toward the snarling brawl taking place so near the boat.

As Da made for shore, I peered over the side for a glimpse of our savior. The rain slowed as I raised the lantern, allowing me a clearer view of the creature harassing the serpent. The *glashtyn's* stallion head and dolphin tail were painfully familiar. He bared a set of impressive teeth at the agitated monster.

"Fynn!" Though he couldn't possibly see or hear me, I stretched my arms toward him. "Get away from there! We'll be fine, we'll—" The words died in my throat.

The serpent rolled its good eye, apparently tired of Fynn's taunting. It surged forward with lightning speed, snapping its jaws around his middle. The monster jerked from side to side in a celebratory dance, with Fynn flopping in its jaws.

I tried to scream, but couldn't get enough air. There was so much red in the water, spreading from the spot where Fynn and the serpent were struggling. There wasn't even that much blood in my body. I hoped the grisly sight meant Fynn had wounded the serpent.

At last, I found my voice. "That's Fynn!" I grabbed Da's arm and pointed to the spot where the serpent threw my dark-haired lad around like a child's toy. "It's Fynn! We have to help him!" I attempted to wrest the paddles from Da.

His grip was unyielding, but he spared a glance for the fight. "That's not Fynn! It's a horse-seal-dolphin—Hell, I don't know what that thing is, but it's no lad!"

"It's him." I patted my Bollan Cross and swung my leg over the side of the boat. There wasn't time to convince Da. I would have to jump in, and trust the cross to help me ride the waves to Fynn. I took a deep breath, preparing to swing my other leg over.

Da seized my arms. "Look," he commanded hoarsely.

There was no longer a *glashtyn* dangling from the serpent's mouth. Fynn, with his shaggy hair and tanned skin, was human once again, but still caught in the monster's teeth. His chest rose and fell shallowly.

Liss gasped, raising her brows at the sight.

"Merciful angels," Da breathed. He changed direction, paddling back toward the fight.

I leaned over the side of the boat, holding the lantern aloft for Da. "We're coming!"

The serpent shot around our boat and rose into the sky. Da hesitated, torn between helping Fynn and fleeing to protect his daughters. I elbowed him in the ribs, urging him to keep rowing to Fynn's aid.

The serpent hadn't yet spotted us. Fynn was now awake, and he was clawing at the monster's remaining eye.

"We're down here!" I yelled. "Jump! Hurry!"

Fynn's exhausted gaze met mine, and he shook his head. "Bridey," he coughed. Then he twisted in the serpent's jaws, digging his fingers deep into the rim of the monster's eye. The serpent thrashed and howled, but Fynn gouged the eye with a sickening pop.

A deafening wail forced Da, Liss and me to cover our ears. With a bone-chilling screech, the blind serpent dived beneath a swell, Fynn still trapped in its mouth. Water from their violent descent smacked me in the face, masking my tears.

Da moved cautiously toward the spot where the monsters had vanished, paddles cutting through the reddened sea. We sat for several minutes, the boat bobbing on the storm-charged waves in the darkness, but neither Fynn nor the serpent resurfaced. The only sound other than my sobs was the mournful keening of the wind.

"Where is he? Where's the serpent?" A woman's rough voice called from a distance. "And the glashtyn boy?"

A blurry speck of light, another lantern hanging from someone else's boat, headed toward us. Morag, no illusion with her sodden clothes and sea-foam eyes, feebly dug a paddle into the angry sea. In her other hand, she clutched a shining spear.

"What happened?" she demanded, pulling her boat alongside ours. "Fynn—?"

"He's gone." Da hung his head. "Whatever he was, he's with the angels now." I sobbed harder, and Liss draped an arm across my shoulders.

"And the serpent?"

"It's down there somewhere." Da waved a hand at the red stain over the water. "Blind, though, if it's even still alive."

"That's something." Morag's gaze shifted to me, and the fire that seemed to animate her sputtered and died. "I'm sorry, girl." Her voice was thick with unshed tears. "I'm too late. I wish I had a way to bring him back, but the greedy sea claims whatever it can."

I stared at her, numb with cold and shock and disbelief. "You shouldn't have come!" The words sounded strange, as though someone else had spoken them. I seemed to be watching everything from a distance, like a spectator at a game of *cammag*.

"What if the serpent had gotten you, too?"

Despite her intense fear of the sea, she had come ready to do battle. She had come for me, for my family, and I couldn't have asked for anything more.

Morag closed her cold, waxy hand over mine. "Don't worry. We'll find a way to make things right, you and me. We won't stop trying until we recover everything the sea has taken from us."

I squeezed her hand. Words still eluded me.

"Bridey." Da laid a hand on my back. "We have to go. Liss needs a doctor."

I nodded, burying my face in Liss's shoulder. The sea had stolen another piece of my heart, and I couldn't bear to watch the crimson water churning in our wake. The serpent had won today, but now that Fynn lay beneath the ocean's dark surface, I would never stop fighting.

CHAPTER TWENTY-FOUR

"Ready, my love?" Da rumbled in my ear, his whiskers scratching my cheek.

Without taking my eyes from the gleaming ocean, I nodded. "Remind me what I'm supposed to do, again." I gripped the long handle of the dip net with both hands, letting the mesh dangle over the side of the boat.

Da frowned. "It shouldn't be any different from the last time. Drop the net in the water, and—"

"Da," I groaned. "I'm teasing." I plunged the net into the brine.

In the weeks since Fynn's disappearance, I'd learned how to set a crab trap, how to use dip nets, and how to bait a hook. Looking into the water still made my head swirl, especially when I thought of the creatures hidden in its depths. But I could hold a wriggling fish in my hands and ride in a boat without getting sick.

We sat in silence awhile, Da with two fishing rods and me with the dip net. An early autumn breeze combed my salt-crusted hair as I narrowed my eyes against the glare of the sun. As always, I searched for a sleek black fin, but the only fins jutting out of the water belonged to a school of dolphins.

A week ago, the serpent's body had washed up near Peel. According to Da, pictures were splashed across newspapers, even reaching Mally in London.

Da took me to see the body one morning, thinking it would help. But as the sightless monstrosity rotted under the summer sun, I wept. I'd somehow convinced myself Fynn would be there, too, but there had been no sightings of a lad matching his description reported.

I wasn't sure what became of the monster's carcass after that, nor did I much care. Lugh insisted someone had carved it up for the meat. I pitied the person who found serpent on their plate at suppertime.

Da cleared his throat, and I tore my gaze from the dolphins. "Morag came by the house again this mornin' while you were helping Liss to her room." Liss still couldn't walk unassisted, but she was growing stronger each day with the aid of the healing tonics Morag provided.

"What did she want?" I tried to keep my voice neutral despite the pang in my chest.

"Same as usual. She asked about Liss's leg. And told me to remind you that your job's waiting whenever you're ready to go back." Da shook his head. "She said if you'd like, you can be the boss, and she'll be your apprentice. She misses you, bird."

"I know." I missed her, too.

Morag's cottage would forever remind me of summer, of Fynn. Still, the absence of Morag's sharp-tongued remarks and pungent teas smarted like a toothache. And I couldn't delay my return much longer when more serpents and other monsters yet swam the depths. Whenever they reached our shore, Morag and I needed to be ready to fight them. Together.

My hand strayed to the Bollan Cross around my neck, rubbing the worn bone between my thumb and forefinger. "Did you invite her for supper like Mam wanted?"

"I would have, but Danell Gill stepped outside to work in his garden, and old Morag limped off before I could get another word past my lips. I've never seen her move so fast. Almost like magic."

Da grew quiet, humming gently under his breath while we waited for hapless fish to swim near the boat. Neither he, nor Liss, nor I had breathed a word of Fynn or our encounter with the serpent to anyone in Port Coire. The arrangement suited us well. And though Liss's doctor asked a great number of questions, though Mr. Gill continued to press us for news of Fynn's whereabouts, we kept our silence. I got the impression Da had explained everything to Mam, though, because she hardly let me out of her sight now.

When Da finished the last line of his sea chanty, he offered me a tin. "Kippers?"

I shook my head, carefully balancing the net handle as I reached for the oilskin pouch holding my bread and cheese. "Thank you, but I packed my own lunch."

"I never thought you'd come out here with me," he remarked, a smile in his voice. He wasn't the only one. In a few short weeks, I had gone from being a gossiped-about witch's apprentice to a gossiped-about lass who went out fishing with the men. And, as before, I didn't care.

I pulled a wedge of cheese from my sack. "That makes two of us."

Da grinned. "Now it's only a matter of time until you're begging to try some fresh fish. One day we'll catch something so delicious, you won't be able to resist."

"Not a chance, Da." I held up the tart cheese and licked my lips. "Some things will never change." Like Grayse's love of every creature finned and feathered. Or my slowly mending friendship with Cat and Lugh, who both somehow understood that I wasn't ready to talk about what happened, even though I'd never said as much.

The kipper tin hit the floor of the boat with a clatter, startling me. "We've got a bite!" Da sprang to his feet. "Help me reel 'er in!"

I threw down my net, unable to stop my heart from giving a hopeful leap. The only other time I had assisted Da with reeling in a line, there had been a baby shark on the end. Perhaps today, we'd see a dark, rounded fin and a pair of familiar cobalt eyes.

My heart sank as sharp, dusky gray fins and a white belly appeared. Together, with much groaning and swearing, Da and I heaved a thrashing shark onto the boat. It wasn't more than three feet long, but it jerked hard enough to rock our vessel. Panting, I wiped my grimy fingers on my shirt and sat back to watch Da subdue the struggling creature.

"This is a handsome one. Should fetch a nice price." Da glanced over his shoulder, a huge smile splitting his face. Without the serpent hunting in our waters, fish were once again plentiful. We caught so many crabs and lobsters that we'd been making weekly trips to Peel to sell our surplus in their larger market.

"Sounds like we'll be able to buy some more cloth then. You ought to ask Mam to make you a new shirt." Now that we could afford fine cloths, Mam had been sewing dresses and skirts. She even sold some at the market. She'd lost all desire to paint, but she wasn't plagued by headaches and nightmares anymore.

"She should make a few more dresses for you girls first," Da said at last. He poked his calloused fingers through a hole in the side of his shirt and wiggled them. "This has room for another hole or three." I smiled as he bent over to check on the shark.

"By God! Look!" Da lifted something from beside the shark's head.

Heart in my throat, I hurried to his side.

A glimmer of silver-pink flashed between Da's fingers as he polished the object on his shirt. "This was in the shark's mouth!" His gleeful expression warmed my insides, banishing thoughts of monsters.

"What—?" The question died in my throat as my trembling fingers closed around a massive pearl swirled with silver and pink.

"Keep it, bird. Consider it payment for being my first mate," Da said. He must have mistaken my watery gaze for one of deep gratitude. I nodded my thanks, gripping the pearl. "Now, do you want to head to shore? Or see if our luck holds farther out?"

I shrugged, swallowing around a lump in my throat. Not long ago, I would have given anything to leave the Isle, with its brine and wind and blue-green waters, far behind. Now, I rode the waves like I truly belonged. Like there was a place for me here. Perhaps there had been all along. And now, some stubborn part of me, the same part that clung to a wild hope that Fynn had survived, vowed to stay put until I saw him again.

London and Paris and Dublin could wait.

After all, the sea had taken Fynn away, but the sea had also brought him to me. New treasures rolled in with the tide each morning, perfect ivory shells and starfish that, if left unclaimed, were pulled back into the water by nightfall. The ocean spat out some of the same shells day after day, never allowing them to travel far from the coast. Who was to say the changing tide and ever-shifting winds wouldn't carry Fynn back to Port Coire today, tomorrow, or even six months from now?

Turning away from Da, I clutched the pearl against my pounding heart. The sight of it was slowly dredging something Fynn once told me to the surface of my memory, about *glashtyns* knowing places deep underwater where they might heal.

I brought the pearl to my lips, tasting salt.

And a promise.

I scanned the water again, seeing only the dolphins diving in and out of the blue. But that could change in an instant.

Pocketing the pearl, I grabbed a paddle and settled into place on my side of the boat, eyes on the horizon. "Let's keep fishing."

A Note from the Author

When I think of a place where magic could exist among the everyday, where the glimmer of a fairy's wing could be mistaken for a flash of sun in your eyes, I think of the Isle of Man. That's a large part of why I chose to set my story about a girl's struggle to overcome her fear of the ocean and its supernatural denizens on this unique and proud island. Take a moment to look up pictures of the Isle (go ahead now, I'll wait), and as you drink in its unspoiled beauty, you might agree that it's one place in this world still wild enough that magic seems somehow possible.

The Isle of Man's rich history and culture also made it such a fun location to research. Despite being conquered by the Irish, the Vikings, and later by the English, the Isle maintained cultural traditions all its own, adapting outside influences until they became distinctly Manx.

However, in the early 1900s, around the time that Bridey's story takes place, there were very few people on the Isle speaking Manx Gaelic. Parents at that time felt their children would be better served by learning only English, so Bridey and her friends probably wouldn't have known any Manx. Still, I chose to honor the Isle's heritage by having Bridey speak her native language, and she and her family would be pleased to know that today, efforts are being made to revive Manx.

As for the other cultural traditions you'll find throughout this book, such as Bridey going barefoot almost every day, they are indeed accurate to the period to the best of my knowledge—even the people of the Isle's deeply held beliefs that fairies, or the Little Fellas (as they are never called fairies by the Manx people), existed. Today, if you visit the Isle, you'll find an echo of this belief reflected in the aptly named Fairy Bridge, a place where it is considered unlucky not to greet the fairies as you cross.

Of course, fairies are just superstition. But if you're visiting the Isle and you happen to glance out over the sea, and you spot something dark and scaly slicing through the waves, or something like a ghost hovering above them . . . I'd find the throat bone of a Ballan wrasse and hang it around your neck. Just to be on the safe side.

Peace, love, and sea monsters,
Sarah

MANX SLANG, USEFUL PHRASES, AND THEIR ENGLISH MEANINGS

Across: The British mainland

Aye: Yes

Bonnag: Flat cake-bread, usually made with dried fruit

Cair vie: Fair winds

Cammag: A Manx team sport, similar to Irish hurling, involving a curved stick and a ball

Comeover: A non-native person living on the Isle

Crosh Bollan: The cross-shaped throat bone of the wrasse fish; it was used as an amulet

Cushag: Ragwort, the national flower of the Isle of Man

Fastyr mie: Good evening

Gura mie ayd: Thank you

Herrin': Herring, a common Manx food

Keeill: A chapel

Litcheragh: Lazy

Little Fellas: Term for fairies

Longtail: A rat; a term used out of superstition, often on boats

Mark: A fishing ground distinguished by its landmarks

Moghrey mie: Hello or good morning

Middle-World Men: Another term for fairies

Queenies: Queen scallops

Samson: A beverage made of treacle and hops, believed to give a person strength

Scutch: A quantity of something, e.g., There are a scutch of people at the market

Shoh Slaynt: Here's health; used in place of the American "Cheers"

Snigs: Young eels

Ta'n ennym orrym . . . : My name is . . .

Themselves: Fairies or other supernatural beings

ACKNOWLEDGMENTS

Now it's time to thank all the amazing people who helped bring this book to life, who stood bravely by my side as I fought my way through the daunting quest we call "becoming a published author." Brace yourselves—here comes the mushy part.

To my husband, Chris: You saw this dream inside me, but more than that, you saw potential, and you never let me give up. You're my biggest fan, my tireless cheerleader, and I'm beyond grateful to have you as my creative partner (for intense brainstorming sessions) and my life partner (there's no one else I'd rather fight orcs with on a Friday night). This book wouldn't exist without you, babe.

To Mom and Dad: Thank you for all the bedtime stories, the library trips, and the books you brought home, never complaining about how many I'd devour in a week. Thanks for not letting me read at the dinner table, so I still learned how to interact with people like a normal human. But above all, thank you for the love, and for telling me I could be anything I want to be.

To Lindsey: This story is dedicated to you, which pretty much says it all, but it bears repeating: Thank you for putting up with me. You're my favorite (only) sister.

To my grandparents, Dawn and Dave: From teaching me handwriting and helping with homework, to introducing me to cookies (thanks for the lifelong addiction), you've been more like second parents than grandparents to me. Thank you for everything.

To my grandmother, DeeDee, the extended Peters family, and my loving in-laws Marilyn and Joe Lauscher: Thank you for believing in me and this story.

To the Williams tribe: Thank you for always cheering me on in whatever I pursue. Hey, Caroline and Mac—now your names are in a book!

To Christa Heschke, my agent: You championed this story from start to finish. Thank you for all your hard work!

To Team Sky Pony: In particular, Alison Weiss, editor extraordinaire, who shaped this book with wit and wisdom. Kristin Kulsavage, who first saw potential in this story and made my dream a reality. And Georgia Morrissey, who gave this book such a beautiful cover.

To my fierce CPs, Katie Bucklein (the Gimli to my Legolas), Ami Allen-Vath (my favorite prom queen), Teresa Yea (my brain twin), Carolee Noury (editorial goddess), and Erin McQuaig (artist/librarian/all-around amazing person): I would be lost without you. You all make me a better writer with your brilliance and your red pens, but more importantly, you have all become important parts of my life. Your friendship is a treasure better than pearls or shipwrecked gold.

To my other early readers, Heidi Lang, Hilary Harwell, Rachel Pudelek, Christine Arnold, Sharon Criscoe, and Eve Castellan: Thank you, always, for your friendship and wisdom! To Laurel Symonds: Thank you for believing in this book, and teaching me so much. To Jodi Meadows: It was a lucky day for me when you agreed to grab coffee! The next one's on me. To Martina Boone, Melinda McGraner Allen, Laura Weymouth, M.K. England, Gwen Cole, and Rachel Simon: Your friendship, cheerleading, and commiseration are priceless—thank you!

To Lenore Bajare-Dukes: There aren't words for how grateful I am to have you in my life, so I'll simply say—thanks for opening my eyes to the wonder that is Lord of the Rings, for wizard rock concerts and long talks and crazy fanfic dares. To Erin Manning: From the moment we realized our mutual love of all things ghostly and strange, you've become a lifelong friend, and believed in my work even when I didn't. Thank you. To Joe Sparks: I'm still working on finding you a dragon; in the meantime, thanks for everything.

To my Twitter friends (too many to name!) and my fellow authors in Sixteen to Read, the Sweet Sixteens, and Team Rogue YA: Thank you for giving me a wonderful, strong community that's carried me through the toughest days. And to my friends on Elendor: Thank you for sharing stories with me and shaping me into the writer I am today.

To the bloggers who have shared their excitement for this book, most especially: Becky at BookNerdAddict, Kat Kennedy at Cuddlebuggery, Brittany at Brittany's Book Rambles, Hafsah at IceyBooks, Kit Cat at Let the Pages Reign, Liran at Empress of Books, Nori at ReadWriteLove28, Jen at Pop! Goes the Reader, and Lauren at Live, Love, Read.

And to you, dear reader: Thank you for making my dream possible.